Omerta -
Code of Silence

Omerta - Code of Silence

Luciano Delcremona

To order additional copies of this book, contact:
Xlibris Corporation
1-800-618-969
www.xlibris.com.au
orders@xlibris.com.au
500134

CONTENTS

FORWARD

"OK where do we start? I *guess like anything;* it's best at the beginning. Hello my name is Violino Bruglioni and I am a boss in the family business. I don't mean to sound smug but that is part and parcel of being a wise guy. Fuck me what an expression—who came up with that one! It doesn't matter, the silly prick wasn't me. Things are looking for the better already.

Lately, things have been going very wrong for us in this game we call survival. You see like any games you have two sides with each side looking to outdo the other for outright victory. The opposition I am talking about is law enforcement.

Christ! I should have listened to my father . . . a real Don. He told me to be a boss in the future, (future being now,) you would need to put a gun to your head and pull the trigger; something that actually happened, *although the details of my fathers' suicide seem a little sketchy;* you see he put his point four-five calibre Barretta to his head and pulled the trigger six times, plastering his brain cells all over his most prized possession—the interior of his Ferrari F-40 after which, he put the car into first gear to test its gliding capability and drove it off a very fucking extreme cliff! *Ha fuck me . . .* why didn't Enzo think of putting wings on his creation . . . ? Oh well, they say you have to look on the bright side of things. At least we saved on casket costs. The fucking Ferrari was so mangled fathers' body was completely encased inside of it. So we buried him in it!

You wanted to see the look on the priests face. Hah . . . Anyway back to my little problem.

For years we would run guns, cars, booze, cigarettes . . . anything we could get our hands on and sell it through the black market which afforded us a great living. We were rolling fat on petty theft and the protection racket. Oh sorry—*security*. The sex trade—oops, there we go again—*adult entertainment*, well you get the picture. Our family on the north side of Brisbane was doing very well with little risk. But the family on the South side wanted fame. They wanted more fucking fortune then our Emperor Cesare` of Roma. They were into drugs . . . drugs—fucking drugs . . . Soft drugs—hard drugs it didn't matter, as long as it was illegal and drugs. And with the drugs came the feds . . . the feds—the fucking feds . . . All of a sudden we were battling wire taps, surveillance and aerial recon by unmarked fucking helicopters hovering above our key areas of business.

Now I know what you are thinking, wise guys can over come any adversity. And to an extent this is true. But not when the guys who are selling the drugs are also the best customers for it! They were snorting it, injecting it. Fuck me they were living on the shit to the point of sustenance. Instead of a mother putting her child to her breast to feed, she would put a cone in its mouth and hold its nose so the poor fuck would suck in the smoke!

I was forced into taking a major action. I wanted to save my carefree lifestyle of driving, screwing and eating, (not necessarily in that order,) what I wanted, whenever I wanted. Basically a never ending smorgasbord of need, sleaze and planting my seed ha ha ha . . . . Fuck. I wasn't going to bend over and pick up the soap. No one was going to call me a chicken licker. So this is what I did . . . ."

CHAPTER 1

Sweat ran down Violinos face and chest. The party atmosphere at the nightclub bought a perfect end to a perfect night.

The blonde beauty that sat kneeled before his crotch had become a regular at the club yielding their chatter into something more.

He flung his head backward focusing on the ceiling; swirling under the ecstasy of millions of nerve endings accommodating tongue.

Tammin's knowledge of men didn't start with him; he pondered as he moulded his hands around her sweet soft face filling her mouth with seed, slumping upon the satin sheets.

Shocked by the act she pulled her head away at once dry heaving the ejaculation over her chest.

An annoyed grunt left his mouth quaffing.

"Ah fuck me . . . Couldn't you have swallowed it instead of spitting it out? Fuck it's only protein for Christ sakes! If that's what fertilises an egg inside your body, then it's also good enough to swallow. Here get over here and start again—I have a good supply," patting the bed beside him smiling sarcastically.

Tammin got off the bed. Her beautiful round face shone red with fury. She had thought the man she was seeing was a worldly gentleman, genuinely interested in the type of women she was and not just a quick pick-up to see him through the night.

She thought it cool he was named after the violin, a musical instrument that created the most serene of sounds.

The anger on her face spilled into the atmosphere, as she picked up her clothes strewn across the bedroom floor.

He rolled lazily over looking at her, turned on by each frantic movement. His penis grew long and hard like a sky scraper touching wet clouds encouraging her to jump back into bed by rolling back the covers and patting the bed beside him.

But she replied by giving him the bird while displaying a discussed expression on her face.

Stirring with annoyance he growled.

"Get back in this fucking bed now! Don't make me get up and force you in!"

But to no avail. Tammin just kept on dressing, giving as much space between her and him as she possibly could.

She turned her back on him for but a few seconds only to find his hands clutching her frame at the hips with an angry spilling of words attacking her ears.

"I said get back into bed bitch . . . And I meant it: When I speak . . . YOU FUCKING LISTEN!"

Pushing her toward the bedroom wall, he pinned her against it enjoying the panic and fear imprinted on her face and eyes.

Her breath grew rapid and panicked by the rise pushing against her thighs struggling and whimpering to get away but to no avail—his tongue breached her lips while hands pulled at her panties in frantic attacks.

Feeling complete rage toward her negativity, he threw her on the bed, pinning her down upon it entering her.

Shrieks and groans matched probing thrusts intensifying electrical stabs of arousal deflating resistance.

She gave in for fear he would beat her.

In her panic, time slowed right down elongating itself to extended units of measurement. She had never thought she would become a victim of rape but found herself living the very nightmare. Each plunge of arousal hurt her in ways she never thought possible inventing memories of distrust to thoughts of future words of compliment and triggering alarm bells.

But during the whirl wind of what was happening, her legs opened wider to accommodate more of him while her breath rode deeper waves of pleasure rather than fear.

She found she was wanting rather than rejecting until cramping spasms attacked her navel swelling and reddening her lust in readiness for pools of orgasm to gush.

Her thighs rippled sodden by her release under squeezing tightness of Violinos arousal and her lust ached and numbed, burned and shivered—arching her back enticing a male's response.

He collapsed on top of her—resting his head upon her shoulder.

Her hands cradled his back and shoulders romantically. The sheets stuck to her thighs, stuck there by a pool of protein.

A mumble found eco in her ears.

"Fuck baby—that was great. Do you want to become a regular thing?"

His voice was low and contented.

He lifted his head gazing down into her eyes; the scent on his breath matched that of her body.

Pushing him off, taking his hand rubbing her sensitive area, still full and wet from the encounter, she said.

"I won't be your play thing Violino. I want to be treated with some respect and not just get rolled when ever you feel like it! AND WHEN I SAY NO—I MEAN NO!" Yelling—warm breath spilling from her mouth while beads of sweat settled on her face.

He looked at her with a stunned expression. A smirk curled his lips and in an intimidating voice, said. "Fuck baby. If you're going to be like that you can fuck off!" (He got out of bed strolling around to where her panties had been thrown throwing them at her face with a smug expression.) "There—now get out of bed and fuck off."

Tammin got out of bed and dressed walking her panties on, as she left the room, slamming the bedroom door behind her.

FUCKING BITCH he yelled hearing the front door slam momentarily breaking the sequence of satisfaction after the nights' festivities.

He ran his fingers over the satin sheets, lingering at each spot of wetness created with Tammin while falling deeper and deeper into frustration at being along.

He liked communicating with people; it gave him a sense of what was happening around him.

A familiar stirring tickled his groin under playful self adventure, recalling past victories and notches when he was a foot soldier in the business, just starting out. His father had given him a territory to share with another new blood. A 5' 7—sleek—smooth—brunette, long flowing hair and the deepest brown eyes he had ever seen.

Her breasts were well rounded and firm and abdomen flat and shapely with creamy smooth legs.

She was the most beautiful thing he had ever seen since and beyond school—an oasis of lust and hunger.

He could feel the rhythm of her love making, wiggling and swirling on his lap, increasing the straining of his groin.

The smell of her wet body perfumed each lung of air and the mattress tensed and flexed mechanically mimicking her well practiced movements while mumbles and moans caught the air; *Holly!—Holly!*

The sensation of his hand touching the very core of her desire, sent shivers up his spine.

Sweat and heat mixed, making a lubricant to insight their pleasure, opening his eyes to adoringly look at her, to see a path laid in past time but she wasn't there. He was alone lying in his bed. His hand slid up and down the shaft of his penis—its length straining at the memory of her. For once they had shared a night of lust, only for him to awaken and find her gone.

His lips parted in disappointment and ear drums vibrated to the whisper.

Fuck me . . . where are you now Holly . . .

CHAPTER 2

The floors, tables and bars at Lights & Lace sparkled. Violino knew Chris, his manager, would have stayed back to make sure the cleaners did their jobs to the T.

Chris was like a brother—they had gone through school together and along with a few other faces in the area had bonded like family.

The nightclub had a foreign feel when it was empty; quiet and eerie yet comforting.

The nightclub was Violinos favourite business and his favourite place to do business. It was a place where his feet could dance across each of his worlds.

Climbing the three sets of stairs spiralling toward the office, light streaming out of one way glass, he heard muffled laughter, as he opened the door and entered.

"Is this what you bastards do when I'm not here!?" He queried, closing the door behind him.

Cool air swirled around his body from the air conditioning system battling rising outside temperatures. Some comfort came from looking at the plain green walls and blue carpet until focusing on the wall decorations—nude posters and paintings of women holding various positions, resting up against walls and doors and lying on beaches, tightened his throat.

His favourite was a poster of an American modelling a tartan two piece at the beach. Her body was framed by the sea and crashing waves.

His crew were sitting on recliners, watching an adult DVD—cheering, as one of the ladies on screen rolled over onto her left side accepting the attentions of another man.

Focusing on the images, he asked.

There been any calls come in yet watching the girl accept the second man.

"No—not yet," Mario—his consiglieri answered, eyeing the footage.

(A low murmur of conversation over what was being viewed, lingered on the air.)

Violino made his way to the bar sitting in the back corner of the room pouring himself a tall glass of orange juice, spiking it with two aspirins laughing to himself at Mario.

"Oh Mario isn't that the girl who is moving in with you!"

The other men in the office sat waiting for the punch line.

"Yeah, she likes fucking me," Mario responded, with sign language while looking at Violino and the men sitting in the chairs around him.

"Yeah—she will!" Violino responded.

The comment brought deep laughter and snide remarks.

Salvatore—a short round man resembling the Mechlin man asked.

"Did you see 'Omerta; stories of crime' last night? *That bitch dancing on the bar*..."

"E," Mario responded but interrupted by Seppi.

"Legs . . . tits . . . ass and great lips . . . why can't we turn this place into something like that!"

All three of them simultaneously turned their attention to the young Don who was sitting at the cedar table behind them facing the television, gulping the orange juice down before turning grey at the consequences answering.

"Because my mother would fucking kill me if she knew I was running a joint like that!"

Seppi—a tall muscular very athletic man in his early fifty's got out of his recliner making his way to the table with Violino; a grin decorating his square jaw face sharing a verbal offering *our fearless boss is scared of his mother.*

Fuck you Seppi! Violino responded, laughing.

The other men followed Seppi over to the table.

Violino adjusted his comfort clapping his hands together.

The action reminded everyone of his father, after a round of jokes.

"Right first order of business! Who's buying lunch? There's this girl dance group, *Naughty Girls* from Sydney performing at the gentlemen's club down the road and I want to see for myself just how *naughty* they are!"

"This fucking guy, he's the youngest boss in the history of this fucking thing . . . And his main point of interest is pussy."

Mario stated under erupting laughter like a swarming of thunder clouds.

"Youngest boss in history inheriting the most problems;" the tone on Violinos voice brought silence to the participants joining him around the table. "We have a rat in the family," he announced, running an index finger backwards and forwards across the table focusing on its grains, feeling his eyebrows droop.

His father had always said that that was the biggest problem any boss could face in this era of being boss. Too many guys today weren't interested in spending time away in a rotting jail cell somewhere, away from their families and—pussy.

He grew up watching his father age with the worries that came with the job. All of the risk associated with being the head figure in an association like the Mafia. There were many personalities that would have loved the opportunities to run the business taking command of the links at the disposals of the powers residing at the top of the heap.

He was brought back to present tenths when he heard, Salvatore in the background voicing his shared alarm: *WHAT-DER-FUCK-YOU TALKIN' ABOUT!*

Seppi added. "Who is the motherless fuck?"

Violino ran his hand over his chin thoughtfully and then looked around the room at the others.

"The church was raided last night by undercover scum. It was flat luck Deli's crew were running late—or we'd be planting six grave sights now."

Mario shifted in his chair adjusting his weight from the left hand side to the right. "If anything, that reduces the possibilities," he aired with a bright expression.

"Yeah—but Mario, that's no positive fucking thing. They're all higher up the food chain. Shit—for all we know—it would be one of our crew!"

"Fuck. God forbid kid," Salvatore responded.

"What do you want to do?"

The questioning tone on Mario's voice plunged Violino into a momentary silence.

"Let's just set up that meeting."

*   *   *

"Jesus Christ Holly . . . where you been!?" Ronato quivered, watching her get out of the car in the underground car park at Police Headquarters. "I've been worried sick . . . no one has seen you since the raid on that little church in South Brisbane!"

Holly cried. "We didn't find a thing in that place. NOT A THING!" Her face burned bright red glazing her brown eyes. "Do you understand that?! We didn't uncover a thing . . . after all that undercover work. After putting so many men at risk! Nothing! I'm not quitting on this thing. I'm going to get that bastard."

He held his sister tightly in his arms feeling her quiver.

He hadn't seen her so upset and determined, since the day they found out their father had been killed by his closest and most trusted friend. A man he had in turn grown up with and protected with his own life. A man invited into their home, as one of the family. The man they called compare`. The man their father called fratello—Bruno Bruglioni.

The very same man Holly not twelve months earlier on a special visit to Queensland—pointed her service revolver at—in the line of duty and in the line of family honour and shot dead face to face and eye to eye as a part of an ongoing special investigation into organised crime in Australia.

The chance meeting was to tempting for her to let go and the misdirection of evidence was simply brilliant—now she was after his son the new Don—or as she termed *one more prick in the ruff.*

She looked up at her brother, tears run down her bronzed face and her hair rested on her shoulders, as Ronato patted the back of her head.

She loved her brother very much and vowed to protect him forever knowing he felt the same way for her.

They had had it tough since their father was gunned down. They and their mother were passed down from family to family, living off scraps thrown at them.

When their father was alive, they were treated like royalty but when he was gone, considered as no more than slaves and liabilities, although some positives were considered: Holly for her looks and body—men she called uncle would try to have her in the back seats of their cars. Ronato was viewed for his earning potential and their mother, as a maid—to service their every whim and need.

She took a personal vow to get them all and to do it the way it would hurt them the most, through money—jail time and eventually death.

She could feel him kissing her hair relaxing under warm whispers of his voice while his hands gently cradled her head.

Isn't it funny how things work out?

"Yeah . . . . Isn't it funny," she whispered back.

"Come on. Let's get you home. We can talk there," he said calmly, directing her to his car after locking hers.

"Sorry for dragging you through all the mud Ronnie," she said, sincerely.

"Hey what you talking about..?"

She looked into his eyes. "This endless game of chess we're playing . . ."

He walked her to the passenger side and inserted the key in the lock.

"Don't you have a button?" She asked, complacently.

"Batteries flat," he responded, as he lifted the door handle.

"I can do the rest," she said.

"I know, but I'm your brother," he responded placing her into the car before jumping into the other side. "Let's go home, where I can take care of you."

CHAPTER 3

"Fuck this traffic ha?" Seppi waled, waiting for some forward movement to happen—the sun was beating down dumping temperature onto the streets, turning his car into an oven.

"Hey turn the air-conditioning on will ya..!" Mario complained.

But Seppi shook his head and said. "Can't, cylinders empty. Haven't had a chance to get it replaced yet. Oh fuck me it's hot," he joined in, feeling the heat depression.

"What's the hold up, up there..? Jesus Christ!" Violino moaned, struggling with his tie, trying to loosen it before melting away. "What are we—fucking stupid? We're wearing suits in the middle of summer! Everyone, wind down your windows. I'd love to have something left for the opposite sex tonight . . ." He ordered, feeling his crotch to give his words more punch.

"So you've got something more than a pepper corn down there . . . ?" Salvatore aired.

The smile on his face made light of the frustration.

"Yeah last time I saw down there it was half the size on my little finger, wetting your mamma," laughed Mario.

Violino found little funny with the comment and responded *fuck you Mario . . . Fuck all of you.*

Loud laughter broke out between the others.

*   *   *

"Good morning, constables Austrella. What do I hold this pleasure?" Sergeant Sugar asked, showing them into his office.

Sergeant Sugar was a tall man at 6' 3 inches, short blonde hair and bright green eyes with a slender and very fit build. He ran his department like a sub branch of an army unit, not deviating to far from the book.

"Please take a seat," he said, walking around his desk to face them. Creaks sang from his leather chair at the settling of his weight. "What's the meaning of this meeting?"

Ron shifted position upon his seat sensing Holly's tension.

She said. "I want to go undercover to . . ."

But Sergeant Sugar's voice broke in. His eyebrows narrowed, as his fingers fumbled with page files on his desk.

"In what case constable..?"

Her eyes found his staring back. "Violino Bruglioni," she said, in a reserved manner, feeling her cheeks turn bright red, as the Sergeant looked at her.

Contorting sarcasm, he traced her outline in a—who do you think you are manner that mocked her saying. "What makes you think we need your expertise in the Bruglioni matter?"

"Sir . . ."

But he cut her off. "We have very capable, experienced, undercover officers working the Bruglioni case. What could you possibly do to bring a quicker conclusion to that matter?" He slurred dryly.

(Ron could feel Holly's mood swing from apprehension to downright pissed off.)

Well sir if you could afford yourself the time to listen—I and my brother were raised within' the family. We are apart of the family sir!

Oh shit—here we go Ron squeaked, adjusting his posture again.

"Oh shit is right son," Sergeant Sugar replied squinting at the both of them. "What the hell do you mean . . . you are a part of the family!? . . . Are you both admitting to a crime!?"

Holly felt her face burn. "No sir. We are trying to tell you that our father was apart of the Bruglioni crew with the then Don, Bruno Bruglioni, Violino's father. And that we," (she looked at her brother,) "my brother and I went to school, played and grew up with the other children to which you now call today's Mafia hit list. And if you let me finish! The now Don—Violino Bruglioni, was my then boyfriend."

Ron felt himself slide down into his seat subconsciously complaining of a racing heart beat, while his sister spoke—each beat was a confused statement questioning the will to go on, feeling chills run the length of his spine under the gaze of two green dots like kryptonite, burning holes through his head.

"Do you concur with her statement?" Sugar asked, under concentrated appraisal.

"Yes sir. That pretty much covers it. Sir—yes," Ronato coughed, nervously.

Holly could feel the balance of power shift to her favour, as she leaned forward placing her hands on Sugars desk, making herself more comfortable. The air too, took on a sweeter flavour.

Ron to could feel an equilibrium and corrected his posture.

Sergeant Sugar reached for the telephone dialling a number—fumbled with wording for a few seconds before ending the conversation with; *we'll have to have a sit down and re-think this thing.*

As he hung up—he looked across the desk to the two senior constables opposite him with a different more respectful expression.

"You two are off active duty until notified by me," he ordered fumbling with some case files that littered the desk thoughtfully re-arranging some in a neat pile to the left side corner before looking back at them.

"Holly—Ron. You are both dismissed."

*   *   *

"Thank fucking Christ we're here!" Seppi puffed, pulling off the road to his left. The car park to the meeting place was filled with limousines, Alfa Romeo's, Mercedes Benz and Maserati's. Long had the time gone where the mob drove Holden Statesmen and Ford Fairlanes—the new generation preferred showing of the jewels of the mother lands.

"You've pulled quite the crowd skipper," Seppi confirmed, straightening his suit.

"Yeah they all want to get a look at you. You're a celebrity now," Salvatore continued.

"The youngest boss in history . . . Your father would have been proud," Mario added straightening Violinos tie.

"Yeah . . . . I just wish it hadn't happened this soon . . . ." The young Don mumbled.

The memory of his father lying in his custom casket, lingered a chill up his spine. He was sure the Prancing horse wasn't made for that purpose. "Fuck it. Let's go . . . we've got a rat to catch," guiding the men into the entrance.

The dinning room exploded with applause, as Violino entered. Each man seated at the main table stood presenting the new Don with a fitting welcome.

The restaurant was open in its design. Angels danced in a sea of blue—and gold covered the ceiling. Panoramic views of Italy's Adriatic and Mediterranean coast lines covered the walls. The floors were carpeted in deep blue, mirroring Italy's national team colours with the emblem of the province of Lazio tattooed in neat increments into it. The dinning tables were a decoration of black marble hand crafted and imported from Italy which; were dressed with Celeste blue and white table cloths, bowls and plates all shaped in the province of Lazio.

"I was sorry to hear of the death of your father, Don Violino." Capofamiglia Eduardo Cavalieri, the Boss of Queensland said. (Both the men kissed each others left and right cheeks.)

"Thank you compare`. No . . . Don Cavalieri."

Violino corrected himself, placing his closed fist to his chest nodding to show mutual respect, before heading off toward the other tables to greet the other families and their members while receiving condolences and congratulations, pats on the back and jokes before returning to the head table.

"Come sit Violino. Sit boys," the Capofamiglia welcomed.

The greeting settled the heavy feelings on Violinos chest.

All of the important figures of Queensland and some from other parts of Australia; were there to share space with him, instead of passing him over to get to his father.

He found the experience to be quite overwhelming.

He pulled out the seat next to the Capofamiglia who nodded in approval.

"Tell me Violino, what is news?" Don Cavalieri asked, patting his hand.

The heaviness returned straining his chest.

Like any air-to-the-throne, he wanted to arrive bringing good news and prosperity for everyone to share.

But the threat of a rat in the family could bring a halt to everyone's business. Federal investigations and charges confined good men, earners and soldiers to dark and dusty prison interrogation rooms and cells where there was a possibility of more information being leaked, or God forbid, men being flipped. It was a danger no one could live with.

He took a deep breath clutching his hands tightly on the neatly presented table feeling his facial expression change, opening his mouth to answer the question.

"Not good I'm afraid compare`," (leaning forward closer to the Don lowering his voice.) "We have a rat in the family."

Don Cavalieri leaned toward Violino, patting his forearm saying he was appreciative of the confidentiality.

"You did the right thing telling me this way. We must keep this quiet between us or we will never be able to catch the bastard," surveying the room. "Things must run normally without questions or threat. They;" (The Don gestured inconspicuously out to the other families) "must have full confidence and trust in your abilities to handle things. Or you will face first hand; takeover bids," (frowning, as he continued) "and none of us need that."

Eduardo looked at Seppi, Salvatore and Mario gesturing with his eyes for Violino to pay attention. "You have a great team with those men. I can vouch for each of them personally. They took good care of your father and—they will take good care of you. You see, you are already apart of their family. Not a new comer trying to take the reins. You are the son of their brother . . . . To them, you are like a son. I can see it in their eyes. Treat them well and listen to them. And they will guide you well."

The eye contact between the two Dons was strong and meaningful.

"We will find this piece of shit and bring an end to him." Violino preached bringing re-assurance.

"I know you will," Eduardo said, watching waiters carry plates of food and bottles of wine, ordered by the families (while waiting for Violinos family to arrive) to the tables.

"Now, let us enjoy," the Capofamiglia said, with a smile on his old face.

*   *   *

The evening sea breeze was a welcome relief from the days' high temperature.

Ronato massaged the swirling stress out of his forehead while listening to each wave crash onto the beach in concise sequence—his memory taking his thoughts back continuously to the verbal pasting his sister had given sergeant Sugar.

"Here—drink this," Holly said, placing a tray with two long blacks and two glasses of a blue umbrella garnished substance down.

"What's that?"

"That my brother is coffee."

"And this..?"

"That is booze," she said. A cheeky smile decorated her glowing face.

"You need to learn to breathe better bro . . ."

She placed a coffee and drink; in front of him throwing two bags of sugar thoughtfully his way.

He tilted his head *you like throwing sugar around don't you* smirking.

"Sugar is sweet and spice is nice," she said, looking back at him in a fun way.

He looked back at her shaking his head, feeling a familiar ache return.

"If I were you, I'd drink the blue lagoon first. It'll help you settle," she said, sipping her coffee thoughtfully.

The blue cocktail in front of her sparkled, an inviting condensation under the sun's rays.

All went quiet between them, as the surf turned from solid tubes of glare to excited flashes of shine.

The quiet background awoke with laughter and chatter, as vacant chairs and tables filled with evening goers.

"What is our next step?" Ronato asked her. (The background noise grew louder.)

She leaned closer to the table, resting her palms next to the empty blue lagoon glass peering at him; she hadn't seen him this blank before. It was like looking at a good book with no written pages.

"Well—we are both suspended until further notice. So I propose we get really drunk tonight. Recover tomorrow. And the next day, start stalking Violino."

In disbelief, Ronato dropped his head to the surface of the table, mockingly bashing his forehead against it repeatedly before saying *we're gonna get arrested . . .*

Holly laughed and said. "Yeah that too . . ."

CHAPTER 4

Lights & Lace was a rainforest of sweaty bodies—thudding deep base from the sound system reverberated Violino and Seppi's Adams' apples while dollar signs and lust cash-registered between their ears.

They had taken over the nightclub after Reillo Mendex—the founding owner, severed his own head seconds before plunging himself into a barrel of hydrochloric acid.

Violino and the guys transformed the sleepy nightspot into the most happening venue in the City with Salvatore overseeing renovation plans and construction. There was a stage for visiting acts with catwalks protruding out in prongs (elevated staging areas connected to underground change rooms where half naked dancers would spring from in shifts) utilizing the stealth of black painted walls and ceilings which helped accentuate an array of disco balls and lighting affects—while also providing an embrace of sensuality to the added feature of water and disco smoke sprinklers in the ceiling which when triggered, released a fine mist of myrtle and rose scented fog to descend amongst the patrons: An affect which spread myth and legend throughout the city of wet panties floating to the floor from the levels above.

Violino stated, as he and Seppi climbed the staircase to the third level on their way to the office.

"Jesus Christ there's some pussy here tonight!"

Seppi looked around responding *nothing new there.*

They reached the office door swinging it open; Mario and Salvatore were sitting at the table counting money, refreshments of bourbon and ice sat before them on paper coasters.

Money—booze and pussy Mario grizzled. *What a great combination . . .*

Sal smiled and shook his head asking. "What would your wife say if she heard you speak like that?"

Mario looked at him and laughed performing a seductive jiggle on his seat saying *she would probably lie on her back with her legs spread wide begging me to fuck her. Money always got her off. She'll never divorce me—I'm worth too much!* He added smugly.

"A big dick doesn't go astray though ha?" Violino stuttered sarcastically. (Laughter filled the room.) "Donkey schlong . . . isn't what they call you?" He added, focusing on action, through the office window.

"Yeah that's right kid and don't you forget it!" Mario injected, glimpsing Violinos reflection through the window.

Is there anything interesting out there kid? Seppi enquired.

Salvatore asked. "Feeling horny Sep?"

"Yeah," Seppi responded. *"It's that time of the month,"* before Violino mumbled something heading for the door.

The guys stumbled to the window finding a blonde bombshell of 6 feet something wearing a figure hugging gown of black shiny material leaning against the third floor guard rail looking down at the action below.

Salvatore uttered, while feeling himself grow hard *the latest notch* breaking a sporadic conversation about firearms, spurred on by the action between Mario and Sappi *we should erect a trophy cabinet up there somewhere to celebrate his victories.*

And then Mario added, noticing Seppi's excitement. "Maybe we should erect a bust of you," pointing toward the bulge poking out of his trousers. "Put it away Sep, before you injure someone with it!"

That would be cock Sal corrected in the back play, catching Violinos progress.

With every step he took, he felt his groin press against the weave of his trousers. No women had had such an effect on him for some time wanting to take her where she stood, adding to the legend of the nightclub; the rhythmic motions of Latin fantasy.

They made eye contact and she gave him a sarcastic glare, washing her gaze over his body from head to toe.

He placed his hands around her waist and said *in every town and every club, there's one every minute.*

She attempted to squirm away from his touch speaking *who do you think you are?* (The warmth of his closeness found her as words spilled into her ear under the softness of tickling whispers.)

"I'm the guy who's fucking you tonight." (His hands traced the contours of her thighs and backside through the softness of her evening gown, taking her passed the point of patience.)

He placed his lips to hers parting her lips filling her mouth with tongue, shock waves jolted her body before the tantalising suction of his technique swirled desire to her lust.

Come with me he sighed, leading her to the darkest corner of the floor.

"God I'm so horny!" He said to her, lifting the hem of her gown above her knees, pulling at her panties wet from the encounter.

Heavy breath thickened the atmosphere under wondering hands and lustful sighs; she unfastened the bounds of his incarceration, parting her thighs in readiness under tingles and flushes of blood pressure, guiding him in.

With each powerful thud of base they found rhythm. Her moans were like vocals to the music encouraging new heights of performance. Her long legs wrapped around his waist like a monkey grip wedged between him and the wall while her panties garter belted her knee.

She hit fever pitch, her vagina ached satisfaction, frustration and satisfaction while he arrived at the inevitable filling her with a powerful flow of hot sticky wet under the choreography of her own orgasm, spilling down her legs.

She felt a kilogram lighter as he pulled out of her, leaving traces of lust over her inner thighs and navel, reaching for his length masturbating him—still excited and hungry by the encounter.

Still panting she asked. "What's your name?"

Violino he responded with a shortness of breath dropping to his knees—running his hands up her legs beneath the plummeting hemline.

She was so hot he could feel her excitement turn to steam.

He covered her sex with him mouth, clitoris and tongue twirled a dance of swan-song, as a flow of satisfaction flowed from her vagina.

The sweet and salty nectar ran over his palate and down his throat, igniting a second wind of energy, as her panties fell—the rest of the way to her feet.

He stood before her, placing the wet fabric of her panties into his pocket, then lead her to a vacant booth just off to the side of them where he invited her to lay down, tasting each millimetre of her flesh from sex to mouth all in the while pulling at her dress to disrobe the treasures of her chest.

Her world turned to oceans when she felt his penis stretch her sex once more intensifying sensitivities toward movement and heat until again she felt a wet sticky flow gush within' her.

"What's your name?" He panted, kissing her breasts.

"Annalise," she cried, taking his penis in her hands and running her fingers up and down its straining wet shaft.

Violino couldn't believe his luck. Annalise hovered her mouth over his swollen pink mess taking it in one mouthful.

She was a master at her craft, stopping at every throng to tease him a little longer.

She could hear the strain of pleasure in his voice over the bass of the music and played with him, rolling her tongue around and along his manhood, she was going to drive him to the point of insanity—a place he had taken her twice before.

The throbbing of his penis turned into one large throng which begged for escape.

She closed her mouth around him one last time sucking deeply, tilting her head from side to side bringing him to climax.

Gushing lust raced down her throat in warm spurts and his hands held her head between his thighs until the eruption was over.

She sat herself up leaning against him. Her head rested on his well defined shoulders, her taste buds tingled under the tang of his flavour.

His breath was still heavy from skill, their bodies were wet and sticky, tired yet charged.

He said to her. "That was fucking great," straightening his clothing, watching her do the same.

She slid herself around the booth opposite eyeing the show.

Him watching the twisting tumbles of her breasts.

"When can we do this again . . . ?" He asked, watching her exit the booth. (She turned facing him asking for her panties.) He pulled them out of his pocket. The wet fibres alerted his senses to her again.

"Well . . . When can we do this again . . . ?"

His words were halted by her palm raised in the stop position.

"I'm just passing through. It looked like a nice place, so I stopped," she said, trying to snatch her underwear from his grasp.

"You'll be back bitch. They all come back . . ."

His comment, didn't win her friendship and she stepped forward in an aggressive manner slapping his face.

He placed his hand between her thighs rubbing her wet spot saying *you'll be back bitch* . . . then threw her panties over the railing to the dance floor below.

*   *   *

Holly pulled her brother onto the dance floor chanting *chill out bro—this place is great* amidst bodies of all shapes and sizes dancing to the hypnotic sounds bellowing out of the sound system. It was like being in another world holding a feeling of hot Mediterranean nights in outer space.

Lights were firing off a spectrum of colours from the sea of black covering the walls and ceilings—droplets of sweat filled her clothes, rotating her hips to exciting Latin notes asking questions of love through its rhythm section fluttering under memories of a past time where she wanted for nothing and then laughed as she was brought back to Earth by her brother performing the Tarantella to inappropriate music.

"Let's get a table!" He yelled out to her, pointing toward the higher levels.

She nodded and then pointed toward the bar saying *let's get a drink first!*

They reached the bar on the back of short mingling with thirsty night goers where a voice fell upon their ears *what you have?* (*Sex comes alive to the sparkles in your eyes* erupted from the sound system under stabs of body intrusive base.)

Holly looked at her brother and then at the selection arranged on brightly coloured neon shelves and refrigerators; bourbons and whisky, bubbles and amber ales shimmered for choice calling out her order under a volley of surprise, as the barman called out her name.

"Holly—Holly—shit Ronato! It's me Chrissie! Where have you guys been! It's great to see you both again!" He cheered.

Holly cuddled into her brother and cried *holy shit Ronnie it's Chris—remember* throwing her arms around him.

Ronato shook his hand in male bonding, bedazzled by the turn of events and listening as Chris asked *where have you guys been* struggling over the music.

He pointed toward the stairs and then tapped at the face of his wrist watch telling them he would find them on his break—reaching for two glasses filling them with ice and whisky, pushing away Holly's money in the process, pointing toward the staircase again.

With drinks in hand they headed up the stairs to find a table. The music painted seductive thoughts of human touch in their minds as the atmosphere of the dancing crowd sent shivers up and down their spines.

Chris had brought back a flood of memories of growing up, with a circle of friends and family that did everything together finding themselves reminiscing old times, laughing at each old memory as it came flooding back.

Laughing, she kicked Ronato under the table.

"I remember you had a big crush on Chrissie's sister . . . you had many productive dreams over her, as I recall," she chuckled, beaming with love.

"Being back in the old neighbourhood is filling us with what's been missing all these years, do you feel that?" He asked, kicking back with brotherly affection. "And it was more than just wet dreams. Those moans you heard from the tranquillity of your room were us together," exploding in laughter, watching face show a full width of surprise.

She screeched *but mamma and papa!*

Shock painted deeper pictures, while watching Chris approach from behind her brothers' head, wearing a huge smile and carrying another round of drinks.

"Papa knew but didn't say anything, proud father and all that. But mamma had no idea we were together like that but knew we liked each other."

"Did Chris know?" She asked, directing a smile over his shoulder.

"No—it would have made things between us different."

"What? This place is different?" Chris asked, placing the drinks onto the table while scooting Holly over a place so to sit down.

"Yeah—maybe cosmetically but not deep down, you know . . . the sum of the faces may change but the place is still the same . . . where have you guys been!?" He asked, the excitement at seeing them was too much for him to overcome leaning over into Holly giving her a big warm squeeze. "God I've missed you guys!"

Holly and Ronato looked at each other for a moment and in a micro second—the feelings they shared for their friend in the past, came flooding back like a tsunami flooding their hearts.

"After dad died, everything changed for us. Mamma just wanted to take us away and start again . . ."

"And it was good for us to get away . . ." Holly stated, cutting her brother off.

"Well. Just so you know . . . Your friends really missed you when you left." Chris's tone deepened. "It would have been nice to say goodbye . . . You know?"

He touched their hearts.

"It would have been wasted breath because we're back. So it's more like hello," Ronato said, his broad smile lifted Chris's spirits.

"Yes! Hello—ciao`!" Chris cheered, lifting his glass to salute their re-union asking facially *are you here to stay.*

The Austrella siblings nodded yes charging their glassed to his.

Chris elaborated. "Well then, toast to old friends becoming new . . ."

And the Holly broadened *to old friends re-acquainting.*

In agreement, they touched glasses again saying *to; reacquainting* drinking to the toast.

Chris asked in jovial tones.

"So what do we do for a living?"

"Well . . . . Ron here is in security and I model fashion."

"A super model..!" Chris broke in, gasping each syllable.

"No just a modest fashion model. There are some things I won't do," her hand actions and vocal tone stirred laughter between them.

"Security Ron . . . ?" Chris's eyebrows rose to sit high on his forehead. The expression painted on his face was of complete interest and admiration.

"It's not something I can talk allot about. We have to sign confidentiality agreements with each new assignment . . ."

Chris nodded. "That's cool man . . . It's obviously something you enjoy..?"

"Yes I do . . ." Ron answered confidently.

The easy going nature of talk mirrored the atmosphere.

"What about you Chris? How long have you been working here!?" Holly asked, trying to carry her voice over the loud music tapping her fingers on the table to a song with the lyrics—*I Surrender.*

"Since it opened about a year ago . . ." Chris answered, lifting his drink from the table taking a mouth full. "But I've been working for the Bruglioni family since I left school . . . . Bar work and the books. I actually manage this place for them. I'm the only person they trust to do it properly. Honestly..! They do the hiring and firing and I do the rest," he confided, following the actions of Holly and Ron, taking a sip of their drinks.

Breaking a pinch of silence resting over the booth, Ronato asked. "What is everyone else doing?"

The silence part and parcel of the years they had been apart.

"Well, Sarah—is working for a computer programming company in Sydney. Pauli's a self employed brickie. Lisa is an architect currently on holiday in Europe, lucky thing."

"Yeah I'll say." Holly interrupted.

Chris continued. "Donna is in the police force," (laughter broke through the sentence.) "Dimity made it as an investment banker. As you would remember, it's all she had ever wanted to be. Give that one a couple of years and she'll buy out Brisbane, lot-stock and barrel" (a smile lit Ronato's face.) "And Violino runs organised crime in—Brisbane!" Chris's laughter forced his head against the padded vinyl behind him.

Holly and Ronato, sitting facing each other, swirled alcohol across their palates, giving each other a thoughtful stare.

Chris corrected his posture swirling his finger around the cold glass holding his drink.

"You know Holly; he was devastated when you left." (Holly took particular notice of the way Chris held his glass.) "It was like a part of him had died."

Holly and Ron looked at each other again thoughtfully. There had been allot of water under the bridge when it came to the subject of her and Violino, as the mood around the table changed momentarily from excited to sorrowful.

"You think allot of Violino don't you?"

"Yes Ron I do." Chris swirled his glass focusing somewhere in time.

"Like you guys, he is apart of the family," a wry grin lit his face.

Holly slapped his shoulder and Ron kicked him from under the table, washing away the hint of sorrow.

"Hey!! Come on lets dance ha!? I love this song!"

An electrically charged synthesizer score filled the inside space of the nightclub . . . *in ballare—si si si in ballare* chilled their bodies with life, as they hit the dance floor.

*   *   *

". . . We have to find a new place for storage."

"Why? They didn't find anything!" Mario responded, sending a funny face Seppi's way.

Seppi questioned sceptically. "You gotta ask yourself—hey—why there . . . you know what I mean: How many fucking churches are there in Brisbane?"

Mario and Salvatore looked at each other.

"Salvatore . . . what the fuck you doing..?" Seppi questioned him, exaggerating his Italian accent.

Sal contorted his face squeezing his shoulders *cosa?*

"That fucking tapping..! It's making me lose count . . ." Seppi grumbled, frustrated at the level of speculation and multitasking.

He grabbed all of the notes resting in their valued bundles on the table and started re-sorting them in their denominations, while counting the amount.

"Fuck me! You bastards are always fucking around when there's work to be done!"

A loud thud added to the vibration of the base, as the office door closed behind Violino.

Seppi shook his head in disgust as he re-bundled the currency on the table and started counting from scratch again.

A whimsical frown coloured Mario's hand gestures, as he stated.

"What's your fucking problem? You *should be mellow for Christ sakes.* You just got laid!"

Seppi and Sal smiled at Mario and Violino, anticipating what was to follow.

"How do you know I got laid?"

Mario flashed palms, as he pursed his lips in a pout. "Fuck me kid . . . I felt the Earth move under my feet and then experienced hot flushes!"

Salvatore laughed out loud. "You must have really fucked her," he said, alive with colour. "The Earth moved five points of the rictus scale!"

"Fuck you Sal. You to Mario..!"

"Don't know if I would survive it kid." Mario's answer ran the gauntlet with *he's come again* playing from the sound system.

CHAPTER 5

Holly ambled through the apartment like an old lady and quivered *oh . . . who held the speaker next to my ear last night* entering the kitchen, her voice was croaky and face pale from the intensity of the partying the night before.

Ronato replied, presenting her with a strong long black *you did Holly—you did* concealing a giggle. "But what a time we had hey!"

She laughed shaking her aching head.

"You didn't want to go out. I had to drag you!" She lectured under the pounding of sledge hammers, dropping her head into her hands and grumbling a pitiful moan.

"And I thank you dear sister—and I thank you from the bottom of my heart," he sang, as he stood over the stove stirring something.

"What's your agenda for the day dear sister—dear sister, breakfast?"

"Is that what you're doing over there?" She asked, covering her nose trying not to breath in the aromas. (Her stomach muscles were tying nots.) "That smells disgusting! What is it?!"

"Well dear sister . . . we have a good old fashioned cook up. Fried eggs, baked beans which are cooked in the juices of Pancetta and cheese thrown in for good measure, toast and grilled tomato the way you like it with garlic and basil," looking at her rubbing his stomach the way their mother used to with them.

"Sounds great," she replied, holding her stomach and dropping her head to the breakfast bar.

"Do you mind if I pass?" She grovelled pleadingly under a green tinge.

"No—but you should give it a go. It will help level up the balances between nutrition and toxins," he suggested, imitating a scale with his hands.

"It will probably make me throw up!"

"Yeah—well that to . . . maybe?"

"It sounds great dear brother—dear brother but I think I'll settle for a water and cold press." (Her pale and sweaty face matched equally with her croaky voice.)

"Go on then, go back to bed and I'll check in on you later," he said, taking pity at the sight he saw over his shoulder, as he stirred the breakfast.

A smile curled his lips at the sight of her struggling up from the breakfast bar stool on her way out of the kitchen clad in butterfly print pyjamas holding her head and stomach.

*　　*　　*

"Seppi—when the fuck; are you going to get your air-conditioning fixed?" Violino yelled from the passenger side seat.

Seppi and Mario covered their ears waiting for the traffic lights to change on the corner of George and Adelaide Streets, Brisbane City.

"Christ it must be a hundred degrees in here!"

"It's only 38 outside." Mario aired viscously. (Violino swivelled upon his seat glaring into the back, while Mario tightened his shoulder muscles sarcastically at the look the young Don fired at him.)

And then Violino asked soberly. "Where are we?"

"The City," Seppi responded, keeping track of traffic, tested by the young Dons constant questions. "Fucking kids today . . . we there yet—we there yet?!"

Violino frowned at him saying. "That's why bodies are found in dumpsters."

Seppi returned the look along with a response. "That's how arses get tanned! You're not too big to put over my knee kid . . ."

"I'm fucking boss of this family!"

Seppi rebutted *I'm you compare!*

Acknowledging the statement, Violino reached across the divide between front seats and patted his shoulder.

Mario told them both to shut the fuck up.

And then smirking, the young Don *how much longer?*

The light turned green prompting movement and Mario answered the pending smugness.

Over the Victoria Bridge, along the main road, turn—turn and we're there.

Violino laughed watching Mario's facial expressions before airing.

"Mario, have you ever thought about becoming a GPS unit? You would work wonders in the traffic. Turn—turn and you're there!"

"Yeah..," Seppi choked. "We would make a fucking fortune!" (His laughter filled the cabin.)

Violino hopped back in suggesting. "Yeah, we could clone him and mass produce Mario's to take over the world! We could call them Brothers Mario!"

"Yeah kid . . . you're real fucking funny. You should be a comedian." Mario stuttered, breaking his words into sarcasm *you and the fucking stronzo driving . . . as funny as the colour of that water.*

Seppi and Violino laughed.

They looked down at the Brisbane River while traversing the Victoria Bridge.

Seppi shared his thoughts. "They really fucked it. The beaurocrats: Dredging it. They say once it was as blue as the sky. But now—*fuck . . .*"

The state of the river took the attention away from Seppi's shaking head.

Mario added. "Yeah and now the colour of the sky matches' the river. Fucking criminals the lot of them—they are steadily killing all of us."

Seppi looked across at Violino, as Mario finished his rant. A confused look painted his face.

"Who the fuck you talking about..?"

Mario shook his head at Seppi's aloofness. The index finger and thumb of his hand clasped together tightly shaking his completing the manoeuvre.

Violino stuttered Mario's meaning. "E` ah, the fucking powers that be; Sep. Jesus Christ..!"

"He ain't gonna help you kid. He ain't gonna help anyone." Seppi spluttered; patting his shoulder, as the church came to sight.

"We're here!" Mario gasped, pointing to the building between the two of them, as he leaned forward.

The car travelled down Vulture Street.

"Pull up in Christie Lane," he suggested, unclipping the seat belt.

Violino did the same.

Both men opened their car doors, as Seppi pulled up and stepped out.

"This is a real fucking mess, ha skip?"

"I don't see why." Violino offered, watching Seppi close his car door and straighten his suit.

"Why is it a problem? They raided the place and found absolutely fucking nothing," (smug expressions painted his and Mario's faces, as he continued down his slalom of theories.) "They didn't find anything where confession is held. They didn't find anything in and around the pews. They didn't find anything where the bread is kept and they didn't find anything where the wine is kept. So where is the problem?

We will sort alternative routes to the downstairs chamber to deflect the attention our visitations have caused and continue on, business as usual."

The three men stopped just inside the doorway. Its high ceilings and white archway walls gave way to the baking heat of the suns rays.

Four rows of pews covered the main rooms' floor space with walkways between each.

Mario testified. "I love coming to this place. All of the stained glass, marble and—well everything about the place. How it was built and who built it," (a wave of nostalgia coloured his eyes before spitting.) "*Fucking people today* . . . Before the Italian people came, they had putzie. We give them cuisine, language, architecture, decimal currency, democracy, fashion and the art of making love and these canguri walk around as if they gave the gift of these treasures to us, *bunch of ungrateful fucks*," brushing the air at the height of his forehead.

"It's ok Mario we know the truth, that's all that matters," the young Don sprouted, softly patting his ruffled feathers.

Their eye contact re-enforced the bond only migrants understood living in a country given so much, yet shared so little.

Seppi looked around at the stained glass windows suggesting; seemingly distant. "It always surprises me how much cooler it is in a church. Outside is scorching, yet in here, it's like ten degrees cooler!" (Violino and Mario watched, as Seppi buttoned up his suit.) "Why is it always so much cooler in a church? It's not like they run air-conditioning with all of the doors and windows open all day," finishing his observation, as they watched the pastor approach from his room, up the stairs behind the altar.

"It my son is because this is the house of the Lord Jesus Christ." Father Glynn Options said, relaying a smile on his face to match those of his guests.

Violino, Mario and Seppi offered their hands in-kind greeting.

"Good morning Padre`; come stai?" Mario greeted nodding, taking hold of the fathers hand in a friendly handshake.

"Va bene, very good thank you my son and yourselves? How are you all, well I hope?" The Father counter greeted, shaking each of their hands in turn.

His big smile made them feel welcome.

"I for one, will feel allot better when I know more about this police raid." Violino mumbled, as to not attract too much attention to the conversation, as parishioners of worship passed them to exit and enter the building.

"Let us go somewhere more private where we can talk," the Padre said, placing a hand behind Violinos back to guide him along the walkway leading to his private room, after surveying the surroundings.

Seppi and Mario followed closely behind, looking up at the ceiling and stained glass windows depicting holy stories and miracles.

"I am afraid I can not tell you much about what happened the other night. I was here clearing up after a late mass about to close the doors when a number of police officers came into the church wanting to have a look around. Of course I said that they could—that the doors were always open for those who cared to visit the house of Christ when a; women came in with two or three other gentlemen dressed in suits. She had a warrant which she let me peruse before asking me all sorts of questions about my daily activities and interests; and if I could hurry along and get the parish books for her and her colleagues to have a look at. I said of course she could look at what ever she wanted to. And as I turned to go and get the books, there were uniformed police officers in the confession booths; tapping on the walls and seats. Others were flicking through the Bibles, page by page, as if to find something that wasn't supposed to be there.

I have to tell you Violino, my heart skipped a couple of beats when they entered this room. If not for the respect they showed for the wall hanging of our founder, our little secret might have been found out."

The four men nodded in full recognition and thanks.

They reached the room and entered. The father motioned for them to sit down in the sky blue leather lounge chair, put to rest behind a white marble coffee table.

"Please make yourselves comfortable. Would you like a drink?"

The men shook their heads in agreement.

No thank you. Please continue . . .

"Of course, where was I? Oh of course. Then I gave them the financial book of creditors and debtors. They had a look at it and then left," (the Father turned his back on the gentlemen, as to pour himself a cup of coffee.)

"Did they make any remark of what it was they were looking for?" Mario asked. (His question re-averted the fathers' eye contact from the coffee percolator back to his guests.)

"No Mario, they did not ask about the drugs and weapons being stored in the chamber downstairs. Nor did they seem to realise there is such a storage asset on this premises."

Mario pondered. "Begs an interesting question though doesn't it? What made them suspect this place has anything to do with us?"

The comment brought full focus from the four men—their eye contact bounced off one another, as quiet overran the echoes of noise filling the room.

Our donations Seppi speculated.

"All off the books," Father Options replied without delay.

Violino returned his head to his hands in full concentration of the problem.

And then looked up, asking. "Mario—what do you think?"

"We find another way into this place, as to not alert attention to our visitations. Move the drugs to another location, fuck me . . . oh excuse me padre," he apologized nervously, looking up at the ceiling of the church, "give them back to Brescio to handle, they're his drugs—move the weapons, and open this place up as a gambling room. We could have our poker nights here . . ."

Violinos fingers traced each stubble follicle and curve of his chin.

"That's not a bad idea. We could run nights in the main room where any monies and proceeds go to charities—while downstairs, our wales play for the bank?"

"It's an idea." Mario repeated, catching the look on the fathers face, before explaining. "That way it will take away some of the negative investigations placed at your church."

Violino entered into Mario's suggestion. "Who is going to dispute fund raising for charities?"

"There will be suspicion on the side of the police. And they will probably investigate it. But—this is a church . . . . We will give it a go . . . See what happens."

The young Dons face went from an optimistic look, back to a questioning frown, as he laid his eyes squarely on the priest.

"A girl . . . woman you said. What did she look like? Mario—have we had a woman asking questions about us in a leading role before?"

"I don't recall a woman or any mentions of a woman asking questions from any of the captains . . . ? I'll look into it." Mario said, placing his hands by his side.

Seppi now standing; straightened his suit, as he mirrored the others preparing to leave.

"As always Padre`—it's been a pleasure." Violino said leaving the private room ushering his guardians in the direction of the car. "We will be in contact about the changes. Don't worry, everything will be o.k."

Mario and Seppi turned, watching Violino himself, shake the hand of the pontiff. Smiles painted both of their faces under the fathers' return of pleasantries.

"As long as everything works out fine for both parties," the father said.

"It will." Violino nodded. "It will."

The men left the building. The outside temperature felt hotter than when they entered a short time before.

Each of the men felt the need to unbutton their suit coats and loosen their ties.

"What now skip?" Seppi asked, as they hopped in.

The car pulled away from the curb.

"Let's go back to Lights & Lace and wait for Sal to arrive. We have a lot of things to plan." Violino sighed.

His hand brushed sweat away from his eyes, as his fingers rested on the door panel, pushing the button to open the window.

CHAPTER 6

"Come on—come on—where are you leading us *now*," Senior Constable Station moaned, as he followed Salvatore through a maze of Brisbane streets.

He and his long time partner Senior Constable Best had been given the assignment of watching Salvatore around the clock to best gain an intimate knowledge of his day to day dealings; to document and photograph each place of business and premises he visited and document and photograph every person he spoke to so that a special team of investigators and researchers could study and identify the important sights and people for closer scrutiny utilizing electronic surveillance by penetrating domestic properties for the purpose of undercover operations.

Up until a couple of months previously 'the family' had been a closed bracket of business and dealings. An organisation which made money and payed taxes like any other, but for the locked doors and shady personalities that governed their every movement.

It was widely regarded, 'the family' ran two business systems—one where there was an up front cataloguing and accounting system for the authorities to see when questioned. These were their legitimate businesses: Lights & Lace; an inner city nightclub.

The Calabrese Club—a cabaret style premises friendly to families and—La Societa Sportiva, a large piece of land in the Northern suburb of Kedron catering to; junior sport.

Then there were the late night meetings with other known shadowy figures running families outside of Brisbane. The coming and going of transport vehicles of all makes and models, delivering items of all descriptions to shipping ports and airports for sale and storage and the disappearances of personalities whom were known collaborators. And people who were placed under great hardships because of business interests. These were the dealings Senior Constables Station and Best were to uncover so the local officers working undercover and federal police could ascertain and make arrests.

Senior Constable Best asked, watching the attitude of Salvatore's car weave in and out of backstreets.

"Do you think he's made us?"

"No I don't think so," Senior Constable Station replied, slowing the car down to pull into a vacant driveway, as to not raise suspicion.

Salvatore's car made a right turn into Parkview Street, from Heussler Tce.

"Where are we?" Senior Constable Best asked, looking out of every window trying to get his bearings.

"We're in Milton. The Rugby League Stadium is over the back of us a little way," Station replied, putting the car into reverse to continue their surveillance after watching their target make a left hand turn.

"He's stopped on Castlemaine Street; must be that Italian restaurant?" He quaffed, signalling oncoming traffic of his intentions to perform a right hand turn.

"I'll do the block and park facing his car on the opposite side of the street," he suggested.

"Is it lunch time?" Best asked—answering the question, as both men looked down to their watches. "Ha! 11:35am."

Station lifted a small recorder to his mouth recording verbally the progress on their stakeout.

11:36am, Sal stepped into Pizzeria la Famiglia on Castlemaine Street, Milton. Subject piece is in restaurant.

*   *   *

"Sal . . . you never come alone anymore . . ." Vito—the owner of the restaurant said, stepping out from the kitchen to welcome his cousin with a hug.

"Fuck me Vito, these pricks have been following me for weeks," Sal scoffed, opening his arms in greeting. "I think these pricks think I'm a delinquento."

Both men laughed.

He pointed Vito to a table.

Vito's smile was as large as his hefty frame.

"Is it safe to talk here?"

Vito laughed. "Who the fuck you talkin' to . . . ?"

The jovial response prompted Sal to sit down.

"We've had people looking into things, have you?" A serious mood drifted in cooling the air surrounding them.

"Yeah, we've had badges in here asking all sorts of questions. But mainly—are you open on weekends?" His laughed bringing Sal no comfort.

"Vito . . . we've been getting reports by everyone that certain parts of the legal fraternity have been asking questions—snooping around—taking photographs . . . I've had these same two pricks up my ass for weeks taking fucking photos of places and people I talk to." (While Salvatore was talking, Vito, with his hand—order a round of coffee.)

"Sal—you worry to fucking much. This is a legitimate fucking business. We don't practice here. That's what council property is for."

The coffee arrived, brought to the table by Vito's daughter, an attractive brunette with a knock out body.

He slapped her on the backside affectionately and said *grazia amore`*.

Sal greeted her and then opened a packet of sugar, pouring its granules into the Espresso.

"Violino wants us to take action. We've heard there's this chick been asking questions with other unrecognised figures," he took a sip. "Those two pricks out there are going to be lambs for the slaughter."

Vito's face lit up mirroring that of his cousins.

When—he blurted.

"When you're ready: Just like that time with the ships. We'll leave their bodies at the dump. Deli drives their car to the gentlemen's club on Nudgee road and leaves it there. We come back here. When the questions come . . . Hector borrowed the car . . ."

Vito jumped in halfway through the mission brief. "Yeah but wait Sal. Not everything works out the same, no?"

"What happens happens. We'll figure it out when we get to it," Sal said.

Both men laughed, taking sips of their coffees while their eyes were ablaze with anticipation and excitement.

"This will be the first time since . . ."

"Yeah Vit'—and what a time we had hey?"

Vito stood up and pointed a finger to the back of the premises in the direction he was headed.

Salvatore stayed where he sat turning his head around to look out the window where the police were sitting. He knew they were probably photographing the business and making notes of its location.

For Salvatore it was like old times being in the pizzeria. Vito's father had owned it before Vito took it over spending allot of his youth in there helping with cooking the sources and serving the customers.

He looked up to his Zio—and Vito was more like a brother than a cousin.

The silence of the dinning room broke with Vito's voice, diverting his eyes to the kitchen doorway, as he re-entered the room with Deli and two other younger men of which, one was spilling his guts about something.

"Arr yeah yeah yeah; fuck me, this can wait 'till later. Right now we have a special job for you to do . . . Deli! You are going to fucking love this . . ." Vito confided.

Salvatore's face shone of the admiration and respect he had for Deli, as Deli looked his way in full exchange of feelings.

But Salvatore was less than happy with the other two subjects. He had doubts rising up inside his gut at their competency and a grimace erased his colour.

"Deli..! That's right my friend—we have work to do," his voice slid to a stop.

Deli shook his hand after arriving at the table sitting down facing the plate glass window spotting the unmarked car immediately.

"Sal . . . This here is Hector and arr—what the fuck is your name..? Arr fuckin' Thomas! Boys; this is the pride of my youth. My cousin Salvatore," Vito chimed.

The expression of Salvatore's face didn't change and his gut feeling got worse.

"Sal . . . It's ok. I can vouch for these two mother fuckers. They might not look like much but they will do the job we want them too."

Hector and Thomas swivelled chairs around sitting in them back-to-front looking over at Sal—nodding their heads.

"Who the fuck; are these two cocksuckers Vit!" The expression on Sal's face matched his voice. "These two fucks couldn't tug the taffy of Daffy."

Hector and Thomas looked at each other with bewilderment while Vito and Deli tried defusing the situation by raising their open hands at him in a calming motion.

"Deli: See those two fucks sitting in the car out there?" (Deli's face brightened.) "They're it." Sal smiled pointing his fingers at the car mimicking a pistol.

"Hector;" Vito entered in. "You two will follow us out to the tip, taking the alternative entrance. You will use the scoped pieces and blow their fucking heads off," he slapped his hand on the table, making sure he had their full attention. "Hit them in the head."

Salvatore interrupted, as he pushed to stamp authority over the two boys.

"Stay there and wait for Deli to come. Do you understand?"

"Yes. We shoot those two in the head at the alternative entrance at the rubbish dump. Then wait for Deli to come over to us." Thomas answered.

"Thank fucking Christ . . ." Salvatore's sarcasm prompted Hector to shake his head.

Salvatore and Deli pointed at him in a stabbing motion.

Vito slapped Hector on the shoulder grabbing his attention back. "Now fuck off and get ready. We leave in ten minutes."

*   *   *

"Well—fuck me, it's about fucking time." Senior Constable Best said, as he holstered his drink in the drinks holder pulling the seat belt while winding up the window, all in one well practised movement.

"Yeah—it's only been one hour!" Senior Constable Station chimed in, firing the engine. "Get the camera ready—there are others."

"Who are these guy's, ever seen them before?"

Station shook his head answering no, while looking over his shoulder for on-coming traffic.

The officers watched their target slide passed them before Station surveyed over his shoulder once more—performing a u-turn *do you see him* he asked.

"No—yeah..! He's about four cars ahead," Best chided, (settling his head as close to the window as possible, so as to not give himself a concussion over every bump.) "He's turning right here into—arr—Caxton Street."

"Cafe` in the city sin-yor-re`..?"

Sarcasm spilled over the brim of Stations words. "Fucking Italians, they think they own everything."

"Yeah, ha—he's turning left onto the inner city bypass."

Station followed suit, both men eyeing off the pristine Alfa Romeo 156, Salvatore and his friends were riding in. Its neat lines and curls and the way she danced over the tarmac, deepened their dislike for the crime entity.

"Fucking Italians and their style," flew from Bests' mouth.

"I agree mate. Fuck them all."

Best pointed a finger in the direction the Alfa was turning. "Left into Horase Street . . ."

Station aired, ". . . arr fucker . . . what's up?"

"The prick has moved into the right hand lane. He's turning right onto Lutwyche road."

Station indicated his intention to merge right but was blocked out.

"Let me in fuck ya's. Best! Give us ya badge."

Reaching into his pocket, Best retrieved the badge handing it over.

"Thanks mate; NOW FUCKING LET ME IN..," he yelled, flashing the badge to the next car running in a long line drawing level from behind. "Thank you kind sir/madam . . . fucking' drivers today. No respect."

The light turned green and each in turn—turned right.

"Where in the hell are you taking us?" (Passing in thought he added.) "Best is there anything in our notes that can help us identify where this prick is taking us?"

Officer Best reached for the laptop on the back seat.

"Give us two seconds . . ." He responded, looking at Station.

He tapped in a search of the route they were travelling but nothing came back. Then he typed in Lutwyche road and two paragraphs filled the screen.

"Christ it's hard to read. The road is so bloody bumpy," he grunted; frustration was evident by the sound of his voice. "No. No clue," he said looking at the Alfa. "He's turning left into Newmarket road."

Station signalled his intentions and again was plunged into difficulty manoeuvring the car into a slow left bank.

Best clutched the hand rest on the dashboard, brassing himself for a collision with the car beside them while reaching into his pocket with the other hand searching for his badge—but it wasn't there.

Remembering Station had asked for it earlier, he looked down at the centre console finding it in the coin tray picking it up with his left and slamming it against the window with some force.

Station looked across in surprise to see Best holding the badge firmly against the passenger side window with his left hand, and with his right, pointing for the driver to pull over, as their car was moving on a collision course toward it.

Too both of their relief the car pulled over giving them room to merge into the left hand lane.

Right—now—make the bloody turn he ordered under the influence of stress, pointing toward Newmarket road.

"I don't know." Station spat. "I don't know where he's taking us."

The Alfa two cars in front, coasted at an easy going pace dancing over the bumps with effortless ease.

"Turn the radio on will ya. We might as well get settled in."

Listening, watching and searching for you filled the inside cabin.

A sigh left the lips of both the men.

"He's turning left again Station into Enoggera road."

Station followed stealthily behind.

"Strange he's in this area no?" Station pondered in bad Italian, mocking the Alfa's movements in question. "What could possibly be out here for them?"

The expression of his face reflected back to him from the windscreen.

Best shook his head. "Maybe he's looking to acquire property?"

"Yeah maybe, but you would think he would buy closer to civilisation? Not all the way out here in farmer Joe country."

Enoggera road turned into Samford road, leaving the two Senior Constables quiet in a state of question and confusion. Best had asked if they should call in their where-a-bouts but Station thought it a waist of time, wanting to concentrate more on where they were being taken.

It made no sense to him why this wise guy would be interested in the country side of Brisbane. It wasn't because he was growing illegal substances, because the families brought from outside suppliers. Or did they? Maybe, he thought to himself, there was something to Violinos crew that hadn't been uncovered yet. Maybe like the church, there was something that didn't add up, something that they hadn't uncovered or maybe there was something they had found in association with the church, but as yet, were unable to come up with the appropriate answers to the hidden problems.

He's turning right melded with his own thoughts and what he saw behind the wheel as—*I see you, I hear you and I just can't get you out of my mind* finished the track playing on the radio, giving punch to the predicament.

"IT'S THE FUCKING DUMP! WHAT THE FUCK IS HE DOING AT THE DUMP?"'

The surprise of Stations voice swirled in Bests ears.

"Call it in?"

"No—let's wait to see what they do."

*　　*　　*

The Waist Transfer Station was occupied as Sal reversed the Alfa toward rubbish.

"How long do you think they will be?" Deli asked, peering out through the front windscreen at their official shadow.

"How long do you think it will take Hector and the other one to reach their position?" Salvatore asked, looking at Vito in the passenger side seat.

"Not long, they can drive through the public park and park on the other side of that hill," he responded, pointing to a grassy mound just off to the side of them. "There's enough grass to mask their position. So nobody will see them."

Then Deli chimed. "The angles are right. From up there, they shouldn't miss."

Salvatore felt re-assurance. He knew in these matters, Deli had years of experience under his belt. He had never once been accused or convicted in his chosen field as a hit man.

"What do you think those guys will do?" Vito asked openly. "The glare of the windscreen might make it difficult to judge the shot angles."

"No it's ok Vito." Salvatore re-assured them. "They will get out of the car. They have to, this is a dump. Why pull into one if you aren't going to get out and throw things away? There's no council insignia on the doors . . . They won't want to create suspicion."

The two cars pulled away from their parked positions on their way out of the Transfer Station, leaving Salvatore's Alfa and that of the unmarked police car.

Salvatore pointed his finger at the unmarked car scoffing. "Here we go."

"They're getting out." Vito advised, happy to see things go to plan.

And then they both heard Deli say, "Wait for it . . ."

*   *   *

Hector and Thomas pulled into the public park lucky to find it quiet heading for the mound with rifles in hand, dropping to their knees when they reached the summit, crawling military style the rest of the way to their positions. They unzipped the rifle cases simultaneously pulling out the rifles before taking aim at the two officers.

Hector said. "Remember, three-two-one and pull the trigger so there is only one pop. I have front left."

"Ok. I have the other guy." Thomas followed, firming the rifle butt against his shoulder in readiness.

"Ok Thomas, on my mark. We have good shot; Three-two-one."

They depressed the triggers in unison, letting lose the sound of a single pop. Their targeting eyes bulged through the scopes resting atop the rifles and like a synchronised diving event, the hollow pointed shells entered through the skulls of the officers, dropping them to the ground.

"Front right, between the eyes and down!" Hector called, his voice tinged with excitement.

"Front left, through the right eye and down." Thomas joined in quite calmly, resting his rifle upon the ground off his shoulder to wait for Deli's arrival.

*   *   *

At the pop of the rifles, Salvatore and Vito headed on foot for the undercover police car—the two officers had dropped without response by its sides while Deli, headed off to link up with Hector and Thomas, a .05 calibre pistol concealed in his trouser belt rested at the base of his spine, above his shirt.

"Pretty fucking good shooting..!" Salvatore admitted with adrenalin spiking his voice. "To fucking bad we have to waist them," an indifferent expression painted his face, as he completed the comment.

"Si to fucking bad they've got big mouths. These boys have a bigger circulation than the fucking news papers!" Vito declared, as they approached the unmarked car and two bodies. "Plenty of fish in the sea . . . Or should I say fodder," a laugh escaped his mouth, as he playfully slapped Salvatore's shoulder looking down at the two bodies from where they were standing at the front of the car.

"Got a knife on ya?"

A fucking knife..? Salvatore questioned, lifting his shoulders and pinching the air with thumb and index fingers in front of his stomach *where the fuck Vit?*

"Arr don't worry. There'd have to be something around here." Vito expressed looking around on the ground.

"Come on Vito! We haven't got all fucking day." Salvatore grumbled, grabbing Best from under the armpits and dragging him to the back of the car.

Vito did the same with Station, stopping halfway to push the boot release button on the dashboard.

Salvatore lifted Bests body into the boot while Vito dragged Stations' to the back bumper dropping the corpse with a thud.

"Come and give me a hand," Sal nagged under shortness of breath. (Vito lifted a hand and laughed.) "Very funny, help me lift his legs in."

Vito took control of Stations legs, as Salvatore yanked from shirt buttons, throwing the corpse into the boot.

"Right," Salvatore clapped his hands together *that's that. What the fuck do you want a knife for!*

Vito laughed as he watched his cousin search the bodies for valuables and other paraphernalia.

"Decapitation . . ."

"Why in the hell do you want to do that?!" He questioned under Vito's heavy laughter. (Another two cars entered the Transfer Waist Station.)

Vito replied under eyeing glimpses of the new arrivals. "It's a tradition that stretches back to Egyptian, Arabic and European times and means as they screwed they got screwed!" (Both men began laughing.)

"Who in the hell taught you . . ." Sal trailed off raising both his hands, as he stood upright beside his cousin, "never fucking mind. I don't want to know. It's your fucking secret," patting Vito on the shoulder, placing his other hand at the moulded edge of the boot. "Come on, let's go."

Salvatore shut the boot.

"Let's go help Deli," he said, as two additional pops rang out.

The other visitors seemingly unaware and uncaring of the gun shots, left as quickly as they arrived.

Vito and Salvatore jumped into the unmarked car, starting the engine driving over to park beside the Alfa, before climbing the hill to assist Deli in disposing of the additional bodies.

"They didn't suspect a fucking thing." Deli said with a smile on his face. (Two blood soaked bodies lay rippled on the ground.) "If you guys keep watch, I'll load them into Hectors truck," he said, pointing down the hill.

Salvatore opened the long grass looking at the four-wheel-drive parked below. "No Deli, we'll take them down to the squad car and throw them into the back with the others. They are quite small. They'll fit."

Vito kept watch, as Salvatore and Deli carried the bodies to the car tossing them in.

"What we gonna do with them boss?" Deli asked, closing the boot shut.

Thinking, Salvatore looked down to the ground.

Vito laughed placing his hand on his cousins' shoulder. "We'll decapitate them!"

Deli started laughing, bending over, as his stomach muscles contracted to the effort. "The treatment..?"

"Fuck. Not you to Deli . . ." Salvatore stuttered, looking over at him with a disbelieving look on his face.

Deli and Vito choked with laughter.

"Ok. Do what you want to with the bodies. The car must be parked outside of a gentlemen's club somewhere. Doesn't matter where . . . We only want to paint a picture.

Deli—you take the four-wheeler. Vito you take this thing and I'll drive my car. I'll follow you guy's, cause you know where we're going. We take care of the bodies and dump them first."

Vito laughed, hopping up and down like a child just granted $20.00 for good behaviour and then asked. "Deli got a knife on you?"

"Not on me, but I know Hector used to carry a set of secateurs in the truck."

Both men smiled cheekily.

Vito turned on his heal, running up and over the summit down toward the truck looking first at the tray before opening the door flicking back the seat to look behind it.

"Found them!" He called like a child.

Salvatore bemused by the childlike antics of both men, watched Vito run back over the summit of the hill, as if he was seventeen again.

"You got gloves Deli?"

Deli frowned at him *now you're pushing it.*

"There're tissues in the cop car." Salvatore advised, heading toward the car opening the door.

He leaned over the drivers' seat to the centre console, where he saw the tissues while throwing bodies into the boot through the back windscreen.

"You open the boot and start at their trousers and I'll bring the tissues," he called out to them.

They opened the boot and both Deli and Vito started taking down their trousers and jeans.

Vito took the secateurs in his hand and started cutting Station and Bests genitalia and then Hector and Thomas's.

Deli laughed uncontrollably; as Salvatore entered the scene watching what was happening.

Vito took the box of tissues from his cousin, swabbing up the blood slowly spilling out of the lifeless bodies.

"Deli; turn them over and I'll plug them!"

Deli did as he was told watching as Vito plug each mans anus.

"Sal . . . Where we gonna dump them?" He asked, finishing off the process, before re-dressing them.

He closed the boot shut wiping the blood from his hands and the smudges from the boot lid.

"Where would an Arab dump them?" Salvatore's question brought silence to the trio.

"Well fuck me Sal. You don't want to get the Arabs off side. We are talking about cops here, not fucking big mouths like those to facia brutti`." Vito summated, looking at the other two with a concerned look on his face. "I for one don't want to be going to the matrasses with the Arabs over these pricks. Let's dump them in Mount Glorious with each leaning into the other, back to front." (Deli laughed.) "Park the cars in Nudgee and let destiny run its course."

Salvatore nodded in complete ore of Vito's thinking.

"Ok," he said, clapping his hands together. "Let's do it."

Sal headed toward the Alfa, then turned around at the sound of Vito's voice.

"Sal..! You take off. I'll take Deli over to the truck. We'll catch up on the road."

Salvatore waved his agreement starting again for his car. Opened the door, jumped in, started the engine and pulled away.

*   *   *

"Where the fuck is Salvatore?" Seppi asked looking at Mario and Violino, as they sat in the office of the night-club. "He should have been back fucking ages ago . . ." (Anguish coloured his face.) "I'm worried about the fucking prick. He's like my fucking brother . . ."

Violino got up from his chair, walking over toward the bar to refill his glass with whisky and ice saying *he had allot to do today Sep. It's still early. He's doing his job properly.* (The sound of ice hitting the base of the glass rang amongst them.)

"He'll get here soon." Mario entered in. "You know Sal . . . He's thorough."

Mario copied Violino, pouring whisky in both glasses, as Violino added ice.

"Sep you want one?" Mario asked, raising a serving in salute.

"What do you say; we all get laid tonight—which reminds me . . . Is Chris here yet?" Violinos question answered itself right away with a knock on the office door.

He yelled for the person to enter and Chris strode into the office with a bag of money ready to be checked so he could go and float the cash registers at the bars.

"One thing about you kid. You're always on time," Mario celebrated, throwing a bright smile his way.

"Hey kid, you want a drink?" Seppi asked, pointing toward the bar.

Violino placed the bag of money on the table, opening it bottom side up so the contents fell upon the wood grain like snow falling from puffy clouds. Notes of all denominations decorated his eyes, as he and Mario busied themselves with sorting and counting the amounts.

"Ok. Chris, tonight I want you to only pick the best looking bitches. No fat and ugly ones, they can fuck off elsewhere," the young Don snorted, standing next to him, as he patted him on the shoulder. A smile sat on his lips.

"So—only woman like Holly?" Chris answered.

Violino nodded. "Yes . . . Only woman like Holly . . . HOLLY! What made you think of her?"

His face was a puzzle of different colours.

"Well she is very beautiful."

"How the fuck; do you know she's very beautiful? For all we know, she's turned into a fucking barking mutt," he laughed, taking a sip of his drink.

"That's one thing she is not!" Chris replied, laughing back at him.

Seppi and Mario weighed into Violinos look of confusion.

Violino opened his mouth firing a Gatlin gun of words out.

"How the fuck; do you know what she looks like?"

"She was here the other night—her and Ronato . . ."

The young Don grabbed his shoulder, his questioning gaze took Chris by surprise.

"They were here in Lights & Lace?!"

Seppi and Mario looked at each other with surprise.

"Yes. I was at the bar the other night, helping the staff with the rush when Holly and Ronato came up to the bar and ordered drinks. I couldn't believe it was them at first but sure enough, it was. I was so happy . . . They were my best friends in the world," trailing off, looking at Violino—his face resembled that of a chandelier exhibiting a bright glow and complete spectrum of colours. "I thought you knew she was back!?" He asked more than said.

Violino pushed him gently aside making his way to the plate glass window standing at its foot looking out into the large empty spaces that would quickly fill with people, as soon as Chris opened the doors for business.

He remember back a few short years when he and Holly were in each others arms frolicking around together, happy with the successes they shared and the future they were building, when she and her family went away without any word after the death of her father.

His world ceased to exist as his heart broke. A world which spun like a never ending merry-go-round, searching for her replacement but never satisfied with the different models.

"Do you know where she is staying?" He asked.

A look of determination forged a distant path.

"No. She left no address but she did say they would be in touch," lowering his gaze from Violinos, placing the empty glass on the table, scooping up the money for the cash registers placing the bundles back into the bag.

Violino made his way to Chris. His voice wobbled under the surprise of the news.

"If you see her tonight, I want to know about it. Come and get me. Ok?"

"Ok." Chris replied, tying off the bag, nodding respect to Seppi and Mario, thanking them for the drink, turning and walking out of the office, closing the door behind him.

*   *   *

"Any word from Station and Best..?" Sergeant Sugar asked the young office girl, as he was exiting the office at the end of his shift.

"No. No one has heard from them in awhile," her tone was flat and unconcerned.

He placed a hand on his chin, looking down to the floor. His eyebrows imitated a V-shape, the lines on his forehead disappeared.

"Even so, it's not like them to not call in," lifting his chin meeting her eyes, ". . . as you think, probably nothing."

His body started to turn away from her in the direction of the office exit. "We'll know more tomorrow," he walked out bidding her a goodnight.

CHAPTER 7

Holly woke full of life, it had been a few days since her hangover and she had recovered fully.

She could hear her brother in the kitchen singing along to a song playing on the radio while wrestling pots and pans. An aroma of her favourite wafted on the air; grilled tomatoes with basil, fried eggs and pancetta and her tummy growled at the anticipation.

She nestled herself back into the bed covers, running her hands along the warm satin sheets. Each ripple and crease highlighted a sensuality of fibres bending her legs running her ankles along the base of the bed.

A shudder of recognition shook her as she yearned for company to break the loneliness.

The clock radio came to life with a catchy tune—under pinning a phrase captured by the mob, like a statement of déjà vu, sending shivers from the top of her head to the tips of her toes. Her thoughts returned to their past knowing her path was to cross with that life again, mixing good times and bad times to bring about the serving of papers or what she termed in her own mind—a divorce in the reality of the mob.

Ronato's voice brought her back along with a gentle knock upon her door.

Holly—are you hungry? He called.

Her thoughts fell to her mother who used to wake her the same way for school; reaching for the robe resting over the bed side chair.

* * *

The Mediterranean cafe` was busy as Violino, Mario and Seppi tucked into a big breakfast. They were famished after the nightclub filled to capacity with a surprise visit from a well known American touring rock band. Female bodies decorated the floor space which enticed a tsunami of horny men to try their luck but none were as successful as Violino and Seppi.

The cafe` held a special interest for Violino; he had a thing for the owners' daughter who worked there during the morning shifts. He'd been trying to snare her for some time, turned on by the chase and constant refusals.

He called out to her as she glided by but for no response, smirking as his eyes rested on the ballet of her hips which prompted the normal hard on.

But the rush was short lived, for he knew if he touched her, her father would cut his balls off. The thought brought him crushing back to Earth with a thud—but his arrogance shone through as she turned and their eyes met, wetting his lips with his tongue.

The atmosphere of the trio was easy going until Salvatore walked in.

Seppi stood up nearly spilling espresso over himself and the others saying.

"Oh Sal..! Where the fuck you been? I've been worried fucking sick!"

Salvatore responded, pouting in a blasé`` manner. "It was late when we dumped the parts," (tilting his head, changing his wording at the last second.) "So I went home."

Violino Questioned. "Where did you take them?"

"Glorious day isn't it," he responded.

A sparkling expression covered their faces.

And Seppi sang gleefully *the ants eat well tonight!*

Shoving Seppi over a place to sit down, Sal ordered a coffee from Clara, waving his hand.

"What we doing today?" He asked.

"We are going home to bed, we've only just shut the shop," Violino advised, fighting back a yawn.

Salvatore eyed him with greater detail before laughing under suggestion. "You've been fucking all night . . . that's why you look so . . . fucked."

Mario laughed along with him.

"You'd better believe he got laid last night . . . four of em! Says a lot for Italian stamina . . . They see him coming and fall onto their backs with their legs spread in the air panting for it." Seppi said, performing sign language. "Me, I settled for the blow job of the century, sprawling upon the table. I had to check my dick to make sure there was still skin attached."

Salvatore raised his palms above the table saying *enough enough—too much information!*

The guys' spurted into laughter around him catching the attention of other patrons.

Salvatore thanked Clara as she delivered his coffee understanding Violinos attraction to her, the closeness and scent of her body and then a glimpse of her cleavage ignited its own race to the starters' blocks chuckling, as Violino probed.

"What you doing later baby?" (The question provoked a snide look from her closely followed by a stabbing comment.)

Nothing with you . . .

The young Don groaned seductively saying, eyeing her sumptuous legs. "Want to come home with me? You won't be disappointed."

Blushing annoyance she responded. "Where are you from?" (Smiling sarcastically . . .)

"Caserta," his answer delivered an instant reaction to her lips.

"Arr—the south of Italia . . . I'm from the north, a city called Cremona where the term man comes from," (turning facing the counter, flicking her hair over her shoulder in a seductive manner gliding off.)

Oh! Seppi and Salvatore swooned, laughing openly at the show.

Mario leaned in toward the young Don stating under an ore of his brightly lit face.

"Violino . . . check you balls—are they still there?"

*   *   *

Sergeant Sugar arrived to find the station in a state of pandemonium—Officers and office staff scuttled about with documents in hand, filing and processing each.

He dropped at his desk overwhelmed by a stack of sticky notes littering it, the telephone was glowing red from all connecting lines and the computer continuously sang *you've got mail.*

Starting to filter through the sticky notes, he found they all touched on officers Best and Stations' disappearance with names and numbers asking for contact.

A tap at the door stole his attention and he looked up to see his secretary standing in the doorway wearing a concerned look.

"Sir," she spoke. "Station and Best haven't reported in yet."

"Have we located last known position?" He asked.

And she responded. "Yes sir, a pizza place at Milton."

There was another tap on the door, this time a senior officer entered dismissing the secretary, making his way over to an empty chair opposite Sugars' desk.

"I gather you know?" Detective Sergeant Doodle enquired, meshing his fingers together.

Sugars facial expression reciprocated understanding.

"These men haven't communicated with us for over twenty-one hours. There is no sign of them at . . ." (The Det. Sgt opened a police issue note pad he pulled from his top inside blazer pocket reading from its face page.) "Pizzeria la Famiglia on Castlemaine Street, Milton . . ." (He closed the pad placing it on the desk.) "We then tried to track the car using satellite Intel," taking a deep breath, releasing the volume of his lungs slowly *but no signal registered which means* . . .

Sugar broke into the conversation.

"The tracker has been disabled," a grimace shaped his face.

"Talk to me," Doodle said, eyeing him tilting his head to one side. "How well do you know these men?"

Sugar leaned into the desk making eye contact.

"These men have immaculate service records. Not a smudge on them."

Doodle rested against the chair, diverting his gaze to the floor. "The search for the car is in full swing. We are also looking for cell phone signals. They must have taken a laptop to enter their data but as of yet, no case studies have been found," (he shifted his weight to the left side of the chair, resting his left arm atop its armrest.) "You have two other personnel at your disposal?" He questioned, showing the palms of his right hand *pardon the pun.*

Sugar too adjusted his seated position. "We have had fall into our laps; two lower ranked officers with useful knowledge," suggesting under meaningful eye contact.

Doodle nodded. "Well promote them. Brief them and send them out . . . up stairs wants to turn the heat up."

*   *   *

"What are your plans today?" Ronato asked.

Holly sat down on the four-seater lounge chair after a shower; her hair was still damp, as she brushed it.

"I thought I would do some—off the cuff investigation. You know, see how many of the old guard are still on the books and where they are now," she paused—a look of excited wonder covered her face, "but you know what would be truly glorious!?"

Ronato sank into the single seater holding his comfort. His rosy coloured cheeks turned off grey, as she burned a hole of enthusiasm into his aura.

"*No; what?*"

"If we could find Donna; remember what Chris said?! She's a police officer! I bet she knows some things."

"But how would we find her without running a search through the department? It's not as if we can go to Chris and say—*hey Chris, where's Donna? We need to speak with her urgently!*"

Holly's earlier excitement dowsed—her brothers' reply flickered; her flame dimming the light.

The hair brush built static electricity, cracking through each stroke, as she voiced an idea.

"The only way we could start doing the ground work is if we re-entered the family fold," (her eyes fixed on her brothers.) "Yes . . . we go visit Violino . . . everyone and let them know we are back and that we would like to re-attach our bonds," she suggested, placing the brush on the coffee table.

"Yes but that will be difficult for you because Violino was red hot for you."

(Her face flushed.) "He will probably want to get back with you. Will you be able to handle that? I know you liked him too—until the death our father," studying his sister.

She looked away from his searching stare.

He remembered the hurt, finding out about Bruno's betrayal to their family. But he could only imagine the pain Holly felt when she found out the man she loved so much, was the son of the murderer of their father.

"Holly . . . you know if you slip up, he will kill you. If we start doing this . . . it will be very dangerous."

"What else can we do Ronnie!?" She pleaded.

He squeezed his shoulders together, mimicking a question.

"If they are ever going to be taken down, someone has to take a risk. And yes, it will be bloody dangerous, but as you said—that family killed our father and not just them but the rest of those cowards too. I want to get them all for the way they treated us and OUR MOTHER!"

Ronato looked at her under a blaze of hot rage. He got out of his chair and dropped down next to her, their eye contact was unrelenting while tears rolled down both their cheeks.

"So we do it? We bring them down?" (His hands rested gently on her shoulders.) Strength floated his voice.

Holly nodded. "Yes we do it," sinking her head into his shoulder croaking *an eye for an eye.*

*   *   *

Sergeant Sugar sat waiting to commence his meeting with police high command and the Federal agents assigned to the Bruglioni family matter—the heat was being turned up in the pursuit of taking the family into custody to answer for their crimes.

He still had no account of senior constables Station and Best as sweat started running down his face and stress built inside his chest.

Sergeant Sugar the Chief Inspectors' secretary called. "You are invited to go in now."

Her pleasant smile and beaming face ran a chill of false security up his spine.

He smiled back at her, as he got out of his seat making his way to the office entrance.

Seated around the back of the Chief Inspectors' desk facing a window that looked out across the Brisbane River were a lady and gentleman wearing give-away Federal Police type dress, sitting to the left side and on the right, an empty seat sat next to a familiar face owned by his superior officer of the Bureau of Criminal Investigations.

"Please take a seat," the Chief Inspector directed him.

The Chief Inspector opened a manila folder file perusing pages, turning them as he went before re-organising them in a neat stack—resting snugly in his leather chair.

"Right then Sergeant Sugar" (the Chiefs' eyes held his) "the raid on the church was unsuccessful."

"Yes sir." Sugar replied, looking around at the other participants.

"This officer you placed in charge of the raid—a Senior Constable Holly . . . arr..," (the Chief leaned forward flicking the pages of the document looking for her name) "Senior Constable Holly . . . Austrella. You gave her the raid after only a couple of months under your charge . . ." (The tone of his voice rose under preparation of his query.) "Why? Normally an officer who has been working on similar cases over a period of two or so years gets such an assignment. Why use her?"

Sugar adjusted his seated position. The other faces in the room turned their attentions to him, taking in his features.

"Well sir, when she had arrived via transfer to my department, she showed great interest in this type of investigation. I checked her credentials and made contact through telephone to her superior officer in Melbourne, where she transferred from and he had nothing but praise for her skills and abilities concerning this form of investigation.

He highlighted her interest in investigations concerning organised crime.

After my discussions with him I decided she was the best way to go after sharing my thoughts and concerns with the direction of the matter with my superior. *This distinguished gentle sitting next to me to my right.*" (Sugars head turned first to his right in recognition of his superior officer and then back to face the front taking in the features of the Chief inspectors—their eyes fully communicated each other's presence.) "She was a fresh face sir."

"And nothing was found?" The Chief Inspector re-iterated.

"No sir. That's correct, nothing was found." Sugar replied.

"Now we understand after further surveillance of the Bruglioni crime family. Two of your officers working the case have gone missing?"

Sugar could feel his rib cage wrap his upper torso tightly, crushing his ability to breathe.

"Yes sir, Senior Constables Station and Best from my charge of Criminal Investigations. That's correct sir." (His attention was taken away by the Chief briefly, as he looked around at his surroundings, taking all other movements and facial expressions in.) "They have been investigating the movements of one of Mr. Bruglioni's most trusted men, a Mr. Salvatore Umbrotti for six weeks. They were to document each place he visited—and the people he had contact with; either on his own or with Mr. Bruglioni and the other leading figures in association to the family."

"How long has it been since last contact sergeant?" The Chief Inspector asked.

"It will have been over 24 hour's sir."

The Chief, while resting in his chair, mirrored the heavy air of expectation filling the office on his face.

Sugar continued along the Best and Station, situation. "We have tracked the cars every movement using satellite surveillance. The unit held position at two locations before the tracking system failed."

"Where were those locations?" The Chief asked.

The sound of rustling paper broke the heaviness of the air, as Sergeant Sugar answered the question. (The flicker of shine from a pen dancing across paper caught his peripheral vision and his words painted the answer.)

"Pizzeria la Famiglia; Castlemaine Street, Milton . . . And the Transfer Waist Station on Samford Road, Enoggera."

The Chief Inspector averted his glance over to the right side of the table, as did Sergeant Sugar and his commanding officer, Inspector Weltshire.

"What's your take on this, Detective Senior Constable Fiorella?"

The body sitting next to Sergeant Sugar opened a file that rested on her lap crossing her legs to give it a better viewing angle.

"The Bruglioni family have close business links with the leader of the Queensland crime syndicate, the Cavalieri family that reside on the Gold Coast. We believe, if we apply enough pressure on Mr. Violino Bruglioni, the house of cards in Queensland will come crashing down sanctioning hefty sentences in custody and as we discussed before; to make this happen, we would like to work closer with Sergeant Sugar and the officers under his charge; to plant surveillance camera's; tracking systems and listening devises to all or any people and premises associated with this crime family."

Donna leaned across the small gap between her chair and Sugar's extending her hand in introduction.

"I'm sorry Sergeant Sugar, we haven't been formerly introduced. This is my partner Detective Senior Constable Eric Nadalle; and I am Detective Senior Constable Donna Fiorella."

The Chief Inspector apologised for not giving them an introduction while Sugar shook hands with Donna and Eric. The stress filling his chest subsided, as his breath returned freely.

"What area's of the family are you most interested in pursuing?"

Sugar relaxed his posture feeling more at ease to ask questions.

"All of them," Eric replied. "We have a secret weapon in this room with us."

(Sugar looked around the office for the suitcase or container he had missed while earlier entering.) "Donna here—grew up with Violino Bruglioni. She knows most of the figures inside his family which is handy because from time to time when we need to—Donna dresses in police uniform and visits the family haunts," a knowledgeable smile filled his face.

"The family still regard me as a friend. Well . . . more family really . . . apart of them despite my occupation. It is how we've gotten allot of our information."

"Well Donna . . ." Sugar chimed in. "It seems you are going to have a re-union with one of your own," his eyes lit taking in the features of the lady that sat to his left. (A jigsaw puzzle of confusion drew her face) and he continued. "Holly Austrella" (he looked at the chief) "and her brother Ronato are about to go fully undercover in this matter."

Donna's face lit, as her full facial regard met Sugar's.

"Holly and I were like sisters at school! It didn't occur to me when the Chief Inspector said her name, it was my Holly. But you mentioned Ronnie..!

My God . . . She was Violinos girlfriend! It nearly broke his heart when she went away after the death of their father. You see her father was Violinos fathers head body guard and family hammer."

She shook her head in disbelief.

"Well then. Let's make this union happen, effective immediately," the Chief Inspector ordered.

Confidence sang from his voice, as he stood up offering his hand to each person in the office.

"To the beginning of the end," he said, shaking each male hand on his way to Donna.

"To the beginning of the end," she replied.

*　*　*

"Tammin . . . what the fuck are you doing here?!" Violino spat with an annoyed twang.

Her perfect posture slouched at his scornful question and tested look.

A feeling of butterflies filled her stomach, as she questioned herself over visiting him tilting her head to one side dropping her chin to her chest before directing her eyes up to meet his—giving him a coy look.

He continued at her *I'm fucking tied . . . I've been up all night . . . And I'm not in the mood for shit.*

"I got lonely," she said, standing her ground as he approached her.

"So you like guys who treat you like shit?" He questioned, running a hand down the fabric of her clothing from navel to panty line.

A sigh escaped her lips under a stirring of red flushes looking toward the neighbourhood, watching cars; flash passed leaving her dizzy with the thought strangers were watching them.

Violino she squealed, dropping her hand to that of his, tracing the opening of her vagina in full view of passers by.

He positioned his firming frame in front of her, directing her through the open Italian archway to his front door.

"There, no one can see us now," he spat.

His voice was low and lusty.

Violino . . . Not here she squealed, trying to push him away.

Her breath rate climbed rapidly, as she tried to squeeze her legs together stopping his fingers from entering her.

"People might hear us," she gasped, with fear.

He withdrew his hands from between her wet legs steering her to the brick wall adjacent to the front door—the cool damp wall sent chills through her, as hot and cold flushes affected her breath.

He leaned into her face to face, attacking the bounds of her clothing stirring under the ach of his groin pinning her hands to the wall, kissing her neck wildly and chest wetly under a full exploration of her body.

The hemline of her skirt rose and fell with frustrated irregularity under searching raids for fasteners until impatience drew the ruling straw and her clothing gave way to violent grasping.

Her breasts like pendulums into the morning air fell; prey to his powerful hands and hungry mouth, sucking and biting them.

Her nipples swelled at the touch of his tongue dancing atop their mounds, as *Holly* circulated in warm breaths between the breaches of her breasts.

Who the fuck is HOLLY..! Fired; angrily from her mouth as her panties gave way to his power.

In one movement he unbound his manhood rubbing and teasing her lust, his voice became stuttered and uneven and he struggled; *Holly . . . part your thighs baby*—hot breath spilling into her ear.

She opened her legs instantly feeling the power of his thrust lift her off the ground. A muffled sigh escaped her lips.

He grabbed and pulled, sucked and bit at her body in violent actions while each deep penetrating thrust of his hips tenderized her flesh against the brickwork until the inevitable shower of sperm filled her lust.

Streams of hot protein trickled beyond the entrance of her sex showering her inner thighs—a gaping hole settled after pull out.

Violino who is Holly she demanded; her face was awash with colour and sweat.

He grunted, pulling his trousers up, rummaging through his pockets in search of house keys, the smell of sweat hung heavily over his body.

"Fuck me . . . it's always the same thing with you!" (He opened the door.) "You should be grateful I had the energy to see to you, for fuck sakes . . . I had four before you—you stupid bitch."

Entering the apartment he turned around and said under observation. *Fuck me you look a mess . . . go home and clean yourself up* slamming the door behind him.

*   *   *

"We'll have to make a list of who was at the top of the tree and work our way down. What do you think?" Ronato queried, opening a police issue note pad.

The sea breeze flapped at the paper turning blank pages one after the other, as his fingers searched his top pocket looking for a pen. "Holly?" He looked at her beautiful face, looking out to sea.

The breeze blew silken hair back beyond her fringe.

His mind fell upon to true stories of children in the U.S, who's father had led a wanna-be wise guy lifestyle, making their families pay for his stupidity for the rest of their lives.

The similarities of their situation to that of those children, was scary. The major difference in his eyes being, his father was a good man: a soldier fighting for his family.

"I like it here," she said, her fingers tracing hair strands away from her eye.

Her and her brother had jumped into his car to drive to the academy of policing in the south of Brisbane to start their investigations and stir the saucepan in search of Donna but instead found themselves in the opposite direction, parked at a beach side cafe` in Redcliffe partly sunned under a beach umbrella and sipping espresso and soda water while nibbling on Savoiardi biscuits, listening to the waves' crash on the beach and the excited screams of children at play.

"Holly: The order of investigation?" Ronato asked once more.

Her smiling eyes took in his handsome features wondering what type of girl he'd marry and what her nieces and nephews would look like.

"Holly . . . *The list* . . ."

Ronato's voice serenaded her ears again, as his hand crossed the table and rested on hers.

"The; what..?" She replied hazily, as her spirit rejoined her body bordering the point of reality.

"The list Holly: The list!" (Both their bodies jolted in fright, as a sudden alarm bellowed from the centre of the table.)

"What the hell is that?" She squealed—croaky from the fright.

"It's my mobile," he replied, recovering from the unexpected bellow of its ring.

"Well who is it?" She asked, watching him lift the cell phone looking at its display.

"It's the office," his reply brought interest and silence from her, as she watched him answer.

His ever changing facial expressions drew her closer to the table—tilting her head to one side returning a look of interest, as he lifted his right hand, showing his palm.

She meshed her hands together on the table top waiting patiently for his response.

"Yes sir, first thing in the morning. Ok sir. Bye-bye."

Again, Ron pressed the index button, placing the cell phone upon the table—his face was awash with curiosity, as he searched for the gaze of his sister.

"Who was that?" Holly broke the silence.

"Sergeant Sugar wants to see us both in his office first thing in the morning."

Her eyes narrowed at the news.

"We will be on official assignment," he said, reaching for his espresso to take a sip.

"Do you feel like something stronger?" She asked.

He nodded yes in response.

"The licensed cafe around the corner from home..?" She suggested.

He nodded for yes again.

"Well then brother let's go."

They both got up from the table and left.

CHAPTER 8

Music cut through the air-conditioned room at quarter volume—Violino entered the premises through the rear entrance witnessing bar staff ready tills and booze supplies igniting a chill of pride to reverberate the length of his body in recognition of the accomplishments they had achieved in such a short time.

A comb of fingers ran through his hair like a harvester changing scenery changing his pattern of thought and in nothing more than a heartbeat he realised everything they had built could be lost if certain members under the omerta continued to procure the dirty business reddening a realization to his face.

He considered prison life and a life without freedom and then queried the loyalty of the three men who stood by him, not as brothers but more as father figures—deleting any suspicion away.

Yet a sick feeling of change stirred his stomach turning his reddened face off grey as he made his way up the staircase toward the office.

Seppi announced excitedly under a minstrel show of movements. "Shit here he is . . . the prodigal son!"

Yeah the prodigal son he mumbled, waving greetings around the room.

Alerted to his dark mood, Mario asked. "What's up kid?"

Seppi and Salvatore joined the moment watching the young Dons movements toward the bar.

What is it dad said he asked, turning to face Mario. (Stress lines ran the width of his forehead,) as the glistening sparkle from Mario's scotch and ice reflected to the tables surface *to be boss today.*

He took a sip from the stress relief; condensation dripped from the glass and fell upon the wood grain surface while the liquor went to work on his tightness.

"Mario," he said resolutely. *I think it's time we made some changes* and then clarified the statement.

"And if we do it right, we will lead Queensland over the finish line," taking a long mindful sip of the drink, cleansing the quality of colour upon his face while Seppi and Salvatore closed the circle.

"Guys," he said looking at each, "we have Brescio and his people selling drugs openly; police, following our every movement; associates being arrested and flipped because they don't want the penal experience—*fuck me, like they didn't know the risks.*" (Sombre looks addressed the other faces.) "As dad said, to be boss today," mumbling his fathers' memory.

"He's right." Mario chimed.

His support was much appreciated.

"Sal, there're four bodies in Mt: Glorious that testify to this.

Seppi, you've been wanting the easier life for years."

Seppi nodded agreement, as all eyes ran back to the young Don.

"Guys we're not retiring as such because there are still our legitimate businesses to run. This place is making us a fortune: The sporting ground and the Calabrese club and our holdings in Parklands are all leaping ahead but if from time to time certain entities make trouble for our enterprises, there is always the option of communion and conformation, or we can frame them," (a sly grin shaped his lips and his eyes blazed a palate of colours, highlighting a multiplication of meanings.) "We will be off the books," his tone dropped factually, as his hands danced a wave of manoeuvres atop the cedar table.

"How do we make this happen?" Salvatore asked, pushing his empty glass along the table—averting his eyes to Violinos.

Violino winked at him confidently and responded.

"Two people, Donna and Brescio."

Seppi and Salvatore shook their heads in disbelief.

Mario sided with the young Don.

A disappointed yet satisfied look covered his face saying. "Well, allot of things have been coming back," tilting his head with conviction.

Violino opened his hands to Seppi and Sal. "We are going to use her guys. USE HER. Not kill her. It's Brescio we're going to clip."

A large grin coloured his face.

"But he's Cavalieri's' tool . . . !" Salvatore spoke with concern.

"Sal . . . Brescio and his representatives use more substance then they sell. Their fucking brains are mush. We'll make it look like they were planning take over bids against each other and us. Fucking shame, two of the bitches working for him, I wouldn't mind fucking . . ." (Laughter rang out around the table.)

"Mm Loretta . . ." Seppi slurped, rubbing his balls openly.

Getting to his feet, Violino made his way to the bar replenishing his drink—offering when he got there to replenish the others as well.

"We keep going as normal. We take great care in identifying our tails and plan each confirmation—communion and framing as we go. We spill the names of the Cavalieri family to the authorities, removing any future threat taking over the control of Queensland running things our way.

We run this fucking thing like a legitimate business. The people under us do the underhanded stuff and then if need be—we get rid of them."

"Sounds like an accomplished plan . . ." Seppi verbally applauded while rubbing his hands together.

Salvatore and Mario nodded their heads in unison, as wide smiles covered their faces.

Violino raised his replenished glass watching the others raise theirs in agreement.

*   *   *

"Good morning Constables," Sergeant Sugar greeted closing the officer door behind him.

"Good morning sir," Holly and Ronato replied, re-sorting comfort in their seats.

"When a superior officer enters the room in other military type branches, what happens?" Sugar pressed hard edged. "The sub-ordinance in the room stand to attention," answering the question in a school teacher manner.

Holly and Ronato stood up each focusing on different points of the opposite office window.

Sugar walked around his desk sitting down, shuffling folders and papers.

"You may sit."

A cold chill ran the length of Ronato's spine, as they followed Sugars order wondering what they were in for after the last meeting.

Sugar cleared his throat, opened a thick manila folder full of documents and flicked through its pages one after the other, as he re-familiarized himself with past events.

"Officers Austrella," he lifted his head looking across the desk at the two sub-ordinates. "You are here to add to the discussion we had the other day. The Bruglioni family matter. The officers working this case, and myself," (he said matter of factually), "feel that you would both be of great asset in the apprehension of these crime figures," his face cracked allowing himself to smile. "And we have a surprise for you." (The sick feeling returned to Ronato's stomach). "You will be working very closely with an old friend of yours."

Holly's eyebrows rose as she waited for Sugar to identify the old friend.

Sugar looked down at the open page that lay at rest on his desk. "Donna Fiorella?" He lifted his chin surveying Holly and her features. "You grew up together!"

Her face lit like a hundred Christmas's glowing as one.

And Ronato held a smile a mile wide on his face.

It was like the ends of their circles were meeting again.

"You will be working very closely together undercover." Sugar advised reclining in his chair meshing his fingers to his chest while deeply watching each response.

His thoughts travelled to a future time where he wondered if their faces would still reflect the light of day or decompose in boxes in dampness and darkness.

He drew his body forward. "This won't be a trip down memory lane. You will be working undercover against the Mafia. It could get you both killed!"

Concern ran down his face like a cascading waterfall feeding a cemetery reclining in his chair.

"There's not too much more I can tell you now. But have your plans open for this evening—we are all having dinner here," he looked down at his wrist watch. "I will expect to see you both at 7:30pm. Donna and her associate," (returning to the manila folder) "Eric Nadalle, will be here where we'll be going over everything. Until then, you are both dismissed."

Holly and Ronato stood to attention.

Sergeant Sugar dismissed them again.

Her eyes met Ronato's, as they turned and faced each other on their way out of the office remembering to close the door behind them.

"Ronnie!" Holly said. "Donna!"

*   *   *

Parklands; was awash with Italia Fest celebrations. People from all walks of life and parts of the globe filled the Pastaccerias', Gelatarias' and Pizzerias' partaking in provincial specialities, while others baked under the bronzing sun, carpeting grassy mounds overlooking a man made beach and salt water pools the park was famous for.

Night Spot Italia was a piano-bar, restaurant, nightclub owned by the Bruglioni family but run by Brescio Caratella, as an agreement of good faith between the Brisbane and Gold Coast families.

Brescio, the nephew of Capofamiglia Eduardo Cavalieri was a very unpopular figure amongst other family members. He was considered loud, un-respectful and loose in his dealings. And power hungry.

His main role in the business was drugs—a position he nominated for as a child by selling cigarettes for fifty cents a throw at his primary school behind the principal's office before graduating to marketing marijuana at high school where he took an apprenticeship in his God Fathers family.

He was becoming a major thorn in Violinos side because he believed in the drug trade *considered by the older members in the family* to be the dirty side of the mob. Violinos main bread and butter came from black racketeering. A consolidation of many small hits which produced big results but Brescio wanted it fast using, as was agreed by all in the family (assets acquired solely for the purpose of dealing) drugs.

Violino believed it was Brescio's loose dealings that brought about the unexpected raid on the church; spreading the word to anyone who would listen, that he stocked and sold drugs through a network of *representatives* as he called them.

Violino knew it would only be a matter of time before the police knew who they were—taking the entire family out. But he was also very smart because he knew he could manipulate the stupidity of Brescio—frame him and have him taken out by either side of the fence.

Night Spot Italia was packed, as Violino and his guardians entered the front entrance on their way to the office. Every available space was taken by happy faces charging a fun atmosphere.

Stefano Picci, Brescio's closest associate, weaved in and through tables, chatting to the clientele picking up empty plates and glasses as he went.

As normal, Violino didn't knock on entering the office but swung the door open to find Brescio banging Loretta his secretary doggy style facing away from the door and then quietly turned to face the guys placing an index finger over his mouth in sign language for silence before leaning against the door to show the action.

Loretta was an attractive girl, her body shaped by years of beach-volleyball; she could make a man stand to attention at 50 paces. And Brescio was at attention diving in and out of her pronounced vagina—their moans and groans were only interrupted by the sound of skin meeting at each interval of thrust.

Seppi laughed, watching Brescio tighten his grip around her hips saying.

"Great action she has the way she lifts her opening to assist a match stick."

"Yeah Seppi . . . they should swap position, they might have more access that way." Salvatore scoffed, finishing Seppi's mocking suggestion.

Brescio pulled out of her in shock—his groin retracted into his abdomen.

"Now guys don't be too hard, it's not his fault he should have been born a woman."

(A steady run of laughter brought on by Violinos comment broke, when the sight of Loretta's' moist vagina smiled at them. Her body lay forward atop the desk.)

Salvatore licked his lips in appreciation.

"Well, relieve my dick before it explodes. Come sit here darling," he said, patting his crotch.

She adjusted her position balancing her weight on her legs; her breasts danced a pendulum of movements, as she squatted for her panties—pulling them up over her knees.

"Fuck me she's the full package!" Seppi panted.

His bulging eyes expressed the thoughts running through Violinos mind.

"Go and help Stefano sweetheart." Violino suggested, heading toward her.

(She stood flush faced at the desks edge.)

His hand took hers, gliding it down his crotch. "We have business to discuss. Come by the club tonight."

Her eyes focussed on his private area and then his eyes.

"Have a shower first hah," he uttered dryly.

She left the office a titillated flushed faced blur closing the door behind her.

Salvatore and Seppi continued laughing watching Brescio straighten his clothing, wiping the sweat from his face with a handkerchief he'd pulled from his trouser pocket.

"You look a fucking mess Brescio," Violino stated, sitting in Brescios chair, watching him get himself in order. "You look a fucking mess."

Brescio returned his gaze, an unimpressed look painted his face. "If I knew you were coming . . ."

You'd have baked a cake Salvatore finished the sentence.

"That's the beautiful thing about being boss. You get to turn up whenever you like and by the looks of things we turned up just in time. Shit Brescio, I thought I was the only one you fucked," the young Don reclined upon Brescios chair lifting his feet onto the office desk top before speaking in a lower octave. "What else are you fucking with Brescio?"

Brescios pale face showed discomfort, as Salvatore and Seppi laughed sinisterly.

"What do you mean? Fucking with what?" He answered asking in turn.

"The books Brescio; show me how you are fucking the books!"

Laughter broke out between Sal and Seppi once more.

Brescio covered the office floor space from one side to the other sliding his feet on the carpet like a spoilt school boy. The static charge he built released when he placed his hand on the filing cabinet.

A loud clap of sound sparked more laughter from Sal and Seppi.

Violino dropped his head in disbelief.

"That's cause of Loretta. I'm feeling that myself," Salvatore aired.

Brescio opened the top draw, sliding it outward on its steel runners reaching in for the ledges.

Violino watched with amusement the frumpy movements happy to benefit from his misfortune.

"What Brescio . . . You don't keep computer files?"

Brescio looked back at him with confusion and *no* passed his lips in response.

"Just checking . . . You can't be too careful with the hired help these days." (The ledgers slid across the desk toward him.)

Violino thanked him, as he opened the first one.

Mario grabbed the second and positioned himself by the corner of the desk.

"Shit! Drugs sell good . . . How much of it do you and your people snort?" He fired, with a determined stare.

Brescios face turned whiter then a bleached blonde. "Not much," he responded.

"Not much . . . should be none; at all!" Violino fired sharply, as a glow settled around Mario's face.

"Someone's got to test the merchandise," he offered, his facial features locked onto Sal and Seppi's. "Think of it as—quality control."

Sal and Seppi shook their heads.

"What the fuck did you say?" Violino snapped, throwing the ledger onto the desk aggressively getting to his feet grabbing him.

Mario followed close behind—*what the fuck did you say, you slimy little prick?*

Brescio felt Violinos hands grip firmly around his neck. "You get pinched; we all go down!"

Capofamiglia Cavalieri would be most pleased Mario said, drawing his face millimetres from Brescio's. "Wipe your nose son. It doesn't snow in sunny Brisbane," (his breath was hot on his face.)

Sal imitated the action of wiping his nose, as Seppi ran an imaginary blade across the width of his neck.

Violino stepped closer intensifying his grip.

"You just run this place and keep your nose out of the stuff," slapping his face.

Mario took a step backward pushing him into the filing cabinet, pointed at him warningly adding *he shouldn't push his luck.*

Violino picked up the ledger from the desk handing it to Mario alerting Sal and Seppi to the office door.

Brescio stood tentatively next to the filing cabinet nervously twitching, as each of the men filed passed, skipping a heartbeat when Violino stopped.

"I'll return this after I've studied it. You be a good boy. I wouldn't want to have to spank you for being bad," he warned, closing the door behind him before Brescio wiped his frustrated face.

"Fuck you Violino," he said, looking at the closed door.

*   *   *

"I wonder what she looks like now!" Ronato pondered.

City lights danced in reflection across the bonnet, as his face painted a portrait of concentration scanning each part of road on their way to the police station.

"Who..?" Holly asked looking at him.

"Donna."

"Did you have a crush on her as well?" She asked, giggling.

A grin appeared on his face. "I always liked her. She was always nice. Not movie star or centre of attention nice," (shrugging his shoulders) "just nice—down to earth . . ."

She laughed and teased *he likes Donna—he wants to be with Donna* watching her brothers' reflective mood.

"So you like—like her?" (Her mind's eye took her forward passed present tenths, as she saw their children playing on swings. His son (probably to be named Massimilliano) was kitted out in F.C. Gladiators colours kicking a football around the back yard.) "Well your children will be beautiful," she suggested.

"Our children..!" Ron screeched; his attention adjusted itself momentarily from the road to his sister. (Her head was tilted in daydream.) "You don't muck around do you . . . you've already got us married with children!" He laughed, searching his finger for a wedding ring. Headlights of traffic approaching from the opposite side of the road froze his response in still frames. His laughter negotiated a number of questions locked and loaded ready to enquire.

"You'd better look into your crystal ball and see if it's by our chance meeting tonight, that I get down onto one knee extending my left hand out to hers—asking for her to share her eternity with mine," laughing deeply.

They entered the police stations sub level car park while Holly imitated rubbing the sides of a crystal ball under an intensive stare like ping-pong balls at the glove box.

He shook his head playfully.

"Well?"

The car wobbled over the entrance speed bumps, as his left forearm recoiled.

She answered the question. "Arr . . . Sisterly love..? It's so warm," pointing toward the closest available parking space.

"*Just park the car.*"

He carefully pulled into the space, applied the parking brake turning the ignition key to the off position.

*   *   *

"Good evening constables," Sergeant Sugar greeted watching them make their way to his position at the conference rooms' entrance. "Right on time, I like that. Holly you scrub up very well," a smile painted his face.

He directed them to make their way into the conference room with the wave of his hand. "Donna and her associate should be along presently."

They entered to see the conference room table dressed with a blue table cloth, plates, glasses, knives and forks. Bottles of wine stood pride of place inviting the penetration of a corkscrew.

Holly and Ron looked at each other wondering if they had somehow walked into the wrong place, as Sugar's voice drifted through the wall.

Good evening Detective Senior Constables Fiorella and Nadalle. How are you?

The siblings held hands in anticipation taking a couple of steps forward.

Ron's hand was being crushed under the grip of his sisters.

"Here comes' your future wife, brother dear," she said. A nervous giggle brought truth to her state.

The conference room door opened and an attractive man with an athletic built caught Holly's eye. Two metallic briefcases hung from his hands, as his suit hinted a V-shaped upper body while his smile hinted at a friendly soul.

"Maybe we will both get fixed up," Ron hinted under his breath.

Behind him a brunette beauty entered with an athletic hourglass figure; her smile was as welcoming as her opened arms.

"Oh my God Donna..!" Holly cried, running toward her, "look at you! How have you been?" Her voice was croaky with emotion.

She took a step backward for a better look, when Ron's voice entered Donnas' ears, introducing himself to the gentleman that entered with her.

"Ronato—oh my God look at you! After you left that time, I thought I would never see you both again," Donna stuttered, as he approached giving her a warm hug and kiss on the cheek.

"It's good to see you again Donna. And may I say you are as I remembered, very beautiful."

Donna laughed coyly. Her cheeks flushed pink.

"Holly. Ronato this is my associate, Detective Senior Constable Eric Nadalle. Eric these are two very old friends of mine, Holly and Ronato Austrella."

Eric approached and shook Holly's hand nodding his welcome back to Ron.

"I cannot believe you are here. And I cannot believe we are going to be working together!" Donna stuttered.

She stepped between Holly and Ron placing an arm around each of their waists.

Sugar interrupted. "Well now that the introductions are complete. We should find a seat and get down to business."

He made his way to a vacant seat at the table.

The other officers followed suit as Eric placed the two cases upon an adjacent table.

Sugar opened a bottle of red filling each empty glass before his own.

"A toast to a successful investigation," he implied, tipping his glass to each of the officers in the room.

Each of the others echoed his good intentions honouring the salute.

"Have you been working undercover long?" Holly asked, placing her wine glass thoughtfully on the table.

"About five years. I've been on the force for nine," Donna replied. "We've been investigating the Cavalieri family for the last 14 months, with varying success," (focusing Eric into the answer.) "It's only been the last couple of months that we've been digging into Violinos family. He has quite a loudmouth working for him—a drug dealer . . . *same old same old*," she nodded.

A knock on the door alerted Sugar to the arrival of their dinner.

"I hope you all like roast Lamb?" He asked, greeting four happy faces getting to his feet heading for the door.

The aroma of the Lamb filled the air, as the catering people carried food containers to the table.

Sugar thanked them and showed them out of the room as quickly as they came.

As he closed and relocked the door he turned to return to the table, inviting the others to tuck into each package and take what they liked.

Donna consoled the siblings. "Everyone was sorry about your fathers' death."

Holly and Ron looked at her nodding their heads.

Holly replied. "It was Bruno Bruglioni that killed our father." (Ron nodded.) "Our father was betrayed by the one person he trusted as much as our mother."

"Is that why you came to me requesting participation in this matter?" Sugar asked Holly, (adding Ron into his stare.)

"It had allot to do with it sir," Ron answered. (Donnas' hand rested on Holly's as she saw her eyes fill with tears.)

"Everyone we trusted turned against us. I had people I once called uncle try and force sex with me in their cars," Holly whimpered, wiping her eyes.

"Mamma found a job and we moved away. She told us not to tell anyone we were leaving. Early one morning while it was still dark, we packed up the car and just left." Ron confessed.

"Now you are back to get your revenge?" Sugar cut in with a questioning attitude.

"Well sir, in a way, I suppose you could say that. I know I won't cry if I know Violino is in jail picking up the soap," (he took a sip of his wine). "But the bigger picture is—their business revolves around deception and I suspect that that's what we are doing here." (Sugar nodded his head meaningfully). "We have the inside knowledge to help you," Ron fell silent, surveying his plate full of roast Lamb and veggies.

"That you do. You three are the sword that will penetrate the heart of organised crime in Queensland. Donna has been working undercover for some time tracking the Cavalieri family but she found that the Bruglioni family ties were too big to work around. So for the past two or so months, has been staking out Violino and his trusted figures in the very places you frequented while growing up. Is that correct Donna?"

Donna rested her knife and fork upon her plate wiping her mouth with a napkin, as Sugar placed his wine glass on the table, waiting for her response.

"Yes that's correct," she took a sip of wine to cleans her mouth. "I have been visiting our old haunts while Eric has been sitting in an unmarked car outside, monitoring surveillance recordings, and the comings and goings of family figures."

"Donna . . . Aren't you afraid they will hurt you?' Holly asked with alarm.

"I am—but at the same time I feel quite at ease. Violino knows I am a police officer but thinks I am only a uniform cop *parking tickets* and that type of stuff. I go in wearing a police uniform and order a coffee, or whatever—and just sit down and do my thing. What they don't know is that I am wearing surveillance equipment; Microphones, nanny cam, pen and paper. From time to time the guys come and talk to me but never anything serious about business. They throw some stuff at me sometimes, but only in good humour," (she looked over to find Holly and Ronato sitting in horror and disbelief.) "We grew up together. Mario, Salvatore and Seppi bounced me on their knees as they did with you and the others. Mario and I played on the swings and in the park, just like he did with you. And while that is strong in their memory, it seems they still think of me as one of them."

She took another sip of wine resting upon the chair, her hands found the napkin that rested under the left lip of her plate and dabbed at her mouth.

"We have brought some of the equipment we've been using in our investigations and some other stuff we intend to use as soon as possible. Car taps, phone taps, that sort of stuff . . ." Eric stated.

"Holly will be getting somewhat closer than that. She was Violinos girlfriend. Apparently he was quite cut-up when she left and we are

Luciano Delcremona

hoping he will want to reconcile his trust in her allowing her back into the fold. She is not to wear a wire. I will be the one who wears the surveillance equipment," Ron ordered.

Sugar wiped his mouth with his napkin reaching for his of wine glass.

"I suggest after dinner, we start planning our strategy. For now though, let's re-acquaint. I'm looking forward to hearing your stories about each other . . . cheers," he saluted focusing good intentions.

*　*　*

"What you thinking kid?" Mario slurped, after a fork full of pasta.

"I'm thinking it's time to clip Brescio," he responded under a settling sigh, the admission lifted a world of weight of his shoulders making the plate of Linguini Alfredo in front of him more appealing.

Fucking drug business . . . Mario sniggered.

Seppi and Salvatore simultaneously leaned into the table with a question painting their faces.

Violino laughed pointing in their direction, while looking at Mario.

"Oh . . . ! Fucking Dobermans here," he said, watching Mario's head nod proudly toward their two compatriots, while celebrating the good-old-times feeling circulating the table at his admission to the Brescio problem.

He suddenly found himself split from the reality of the restaurant to the old days when he would listen to his father and the gentlemen talk about getting rid of certain problems they were having with figures in the family recalling the feeling of cold painted diecast metal in the form of his matchbox cars rolling over the ruff shag pile carpet that lay in the den of the family home, powered by his fingers as a child; the focused look on his fathers face and that of his crews', as they toyed with each solution as it came to mind and the laughter and festive atmosphere that electrified the room as each part of their plans would fall into place and the after-mirth of each successful stage. It always felt like Christmas. And as he found himself stirring back to the recognition of the table and his company—that for him, the feeling of surprise and the unknown were the same.

He enjoyed another mouth full of linguini. Adrenalin filled his veins, as he felt a shiver of expectancy and excitement force-field his body. A flutter of laughter shook his stomach drawing back to his memory, every word Brescio had uttered to him about his drug dealing exploits; where he had it processed and where he sold it. The people he associated himself with while marketing it or used it and; his next big shipment and the layout of the building.

His mouth explored the textures of pasta and sauce, rolling the flavours over his palate while taking pleasure in seeing the same pleasure emitting from the others.

"Drugs are a very dangerous business . . . very dangerous," he said with ringing confidence. "Brescios next big shipment comes in next week. We should use that as the basis of his demise."

Mario tilted his head toward Violino while waving small circles along an imaginary line with his open hand.

Violino swirled the fork merrily through the linguini, a movie-star smile painted his lips, as his stomach uncovered another small laugh. Then a wave of pride washed over him taking his glass of wine in his hand raising it in a toast to his father and as the others echoed his words, the song *Cats in the Cradle* filled his head in a ghostly rendition. His dream had come true. His footsteps were as Gemini to his fathers.

Darting forward upon his seat, Seppi asked. "When you gonna do it kid! What time of night is that fucker gonna kiss dirt?"

His eyes were open and alive to the possibilities while a number of merry images ran amongst his thoughts.

"Been out of the game for awhile Sep?" Mario asked, a giggle croaked his voice.

Seppi adjusted his seated position creaking; the dining room chair he sat upon. "I've been hungry to clip that prick for some time," meshing his fingers on the table cloth before taking advantage of the chairs backrest.

"I was thinking about using Deli." Violino advised, resting his fork on the plate.

"Fucking Deli again . . ." Seppi said, in disappointment.

"Lucky prick . . ." Mario sniggered, watching Seppi's happiness deteriorate.

Violino laughed taking a sip of wine to clear his throat, "well there's a number of ways he can do it Sep."

Seppi raised his chin in a questioning manner.

Violino promoted. "He can shoot him, stab him, or fall on the pr-ick." (The table erupted, as the young Don rested upon his chair taking another slurp of wine.)

"What a way to go hah?" Mario chuckled.

Crushed beyond all rec-og-nition Salvatore contributed.

Drawing closer to the table, Violino took his fork to stir the contents of his plate.

"He knows his stuff . . ."

Mario finished the Dons views as family consiglieri, a cold edge blunted his voice *no mistakes.*

"Stefano Picci?" Seppi asked—excitement washed gold back into the grey of his disappointment.

"Fuck no..! Deli gets to do them both..?" Violino confirmed, watching the grey return to Seppi's colour, finding a new level of disappointment.

Salvatore weighed in. "What about Loretta?"

Violino laughed, a vibrant colour of lust shaded his defined features. "This is a public place Sal. Keep it in your pants," (his laughter spread around the table like an infectious decease.) "I can think of a few good uses for her. What you think Sep?"

"She eats snow too . . ."

"I know Mario, don't worry she won't live a lifer. She's like a candy apple. First you lick the outside and sample the sweetness of the toffee. Then you get to the middle and drink the juice—enjoy the wetness and satisfy the craving. Then you dispose of the body, when you've had enough and bury it in garbage," swirling the last of the linguini around his fork feeding it to his mouth sexually.

"Yeah but do we all get to taste the candy apple..?" Seppi asked. His face matched the shade of Violinos.

"Does a cone of trifle feed one man?" Violino gestured.

Seppi clapped his hands together happily. "Oh I can taste her now!"

He swallowed in sweet anticipation.

"You will be her last Sep," Violino confided. "Find her a nice resting place."

"I will I promise. She'll die happy," he sighed; rubbing his balls under the table swelling his groin to the porno screening in his mind.

*   *   *

After dinner, Sergeant Sugar and the other officers' cleared away their plates and food packages settling down to talk over the remaining wine—the mood of the room was a combination of frosty anticipation—the possibilities of grave circumstances were real, as collectively, they looked into their uncertain future and felt the electricity and familiarity of the friendships they built as children.

Holly, Ronato and Donna found themselves in a close huddle, talking and laughing the same way they had done as kids.

Ronato, Violino and Chris were the three Musketeers (*Italian style*)—Donna and Holly partners in crime inseparable to most of their collective dealings.

All of their exploits flooded back to life through shared laughter and memories and from time to time, the laughter of Sergeant Sugar and Eric would be heard by the trio—their questions of where and why adding to the hilarity.

Holly and Ronato leered at the metallic cases with baited breath, as the glow and smoothness of their surfaces stole their thoughts and curiosities.

Sparkles of disturbed light danced over each silver surface under the guidance of Eric's control, as from table to table he moved them in preparation of induction triggering each lock.

"Curious aren't you?" He asked Holly.

His smile ignited sparks of interest in the pit of her stomach.

"Yes . . . Your equipment has me curious . . ." She replied, turning pink when she realised her choice of wording.

Eric finished unpacking the cases, periodically taking quick peaks at her to see if she was watching, eager to spill another clever line.

Sugar made his way next to him helping to unpack the equipment, his mood changed, as his face turned a deeper shade of concern leading him back to days when he himself was an active officer taking risks in the pursuit of justice.

"Right everyone, gather around," he said, opening the viewing screen of the nanny-cam he selected from the table. "You all know what this is. It's a nanny-cam. This little thing is one of the most used tools in private investigations the world over because of its size and weight. It's easy to conceal. The electronics available in this model can be viewed real-time through relay to our offices here, or to other security chambers around the city," he fell silent.

Eric continued the briefing. "This is a micro-cam. This little private eye can be placed anywhere your imagination can think of. We have hidden them in barby dolls; teddy bears *ha* even a slot car set with overwhelming success."

Holly's heart pounded on approach to the table, her wish for revenge was taking shape like an early gift from Saint Nicholas.

With her eyes she took in the efforts of discussion and planning; with her ears she digested the strategic data being modelled for their landing parties—and with her mouth discussed ideas toward the efforts they were discussing.

For a brief moment, her thoughts lead back to when they were simple children, skipping and playing, laughing and running—and for the first time wondered if the children who had moved away, did. *Had those families who suddenly left, actually moved? Or had something more sinister happened to them?*

And then just as quickly, she found herself back in the moment playing out in the conference room. The strength of her brother stood by her side. Sergeant Sugar's voice (low and full of concern over their safety) assured him that she would *not* at any time wear a wire.

Her old friend Donna who shared her need and hunger for justice, re-stoked the flames of friendship they knitted as children and a hunky guy by the name of Eric; carefully; briefed her brother on the technical aspects of the surveillance equipment.

She ran her fingers across the tables' surface wrapping her hand around an x-ray imaging devise, eyeing it attentively.

"When do we start?" She asked, sharp and directly.

"The moment you are ready," Sugar replied.

Holly (in response to Sugars reply) swivelled first to Donna—her smile was radiant and alive and her voice confident and steady relaying she was ready. Then she turned to her brother taking in his stares. The size and colour of his eyes froze her for a moment sensing his fear for her, as he reached for her hand chanting the credo they learned during the security faze of their training '*disarm—disable—disappear*' before turning to face Sugar—and together in time with her brother responded.

"Tomorrow . . . We are ready to start tomorrow."

Once again Sugar uncorked a bottle of red filling each person's glass.

"A toast for each brave soul," he said, raising his glass in salute.

A toast to each brave soul they replied taking a sip of wine in turn.

Placing their glasses to the table a low giggle slipped out of Holly's mouth as she turned facing Donna.

Ronato sensing embarrassment, reached for his sister but before his embrace locked to hers, his head slumped to the back of her neck in embarrassment.

"Donna . . . Will you marry my brother? He's nice, single—and your babies will be beautiful," giggling turned to outright laughter.

"Holly..!" Donna giggled *you haven't changed a—bit . . .*" Her words were full of warmth, as she framed Holly's face with her hands. "Ronato Fiorella has a nice ring," she laughed as Holly framed her face with her hands squealing *you haven't changed either!*

*   *   *

Lights & Lace was a steady hive of activity. Violino and the guys stood around the bar watching Chris brief the bar staff of special drink deals Mario and Seppi had worked out to move more booze from nip measures to mouths, while the band Mario hired for a one off, humped their equipment in through the back entrance like worker ants—prompting the young Don to make a comment.

"Fucking band better be good or we might have to hand them over to Seppi."

The band members met the comment with shaky glimpses.

Seppi swallowed in one gulp the contents of his glass enjoying the vibe of unfamiliarity as he posed. "It's like sex—torture, you just have to have some from time to time," banging the bar with another empty glass. (A full one was placed next to it) raising it in salute of the barman.

"Sep," Violino started. "Guitar wire, if you tightened it hard enough around someone's neck, while in the throws of suffocation. Can it sever it?"

Seppi spread a smile across his colouring face *the head?* He asked.

"Yes, you joking fuck, the head," Violino spluttered.

"If I had that person in a position where my foot is pushing against the back of their neck, yeah maybe . . . Why? You want me to try?"

He called over to one on the band members to bring him a guitar.

Violino raised a hand to the band member who responded telling him to continue on setting up and then gestured for the guys to follow him up to the office.

Seppi slid his arm around Violinos waist pulling him in close.

"I'm horny for sex and sledge."

The young Don nodded and smiled understandingly *tonight my friend, tonight.*

On entering the office, Salvatore did the honours by pouring himself, Mario and Violino a drink.

Violino sat down in one of the recliners asking Sal to call Deli to call around to the club so they could start talking about clipping Brescio and Stefano.

Sal handed the drinks to each of the men and then pulled his cell phone dialling Deli's number.

"Tell him to bring Vito!" Violino added. "Let's have some fucking fun tonight!" (His hands tapped the table like drumsticks.)

"Arr..! What time does the shit arrive?" Mario asked, sitting in the chair next to him, (the coffee table in front of them finding the wet base of Mario's drink.)

"The shipment arrives at Brisbane dock that morning. Brescio will be waiting for the container to be delivered at the warehouse. Stefano will probably arrive later, after he has secured the night staff for Night spot Italia," advising confidently.

"I've been there; with you I think. There's allot of trees around that warehouse, no?" (Mario's eyes danced a circle of memory around the drink at rest on the table.) "Nudgee . . ."

Swirling Whisky around his mouth, Violino nodded stating, "corretto."

"There's allot of cover for Deli to hide during and after the hit." Seppi added.

"There's a short drive-way around the other side of that park. He can park the car off the road out of sight, walk over to the back of the warehouse and sit tight. Make the hit and leave without ever being seen," Salvatore added, sliding his cell phone into his pocket. "Vito and Deli are on their way over."

"Good," Violino said, swirling another sip.

A knock on the office door provoked them all to say come in.

"Loretta, from Night spot Italia called to say she would get here around 11ish."

Chris swung his head around the door advising.

Seppi rubbed his crotch in sweet anticipation. "I can feel the blood running to my balls, as we speak," he aired.

"Soon it will be tucked into her tight spot." Salvatore contributed.

"Just don't come into the shower after Violino is done with her. I'll satisfy her there."

Salvatore asked thoughtfully. "What you gonna do with the body?"

"I'll throw it in the boot and take it for a nice drive to the mountain," he advised, sliding his hand the full length of his dress boat—resting on his knee.

"That's what I like about you Sep. Always the romantic." Mario laughed; his stomach muscles gave the recliner springs a work-out.

"Someone has to bon-voyage her after mini mouse here is finished with her," his laughter and comment earned the bird from Violino. "Don't worry kid. One day I'll teach you about the finer points of performance," rotating his hand backwards and forwards.

The others joined in laughing.

Violino wrapped his fist around an imaginary shaft.

"Masturbation is only apart of it kid."

"Fuck you Seppi," the young Don grumbled.

"Yes but will you respect me," Seppi inquired, reducing the young Don to a shaking mess.

"The last of the wise guys," Mario scoffed, leaning forward to take his drink. Droplets of condensation fell onto the carpet and recliner. "That will be Loretta. Dripping . . ."

"You'll drip to after swallowing seaman." Sal said.

"Drainage . . . The thought always makes me horny." Mario confessed. "Where's my cell? I've got to call my wife."

"What you need her for?" Seppi asked, as Mario sent a strange look, elevating his chin.

"I'm married too Mario . . ." Seppi said laughing. "Things dry up."

"You should see a doctor about that." Mario laughed, pointing toward his groin. (Violinos laughter ran a track of background noise.)

"The thought of my wife cracks the bed—normal no?" He scrunched his shoulders. "We got married!"

Violinos laughter broke out again.

"Let that be a lesson to you young Violino. You can find them and have them . . ."

But never marry them Salvatore interrupted Seppi's finish.

"It's the walk down the aisle that drains all the romance out of them."

Mario's thumb busily pushed numbers on his dial pad as he mumbled—*drainage.*

"Talking of drainage," Violino interrupted, a smirk appeared on his face, as he watched Mario fumble with the cell phone. "When was the last time we had our places swept?" (The office door swung open and Vito and Deli entered the room.) "Oh—what did you do, fly your broom sticks here!" The young Don cried excitedly.

"Fuck no . . . We came via the government," Vito explained, padding himself down. "Go look. They're parked outside!"

"Get over here you cheeky fuck," Violino laughed, as his feet made contact with the floor, opening his arms.

"Fuck me . . . God forbid, there'd be a device here," Seppi cried.

Salvatore, after greeting his cousin and Deli, cast Seppi a question. "What you worried about?"

"I'm not worried for us. I'm worried for the poor bastard who listens. Have you ever heard Mario talk to his wife about—sex?"

Seppi screwed his face, spinning his palms in Mario's direction. "Sickening—fucking sickening," he scoffed shaking his head.

Vito said from giving Violino a hug *Sep—have you seen his wife lately* rolling a palm in circles.

Vito and Salvatore watched Deli approach the table dropping down onto a seat, laughing at its wooden complaint under his weight.

"You; ever been to the warehouse in Nudgee?"

"Where Brescio stores his drugs..?" Vito answered with a question.

"What you know about it . . ." Violino fired at him excitedly.

"Everybody knows about that place. He's got a greater broadcast range than that of Sounds FM," Vito's reply brought a steady nod to Mario's head.

Deli's bobbed up and down in response like a boat riding choppy seas.

"I didn't think you were in the drug business?"

"We're not!" Mario replied.

Violino got up from the recliner joining Deli at the table. "Deli's going to take Brescio out."

Deli's face lit up like the lights on a Christmas tree saying *I've; been wanting to clip that fuck for . . .*

"Another one," Seppi broke in—depression sounded his voice.

"What's wrong with you?" Violino barked. "You get to fuck Loretta!"

"He'll fuck her—then fuck her," Salvatore laughed.

Vito nodded appreciation for the task.

"When does he do that?" Excitement coloured the question. (*Tonight,* Mario answered.)

"Ok—ok," Violino said, as he took control over the session telling Deli he would ice Brescio and Stefano on the Monday night and that, that gave him two nights to prepare.

Mario went to the stationary cupboard pulling out a street directory, flicking through the index, opening the pages to show the area.

"Here you go Deli," he said, lowering the open directory in front of him.

Deli looked at the pages re-positioning the directory under his vision.

Buchanan road he asked rhetorically, his finger traced its path.

"There's a second entrance onto that block around the back—a dirt track stops partly through the trees. Enter there," Salvatore directed him.

Violino leaned forward on his seat pointing toward the position of the warehouse on the page.

"Do not clip them until the police enter the building," he ordered, looking at him. (Shock and silence blanketed the others.) He resort a comfortable position and eye-balled Salvatore asking. "Did you keep the service revolvers of the government you left in Mt: Glorious?"

Salvatore nodded.

Violino shared the plan with the others.

"Deli—on Monday night you will enter the block from the rear. There's a large bay window that looks out at the trees. If you stand in the right position out there, you can see everything in the back part of the warehouse. Me; and Mario will be parked out front, watching the governments' movements when they arrive. When we see them enter the building, we will radio you. You will wait until the shit hits the fan witnessing the government take position," (locking gaze with him once more.) "And then!" He slammed his open palm against the table with a thud, "then you take them both out and get the fuck out of there," his eyes travelled around the table. "Everyone will meet back at the sporting club."

"Why are you going to tip of the government?" Vito asked, rubbing his forehead.

Violino took another sip of his drink, resting the glass on to the table.

"The government haven't found their missing men yet, so if we use their pieces and leave the shell casings on the ground at the back of the warehouse, they will find them and trace them back to their men. Then it becomes an internal investigation of police corruption, not a mob hit. Their car was left outside a gentlemen's in Nudgee," (peering at Salvatore, who was nodding.) "Two missing police officers, an empty car and shell casings belonging to those law enforcement officers," he trailed off, focusing his stare at Vito. "You do the math. In most languages, one and one make for a partnership."

(Vito and Deli shook their heads in full appreciation of the young Dons' thinking.) "And it will give us some time to figure out how we are going to explain things to Don Cavalieri—and plot our next moves," he added.

"That's fucking brilliant kid. Remind me never to go toe to toe with you—you sneaky fuck." Vito voiced, standing bolt upright flashing his palms shoulder height under a purposeful voice.

Mario patted the young Dons shoulder; pride reddened his eyes in memory of his great father.

Two peas in a pod the Bruglioni men . . . Two fucking peas in a pod he sobbed.

Deli nodded extending a hand over the table. "Great fucking plan kid," he looked around at the others nodding appreciation to each one. "It will be my fucking pleasure to rub that Girl Scout out."

"If we keep it that simple, nothing should go wrong," the young Don stated.

He lifted his glass to see it was empty. "The plan is to get out of the drug business. Get rid of our competition and take control of Queensland. If the Chinese, Brits and Skips want to deal the dirty business, they can have it. We don't need to dirty our hands with that shit. You can't trust anyone who uses it. And you can't depend on anyone who sells it," (Salvatore replenished the glass full of whisky) under Violinos salute. "You guys have the pizzeria. We have this place; the sporting concern; the Calabrese Club and the restaurant in Parklands: **Legitimate business and legitimate businessmen**. We also share in racketeering and the black-market and we make a fucking fortune. Next for us is the stock market, who needs drugs to fuck everything up. That's what finished the Omerta—the precious code of silence. All these fucks here following those filthy U.S. fucks. No loyalty and no balls; Capitalism instead of Socialism. We build and grow together! We will re-unite with the Camarra, 'Ndrangheta and Sacra Corona Unita Oro and any other group in Italia offering shelter for man and merchandise, this is a fucking big country, you can lose allot here," he saluted to find all of the guys looking at him with presidential ore.

"Fuck organised crime kid. You should run for the biggest con of all. The Prime Ministership," Deli said with vigour, tapping his heart.

A knock on the door settled the room and Chris's face appeared peering around its edge.

"Sorry to interrupt. Loretta is here," he advised.

"Show her in," Violino instructed, as he stood from his chair running a hand over his groin.

"Shit save some for me," Seppi cried, drool amassed in the corners of his mouth.

"Steady on . . . there'll be plenty left for you. I'm doing you a favour going first. A ticker like yours might find it too much," he laughed.

The others volunteered gears, laughter and claps at the young Dons play.

"Just save me some," Seppi laughed.

Everyone's attention was taken by the sight of Loretta, as she entered the office.

"Shall we go my dear," Violino asked, extending his hand to take hers.

Her fingers ran suggestively across his palm blazing eyes into his.

His groin throbbed at the thought of her wrapped around it.

Yes she said—eyeing his body, tonguing her lips *lets*.

He led her out of the office and down the stairs toward the bar.

"What can I get you to drink," he asked suggestively.

"A quick fuck," she replied.

They reached the bar and Violino relayed the order to Chris, who approached to serve them personally.

"How long have you been working for us?" He asked.

But the question seemed to amuse her and she traced a hand down his flat stomach over his groin.

"A very long time," she expressed, directing her lips toward his, bitting his bottom lip on contact.

"You don't waste any time," he choked under excitement.

Her hand massaged him longingly.

"Let's skip the drink shall we," she said, pulling his hand to lead him away from the bar.

He raised his hand at Chris, telling him not to worry about the order.

"That dress doesn't deserve the flesh it's trying to cover," he stuttered thick with lust, tracing the outline of her bodice, dancing fingers along the soft red material as the sight of her heaving breasts, almost sent him over the edge.

He led her through the side exit and out to the alley pinning her immediately against the brick wall—pressing his lips hard against hers—their tongues jousted hungrily.

"I'm gonna fuck you baby," his voice croaked to the strain of his Adams' apple.

Her hands fort with his belt and zipper, as her thighs parted in readiness for penetration.

In a moment of desperation he unbound his penis pulling at her perfumed panties with his other hand—a hot waxy aroma of need surrounded them as her dress and underwear fell to the concrete ground.

He marvelled at the sight of her full D-cup breasts, pinching and teasing her nipples standing long and erect under raids of her mouth and tongue across his face, (parting her legs rib boning them around him, forcing penetration.) The sound of their sex drummed off the brick wall like a dance beat until in a flash flood from his water cannon—socked her innards sending shivers and shudders through her thighs and hips, convulsing her body into deep breaths and searching tongues.

He took a step back surveying her—his penis dangled like a branch in the breeze swelling to rock hard and rigid at the sight of his sperm drizzling out of her sex and down her inner thighs.

She followed his back pedal, pushing him against the opposite brick wall, ripping open his shirt to servile rippling sweaty muscles.

Hungry, she bit at his chest and nipples exploring with fine details his backside, legs and penis, orchestrating a classical concert between them, dropping to her knees and taking him into her mouth, altering the length and breadth via the subtlety and power of suction until her swallow explained the soprano of his moans.

"I could use that drink now," she gagged, looking around for her dress crumpled on the ground. "A satisfied suggestion would be nice," she suggested under a jerk of forward movement from a push from behind, throwing her hands against the brick work she'd met moments earlier.

Her lust stretched conforming to the length, width and thrust of Violinos throbbing shaft. Moans and groans waled from her mouth, as her stomach and breasts pressed forcefully against the brick work while taking a full work out between her thighs.

His flesh slapped against her buttocks until he climaxed, his breath was hot against the back of her neck and his protein sowed its wetness in, along, and around her sex.

"I could do with a drink myself," he confessed, pulling away from her in search for his clothing. His penis reduced its size in a shimmer of use.

"I think Seppi wants to get to know you to," he advised, pulling his trousers on and fixing his shirt into place neatly, all-be-it without its buttons.

"Well, if he's a good boy, I might decide to open myself up to him," she said, while dressing.

Her eyes glowed with a circumference of titillation.

They headed for the door and Violino said. "A satisfied story . . . I've never heard of that . . ."

His face held a picture of confusion.

"With that thing—I'm surprised to hear you say that," she replied, finding the night-club floor while he closed the door behind them.

He placed his hand on her shoulder and said. "There's a shower here, if you want to freshen up."

She turned and faced him. "That sounds great. Will you bring our drinks, if I go and tidy up?" (Her hand traced the lines of his groin,) stepping into him, washing his lips with her tongue.

His groin mimicked the shape of her breasts.

"Can happen," he said. "Enter the bar and tell Chris it's ok and follow it around to the far wall, just passed the last glasses fridge. Feel around the wall next to its leading edge for a door-knob. The shower is in there. I'll get the drinks and follow you in," finding the back of her neck drawing her lips back to his.

"Ok, don't be too long, big boy," she huskily said, running her fingers along the length of his penis once more.

Violino climbed the stairs to the office, entering.

"She's in the shower," he said, as his face was a sticky mess of sweat and saliva.

"Fuck me kid, looks like you could use a shower," Mario chided, as his voice was a comedy of notes.

"You didn't save me very fucking much did you," Seppi stuttered, studying him.

"There's enough left for everyone," he stated contently. "Go on Sep, go and finish her off."

"I'll give her a fairy-tale finish," Seppi stated, leaving the office. The door closed behind him.

Seppi entered shower meeting a heavy cloud of steam, locking the door behind him before following the small tiled corridor to the cubicle.

"You took your time," Loretta chimed.

His eyes picked up on her smeared outline.

"It's Seppi darling. Violino sent me instead. He said you wanted a drink. He said you earned it," his voice quivered with laughter, as he made his way to her, undressing with each step taken.

"He says you like me too . . ."

Her query was halted by his mouth pressing hard against hers.

Violently cupping her breasts, he forced her against the wet tiled wall with a thud.

The moans she experienced with Violino turned to screams with Seppi. His manhood found her opening—stabbing her insides. His mouth bit at her lips and breasts, throat and chest.

She struggled to get away but his hold was relentless.

He forced her to the floor. Warm water cascaded off his back, over his shoulders and down onto her face, into her eyes. Her screams were muffled by his tongue and her breasts were flattened and squeezed by the power of his hands and fingers while his thrust was more of a forceful drive than a squeeze of buttocks; as he fired a stream from his origin, inside her body.

With her blonde hair sodden and her eyes full of tears—she got up, off the wet tiles. Water still washed over her from the shower head and her company had vanished in the cloud of steam.

She found her heaving breath had been replaced by whimpers, as a hand traced the back of her neck to her throat. A pleading yelp escaped her lips; as again, she found her stomach and chest pressed hard against the wall—expecting to feel the powerful thrust of lust search for her opening but instead tasted a sweet, thick syrup texture fill her mouth.

A stinging sensation across her throat took her by surprise and with her hand, traced the area. The pressure against her back had lightened and the white tiles changed colour.

Her whimpers turned to screams, as her fingers held a palate of water and blood.

A Nile of blood ran the full length of her body to the tiled floor, on its snaking run to the drain and beyond and her mind became light.

Her vision blurred and body slumped, as the stinging sensation turned to burn. Trickling water gave her a sense of place until there was nothing.

Seppi dressed, focusing on the blur of flesh and blood sprawled atop the tiled floor before noticing her dress, hanging on a shower hook in front of him. The poetic symmetry of the garment sent a giggle from his lips, as he ran his palm and fingers down its seam.

"Lady in red," he drooled.

He entered the bar, locking the shower door behind him and kneeled down to an under counter cupboard where the garbage bags were kept.

Steam and disco smoke mixed, infusing thirsty patrons waiting for drinks at the bar to swirl in a frenzy of lust for alcoholic hydration.

"Chris!—is this the best we got?" He shouted questioningly, as he came to service the thirsty patrons. A garbage bag hung in his hand.

"No!" Chris called back barely breaking the dominant music. "There are grain bags out the back!" He pointed to the storeroom door.

Seppi patted his shoulder making his way to the storeroom—the shower room key danced circles around his forefinger while the pulse of the music built an electrical charge powering his adrenalin.

He entered the store room and found the grain bags at rest in the far corner, retrieving them, making his way back to the shower, where the cloud of steam had grown denser containing an added scent of blood.

He entered and shut the door behind him.

Stepping carefully back to the cubicle where droplets of steam turned the white tiled floor into a skating rink—he turned the water off leaning down straightening Loretta's lifeless body, placing her arms and legs together.

Retrieving the red dress—he tied it around her open wound placing a grain bag at either end of her body.

Bit-by-bit, he slid her body into them, until the corpse was completely covered—and then noticed that steamed portions of blood, clogged the shower drain preventing excess water and blood from running into the plumbing. With his shoe he stood atop the drain rubbing semi-circles over the partial openings to force a breakage in the blockage.

With that done, he showered the grain bags containing her body, cleaning all signs of blood from the parcel and then rinsed the cubicle to make sure there was no sign of blood left on the tiles before checking the under-side of his shoes—turning the water off for the last time—sliding the parcel out of the cubicle, laying it to rest by the foot of a black seat-bench bolted to the centre of the corridor floor at the entrance of the cubicle.

As he opened the door leading to the bar, his hands were shaking—the thrill of killing recharged his batteries and his mind ran from the act to the cover-up.

He looked back at the parcel lifting his nose to judge the air—running the shower key around his finger. There were no windows to worry about but pockets of steam still hung in the air so he closed the door again turning toward the ventilation switch, flicking it on, and waited momentarily for the air to clear.

Satisfied with his efforts, he made his way out of the shower room locking the door behind him on his way back to the office, pushing his way through clusters of young and old, drinking and dancing.

The stairs were cold comfort mimicking a climb of Everest—a cold drink played on his mind as he reached the summit and found the door knob, pushing the door open only to close it behind him.

The party of familiar faces surveyed his path to the bar where he over turned a whisky glass throwing ice into it before selecting a poison.

The murmur of the band was the only noise in the room.

He lifted the glass from the bar and made his way to the recliners, selecting the closest one to the television set, dropping into it.

One by one the other men selected chairs around him. The murmur of the band created an out-of-body-experience, as Violino chimed his whisky filled glass against his.

"Is it done Sep?" He asked.

The other faces leaned forward waiting on baited breath for the answer.

Seppi took a long sip of his drink snugly placing the glass in his lap. His lungs filled with air and the discharge yielded the reply.

"It's done. She's lying in a parcel next to the bench." (The other men looked around at each other and then back at Seppi.) "She'll have to stay there until shut-down," he panted, about to take another sip *fucking waste though. Fuck she was hot* he patted Violinos knee. "She died happy," he looked at the young Don with a smile on his face. "Call it experience kid."

Violino laughed at the comment. "Where you gonna plant her?" He inquired, making second base with the whisky glass.

"Manchester Lakes," he replied.

Violino nodded pursing his lips together.

Mario leaned forward and reduced the space between himself and Seppi, his bottom lip drew outward asking. "How good was she?"

Seppi smiled back at him, a satisfied glow emanated from his face and he replied. "Drainage Mario . . . Allot of drainage."

Mario fumbled in his pocket. "Fuck. Where's my phone?"

*   *   *

Sergeant Sugar, Donna and Eric, Holly and Ronato walked down to the car park together, an air of satisfaction lay groomed in their step. The meeting had gone well with many ideas on how to track and servile the Bruglioni family, taken.

Sugar bid them a nice evening, as he shook hands with each of them on his way to his car.

"Feel like a night cap?" Donna asked, fumbling around her hand bag for car keys.

Eric agreed with a nod, looking at Holly and Ronato with Donna dropping her bottom lip in a childish way.

"Yeah—what the hell," Ronato said, digging around his pocket for car keys and wallet.

Where Holly asked; her mood swung toward a tall-cool-Sangiovese red.

"How about Brisbane's' best kept secret," (Donnas' tone was of government conspiracy before excited and happy, raising her hands as if celebrating a football goal) *the club at Newmarket.*

"Would they still be open?" Holly asked questioningly.

"Oh . . . for at least an hour yet," Ronato replied, happy at the choice Donna made. "Can we walk you to your car?" He asked, as she and Eric started the ball of movement rolling.

"No. It's cool. We'll see you there," she smiled back at them.

Ron and Holly started for their car.

In the background they heard Donna ask Eric if he knew where the club was.

*   *   *

Chris shut the doors at Lights & Lace after the last of the patrons exited the building. The band were busy dismantling their set as Violino, Seppi and the others made their way from the office to the shower room door.

Seppi inserted the key twisting the lock.

"Stay here Sal. Make sure no-one comes in," Violino ordered, as he motioned for the others to enter the corridor.

"What the hell did you wrap her in?" Mario asked, stopping at the foot of the parcel that lay at the foot of the black bench.

Seppi replied. "Two grain bags I found in the store room."

"Two bags to one body," Violino mumbled, impressed at the improvisation.

"Where's your car Sep?" Mario inquired, slapping him on the shoulder playfully.

"Out front," he responded.

Violino leaned over and placed his hands at either side of the parcel where Loretta's feet rested telling Vito to get the other end, advising Seppi to park his car in the alley.

"We'll throw her in the boot there."

Vito picked up the other side of the parcel and Seppi searched for car keys in his pocket, starting for his car.

They lifted the body and carried it toward the fire exit.

Trying not to breath, Mario and Seppi screwed their faces while they followed behind.

"Fuck me . . . she's heavy," Vito complained, opening the door finding Salvatore standing security over the entrance.

"It's all clear—the band are on stage pulling shit apart," he re-assured them. (They continued on down the bar walkway to the fire exit door.)

"What the hell is that smell?" Mario complained, placing a handkerchief over his nose, entering the alley. (Seppi's headlights drew their shadows longer against the height of their bodies.)

"The bags warm. It's probably Loretta," Vito stated.

Violino dropped her, feet end of the parcel, as Seppi pulled up.

"Pop the boot Sep!" He called.

Deli stood over the body sucking in a sniff. His reaction was less than grateful.

"She hasn't been dead long. How the fuck can she smell; like that?" Mario complained disdainfully.

Vito responded business like. "Sep probably sliced her open while she was standing under the hot water. The temperature combined with her natural body heat, stuffed into a bag, would start a simmering process,' (taking in Mario's features.) "Hence the smell . . . Chances are he had to unblock the drain. The blood she spilled would have congealed, covering it over."

"Enough!—Vit . . . enough," Violino complained, bending over to pick up the parcel.

Both men walked it around the back of Seppi's car throwing it into the boot with a thud.

Seppi closed the boot lid, as he noticed band members had started making stacks out of their equipment at the fire exit doorway.

"Anyone want to come on our drive to lovers' lane?" He laughed, opening the drivers' side door.

"Just make sure you don't speed. We don't want the government pulling out their battens—do we," the young Don suggested in a British style.

"No prob. I'll pop the boot and take her for a moonlight swim," he laughed, as he jumped in behind the steering wheel, closing the door and pulling away.

A second set of lights ran the brick walls of the alley, as the bands truck, idled up level with the doorway.

"No one broke a leg hah?" Violino laughed, as he followed the others through the door.

Voices behind him replied no, as he announced it was Salvatore's shout at the bar.

Gears and cheers erupted between the men as Salvatore stated *another one bites the dust. Fuck she had nice legs.*

The band members laughed as they packed the truck with their equipment.

"He's worried about one woman, when they pack this place with hundreds of women every night," the bass player stated, shaking his head in disbelief.

The singer shoved him playfully. "There's a heart broken every second," he laughed.

"Isn't that a song?" The bass player queried.

CHAPTER 9

Saturday brought mixed emotions, an uneasy sound of static buzzed Violinos subconscious while he rolled, tossed and turned in bed—images of Loretta flashed like three second still frames through his inner eye; her naked body—red dress—her face—lips—legs—her corpse arrested to the murky depths of a watery grave—a Manchester football club supporters celebrating a goal—a chess board where the pieces were animals; carnivores and herbivores empathizing survival.

He rolled over—silk sheets cried in loneliness and his eyes met the glow of his time piece, 9:48am. At 10:30 he was to meet the guys at the Italian Club for breakfast before splitting ways. By 3:00ish in the afternoon, he hoped to be travelling home in his car with Mario from a meeting with the Capofamiglia of Queensland.

A smile spread across his face—the sound of rubber on road sweetened the air in his lungs.

His body stirred, feet found the carpet floor and an erection stood pride of place between his thighs.

He entered the shower—a blast of water cascaded his body and Holly's name glided on the warmth of his sigh.

The atmosphere outside was steamy and his car smelt of musty vinyl, pulling onto the road joining a long line of others that would follow twists and turns to their destinations, bumper to bumper, like ants from prey to mound.

He entered Foster Drive from Baradine Avenue; the clubs car park lay half filled, locating Mario's, Salvatore's and Seppi's cars anchored in their bays, side by side. An empty bay lay waiting next to Seppi's.

A breeze tickled his skin on entering a shadow caused by the clubs roof collecting suns rays—his feet processed the difference between concrete, tiles and carpet, as a messy sound of music entered his eardrums. Poker machines hypnotised the possibility of chance to happy morning gamblers—finding the guys', wave their tables' position to him.

"We've ordered kid," Seppi advised.

He turned on his heels and headed for the menus bar.

An animated chorus of laughter erupted on his return lifting his chin sharply in a question to it.

"This stronzo thinks," (Mario pointed toward football club situated behind the Italian Club) "that César's' sword will wield and they will win the championship this year."

The laughter continued.

The comment also brought broad smiles from faces sitting at other tables close by.

Salvatore defended his reasoning.

"Sal you shouldn't play with yourself in public," Violino spluttered.

"Why the fuck not..?" He cried.

"Play with yourself?" Violino questioned him. "This is a public place Sal."

"No . . . you prickly pear . . . Why won't they win? Stranger things have happened. No?"

"Sal that's not strange. That's x-files," the young Don informed him, clasping his hands together pleadingly.

The others followed suit under choreographed pleas.

Mario shook his head at Sal, responding to Violinos comment. "They're not hard enough on their players. You have to have discipline to have direction and leadership . . ."

And Violino butted in before Mario could finish.

"If those useless pricks lost a game with me in charge, I would string them up to hang upside down by the girders of that grandstand and fire footballs at their fucking heads until they learned some guts!" (The others around the table and people sitting close by nodded agreement.) "Fucking pussy's . . . They play like skips."

Mario placed a club program in front of Salvatore while Violino rambled on.

Salvatore picked it up flicking through the pages until he came across the squad line-up.

"Fuck me," he said, screwing his face up. "They are skips!"

Laughter found the room once more.

A waitress carried four breakfast plates crossed the floor to their table.

"Parlare Italiana?" Violino asked.

The waitress smiled back at him.

"Si Signore`," she replied, as each breakfast order found the correct person.

"See. An Italian and no fuck ups . . . what's their excuses?" The young Don explained, eying her features.

A diamond ring decorated with pride her wedding finger under memories of advice given from his father *you should never slurp from another man's soup.*

A murmur of voices mumbled in the background in time with clings and clangs of cutlery and china.

The aroma of their breakfast focused his attention back to the table.

Salvatore giggled. "The last time I went to the surf, I got burned."

"Yeah . . . His amante caught him cheating on her . . . with his wife!" Seppi followed on in great humour.

"Yeah I remember that!" Mario exclaimed. "She was going to cut his balls and bolt off. Fry them up in a little olive oil and garlic and send them, fully serviced back to the wife . . ."

*   *   *

The some of traffic on Nudgee Road; had mostly reduced. Deli turned the air-conditioning off activating the power windows on the steering-wheel.

The Maserati purred like a pussycat while his attention was momentarily diverted to a Boeing 767 with its flaps extended and landing gear down on final approach into Brisbane Airport.

The only way to travel ran across his mind, as he recalled childhood dreams of becoming a pilot. He saw himself shooting down F-4U1 Corsairs and P-51 Mustangs in his Fiat with *Ciao` Bella* painted down its sides.

And then Buchanan Road; took his sight and the warehouse filled his memory.

He turned right and followed the road along its L-shape to the block the warehouse sat on remembering the building was covered by tall Christmas trees along its sides and back, pulling up by the front of the building.

An aroma of pine cones filled his nostrils, sparking other childhood memories from his sub-conscious, climbing the curbing following the power cables from the power pole down the right side of the warehouse in search of surveillance cameras or other security measures.

The trees sang an eerie presence orchestrated by a breeze as if confirmation had been made by his sure and steady footsteps, following the leading edges of the guttering with no sign of electronic surveillance.

The big bay window was as big as Violino mentioned; a forest of trees covered its every angle and he placed his hands on the glass like brackets drawn off a page resting his head between they're gap to have a look inside.

Another point's correct he thought.

The building lay shut during daylight hours so he investigated the tree line and beyond in search of this magical angle that covered all inside angles, again proving the young Don correct, as the eeriness brought on by the choir of trees danced shivers down his spine.

He walked along the dirt driveway to the back block entrance noticing if it wasn't for a split in a fence, you would never have noticed it was there but decided he wouldn't use it, instead deciding to park up the street in the shadow of a building where he had a better chance of slipping away un-noticed.

He made his way back to the bay window, through the break in the fence and along the dirt driveway—when and a reflection caught his eyes mirrored off the glass. It was him and the thought *I'll be seen* as he found the angle again.

He imagined himself in the moment—the fire-arm pointed ready to fire at the first of his two targets.

He could see the lights inside the warehouse pool around his body, giving his position away, knowing he would have to find a better position.

And raising his chin—he looked up.

*   *   *

Beads of sweat ran down Eric and Ronato's faces on approach to Pizzeria la Famiglia. Shadows ran the hot pavement stirred by slow moving white puffy clouds as each footstep produced sludge sounds from sweat build up in their shoes.

Tracksuits blended them into a continuous flow of Rugby League spectators entering the Stadium, as Junior Rugby League started their fixtures program.

They had spent most of the morning walking the block, making notes on the best positions to arm with surveillance equipment. Power poles seemed to be the best places, as Ronato jotted down each poles position and the utensil to be placed there.

"You hungry..?" Eric asked, tapping him on the shoulder, flicking his head in the direction of the restaurant.

"Yeah I could do a slice and drink," Ronato replied—a smirk lightened his face.

Ronato opened the door and stepped into the air-conditioned room holding the door open for Eric to enter.

"What you want?" Eric asked, as he passed Ron.

Ron peered up to the order board skimming down the menu—letting go of the door making his way toward the counter.

"Pizza d'Italia and a Chinotto Cola," he replied, watching the guy behind the counter write the order.

"Make that a small Pizza d'Italia, Chinotto Cola and a cold glass of Chianti for me," Eric added.

The guy behind the counter adjusted the order sending it into the kitchen.

A frosted wine glass and soft drink flute slid across the small opening from kitchen to the area behind the front counter along a stainless steal top, as Ronato and Eric turned to find a table.

Again they found themselves well camouflaged. The restaurant was three quarters full of other patrons.

They found a table in the back corner overlooking the large plate glass window that took in the road view. Eric's eyes ran over every inch of floor space and structural design, making mental notes of points of interest.

Ronato took his note book from his pocket and placed it closed upon the table cloth that shared his tracksuit colours.

A feminine hand placed two drinks on to the table from his right side. *Your pizza won't be long* breaking the silence between them.

Eric nodded her presence—admiring her features.

"What you think?" He asked Ronato, while watching the waitress head back to the counter, the sway of her hips glued his eyes.

"I don't think we need to plant listening devises in here. The parabolic lasers will take care of all that out there on—probably that power pole," drawing an invisible line across the street. *Video surveillance..? Definitely:*

Eric nodded agreement, finding the curve of his wine glass while tracing the hourglass figure of the waitress.

*   *   *

Donna pulled along the curb apposite Holly out front of the Austrella apartment, strands of brunette hair danced on the breeze as rainbows of colour washed over her head from the sun's rays.

Holly's face was a glowing artwork of kindness understanding why men were attracted to her.

She wound down the window—watching her lean into it.

"Hello beautiful." Donna greeted.

Holly lifted the door handle sliding into the passenger seat, leaning across the centre console to give her a kiss—her smiling face added to the excited atmosphere of the mood.

"Thank you." Donna giggled. "Feel like a drive?"

Holly smiled and closed the door.

Checking for oncoming traffic, Donna pulled away from the curb.

"What do you have in mind?" Holly asked, her vibrant voice sang anticipation.

"Well. I thought—if we were seen together somewhere in Brisbane before everyone knew you were back officially, it might create suspicion. Some people might put two and two together," she said, checking her mirrors before merging into the left carriageway. "So I thought, why not make a day of it and take a drive into the country. There's this wine region I've heard lots about but as yet haven't checked out," she said, watching Holly nod agreement. "Great, and while we are travelling, we can talk and discuss the case."

"Deal," Holly reciprocated, clapping her hands.

She leaned forward retrieving a notebook and pen from her hand bag before looking at Donna. "Where would you like to start?" She asked.

"How about the church on Christie Lane . . . I understand you found nothing," Donna queried, disappointment sounded her voice.

"Yeah we entered the premises through the front entrance. Other officers waited around the back *as you do* . . ."

Combing her hair with her hand, she followed the road with tunnel vision. The North side turned into the Southside on their way to the country. "We had received a tip off, originally from a concerned parishioner who had on several occasions heard foul language being spoken by a regular visitor of the priest. After several visits investigating the complaint, the uniformed officers identified Brescio Caratella. This of course sparked the interest of the department.

It was flat luck I was given the raid. They had had several officers investigating the family undercover," pointing toward Donna in recognition of her part. *Mine was a fresh face—or so they thought* a giggle left her lips.

Donna interrupted to ask a question. "Who did you have with you?" (Her left hand floated off the steering wheel, excusing the interruption.)

Holly traced a finger over her left eyebrow crossing her legs to interfere with the flow of air-conditioning.

"There were six uniform officers, myself and Senior Constables Station and Best," she stated, facing Donna, watching her pilot the car through Southern Brisbane. "We searched everywhere. The pews, confession booths, altar, the back rooms, and there was nothing. We flicked through the churches records and ledgers: Nothing. We asked the priest if he could understand why complaints had been lodged against a certain regular. He shrugged his shoulders and said no. So we thanked him for his time and apologised for the disturbance, and left."

"What's you gut tell you?" Donna asked, as city roads turned to country.

"There's something not right there," Holly answered.

"Same feeling I get," Donna agreed.

*   *   *

It seemed to Mario the mercury had climbed a point or two, as they climbed out of his car and headed for the casino lobby.

Violino made mention of the canals and how it would probably be a good idea to set up a Gondola and party cruise business.

Mario did some ball-park estimates on initial investment in his head.

The main bar lay mainly full. A few tables by a bank of elevated television monitors sat empty inviting the use of passers by.

Violino pointed to the far one sitting in the corner and they headed over to it sitting down.

"Maybe we should place a bid for this place," Mario suggested, watching an endless flow of people exchange hard currency for gambling chips.

Violino laughed, openly taking in the ballet.

"Chance invites women—invites booze—invites men—guarantees profit."

"Women—money—booze and sex, music to my ears," Mario confessed, catching a glimpse of Don Cavalieri.

The Capofamiglia entered the main bar.

Both men found it very unusual to see him alone.

Violino stood up and straightened his suit making his way over to greet him. His smile was welcoming, yet hinting concern.

"Ciao` Compare`," he greeted, hugging and pecking each side of his face with kisses.

"Buono e tu..?" The Don replied, smiling.

(Mario approached and greeted him.) "What news do you bring from Brisvegas?"

Violino and Mario led him to their table calling a waitress over to order drinks.

"How is business Violino?" Don Cavalieri asked once more, placing his hand on his like a father would a son.

"Business is good. Drugs are not. Our rat sniffs snow.'"

Don Cavalieri dropped his eyes to the surface of the round white table *do you know who* his voice was low with concern.

"Not yet," Violino replied, as the waitress carried their drinks over, the men nodded appreciation.

Don Cavalieri bedded his drink upon a white napkin looking the young Don in the eyes saying *bait the runs Violino.*

"That's not all," Mario added. (His eyes were met by the Dons.) "We've had the government sniffing around the church and the warehouse."

The Don swallowed the drink in one gulp while the early steadiness of his demeanour turned to turbulence drawing his eyes upon Violinos in like a snake hypnotising its prey.

"Get me a name and I'll have him put to rest," standing up and walking away.

"I think he's pissed off," Mario said, rubbing the cool glass of whisky sensually against his lips.

"Brescio runs the drug business," Violino laughed.

*   *   *

After exploring the capital of the South Burnett, the girls settled on a picturesque winery with rolling valley and water views. A sweet scent of Daffodils drifted the mountain air, as they sipped wine from goblets. A low murmur of chatter welcomed the visit, and a waitress presented their order of lunch.

Perfectly braised steaks with potato bake and fresh crisp salad excited their eyes, they both complemented the waitress on the food presentation and ordered another round of drinks to accompany the cuisine.

It seemed to nicer-place to talk about business, the atmosphere was warm and welcoming and the views sumptuous.

Holly looked down upon Donnas plate, her mind firmly focused on the layout of the church and what herself and the other officers had missed when they raided it. She mentally studied the architecture figuring the building must have been commissioned during the war years. Maybe there was an underground access to it. Maybe there was a tunnel connected to the drainage pipe feeding the Brisbane River.

She took the last sip of her first glass of wine fumbling with the cutlery that was wrapped in a napkin speaking her thoughts.

"Maybe we should investigate the blue prints of the church," she took hold of her cutlery eagerly anticipating the first fork full of food. "The State Library would have those records wouldn't they?"

Donna digested with a sip of wine her first sample answering Holly's question. "Yes, good idea. What's your thinking?" Her face asked as much of the question, as the question itself.

"Well. The building might have been built in the war years. If so, most of the structures back then had secret exits or storage space built into them for fear of enemy invasion or capture."

Donna nodded and agreed with her watching her make a note of it in her notebook.

Their second order of drinks arrived and an echo of sound brought truth to a tractor off in the distance, clearing a vacant block of Earth under the constant hum and serenade from the breeze like a violin through power lines.

Savouries had turned to desert and coffee, both women were satisfied with the bounty thus far.

"Do you think Violino uses his businesses to store substances?" Holly's question stirred a contemplating silence in Donna.

She leaned forward crossing her arms upon the table.

"I don't think he works like that," she answered thoughtfully, swirling a sip of wine. "It doesn't stretch reality to much to presume that they plan allot of things together at the Nightclub and probably the other places. But as fare as I've seen, there's nothing solid stored at any of them . . . as funny as it sounds. I have heard criminals testify that legitimate ventures and criminal ventures should never mix. I think Violino follows the same rule.

He isn't going to be easy to bring down. Most of his dealings are physically done by other people. I think the only way we are going to get him is to follow the money trail," Donna pondered, before rolling red comfort around the inside of her mouth.

The waitress served their desert, the smile on her face matched perfectly the serine countryside.

"Well as smart as he seems, he's not perfect," Holly said.

A smile brightened her face as she snuggled herself into her chair with spoon in hand cracking through the solid chocolate dressing of her ice-cream tart.

"Has there been any breakthrough with Best and Station?" Donna asked.

Her face showed delight in tasting her creme caramel.

"No. They are still missing. Their mobile unit was found and recovered but the unit laptop and fire-arms were missing. Internal Affairs found five different—foreign sets of finger prints around the car. Two of the sets were their own;" she giggled. "As they investigated the unit, one set was from the police towing unit that brought the car back to the station. One set, was from a little boy who must have touched the car in passing and the other set belongs to Sergeant Sugar after he inspected the vehicle."

She took a sip of wine and then a spoon full of desert entered her mouth, after asking Donna about her investigation.

"What have you uncovered?"

"Not allot. Basically he gives an order and things get done. We've tried to wire tap him and leave other sensitive surveillance equipment but it is really hard to do without a flipped member on the inside. Any equipment we do get through the door—leaves when we do, because we are wearing it. But I do know he doesn't want the drug business," she stated, enjoying her desert.

"Can't we tie him to that?" Holly asked.

"No. Brescio runs that. We can tie Violino and Brescio together through the restaurant, 'Night Spot Italia,' at Parklands. But there, Brescio is Violinos employee and even though we know Brescio is dealing drugs, we cannot connect Violino to him. But—I don't think Violino likes him. They don't mix in public and if gossip on the street is anything to go by, Violino wouldn't lose any sleep if Brescio went missing," playing with her desert. "We just don't have enough. Violino is too clever," she stated. (A hint of frustration filled her voice.)

*   *   *

The traffic on the Pacific Motorway was bumper to bumper. An accident one and a half kilometres up the road slowed it to inching pace proving the trend for Salvatore and Seppi's movements.

They drove around Brisbane on the 'H' trail, checking all of Brescio's stash drops in hope of picking up the names of suppliers. The move on Brescio was only a couple of nights away and Violino was worried that if they took Brescio out without also taking out his main supplier, there would be white rooftops all over Brisbane with birds skydiving for thrills—pointing a sticky red arrow back to the Bruglioni family.

In the ledger they took from Brescio's office they found all of his entries were written as *Supplier one—Buyer one. Supplier two—Buyer two* . . .

A cold sweat had formed like condensation on the young Dons' and Mario's foreheads, when they opened it at the Calabrese Club.

Salvatore recalled the tone on Mario's voice when he said *what if he runs the restaurant like this.* Violinos reply was *what if his tapped out suppliers mistake the restaurant for his fucking warehouse!*

Their first port of call was Indooroopilly. A captain proclaimed under Brescio's eyes ran storage sheds which were really second hand shipping containers they stole from a charity run organisation.

Brescio thought it was a perfect cover for an 'H' house. He called it his Hyper—Market.

Alessio Nuarima was a second rate pimp when Brescio found him banging junkies in dark alleyways. The two hit it off while snorting snow at rave parties in their early twenties.

In many respects Alessio reminded the guys of Brescio. They both ran their mouths off hoping to gain notoriety for their escapades and as with Brescio, when Alessio saw the guys approach him, his balls retracted into his abdomen and he ran. An act which disappointed Salvatore immensely, as it was over 30 degrees in the shade and a running race up and down hills, he didn't want.

He called for Seppi to assist by following in the car.

After they caught and contained him, they went to work on extracting what he knew but he did something unexpected. He said nothing. So they stuffed him in a rubbish bin, slamming the lid on tight.

Seppi ran to the boot of the car and found some gaffer tape sealing the rubbish bin water tight, tying a knot to the bin-lids handle, securing it to the boot lock of the car—taking him for a little drive, tractor tube style over the bitumen roads of Indooroopilly—a thrill which didn't sit right with Alessio.

After Salvatore punched a hole through the tin, Alessio spilled everything he knew about Brescio's drug trade and how he ran things. He told him about the *Ipswich and Beenleigh connections* and other Cavalieri family rejects running a tightrope of drugs. Even that Don Cavalieri had promised to boot Brescio up a notch or two; level in rank with Violino.

Salvatore and Seppi looked at each other and laughed, as Salvatore reached down into his trouser pocket pulling out his cell phone.

Seppi kicked the rubbish bin onto its side rolling it around the ground for fun while listening to Alessio scream.

Salvatore ended the conversation—pocketing the phone.

"What did he say," Seppi asked, as he gave the bin one last final push with his foot.

Screams of *I told you everything* echoed out of the hole punched into its side.

Laughing, Sal looked over at the rolling cylinder of metal pointing to it.

"Metal, water and falling, mean anything to you?"

Seppi's face exploded in smiles.

They loaded the bin into the boot before jumping into the front themselves.

Pulling away, Sal glanced over at Seppi saying they first had to check out other places Alessio had told them about.

Seppi pulled a copy of the Brisbane Street Directory from the glove box asking partly dazed under circumstance *where the fuck we gonna find a water fall?*

Sal took a moment and then said *who says it has to be water . . . ?*

*   *   *

Violino pushed the brake pedal down with his right foot parking his car between two sheds that stood in a complete row, across the street from the warehouse on Buchanan Road: Moonlight streamed down from the night sky adding extra depth to shadows and dimly lit areas.

Mario watched the left access keeping eyes peeled for any sign of movement coming down the street while the young Don focused his gaze dead ahead, hoping not to see Deli—(the echo of Salvatore's voice still sounded a ghostly warning between his ears) *Ipswich, Beenleigh and the Cavalieri family stood out worthy targets* as headlights danced beams of light down the road.

Four white streaks split the darkness before disappearing like an unfinished dream, collapsing under the weight of night.

Violino lifted a walky-talky to his mouth pressing the communication trigger to release a perfect score of sound into its mouth piece.

"What you see Deli?"

"Fuck me kid, this fucking Barbie doll; he's snorting the shit in bucket loads!"

The young Don nodded in full recognition of Brescio's practises.

"Do you have them both?"

Fucking dope heads Mario rang a comment in the background.

"Don't worry kid. I've got an Owls view. *Gertrude* and *Annie* are right in front of me."

Screwing his face, Mario appreciated the jovial description.

"It's about to happen kid. The police are here," he informed them.

Violino and Mario looked at each other.

The atmosphere in the car trembled like a heavy duty wash cycle.

Mario questioned. "How can he see them?" (Violino shrugged his shoulders.) "We are sitting right in front of the building and I don't see a fucking thing!" Mario urged, as he and Violino bobbed their heads up and down and from side to side looking for the best vantage angle—and then slapping the young Dons' arm, asked excitedly. "Where the fuck is he?"

The cars suspension acknowledged each movement.

"Don't be seen Deli!" Violino ordered.

The message vibrated out of the walky-talky into Deli's ear.

"Don't fucking worry kid. They will never see me. I'm up a fucking tree."

What the fuck fell out of Mario's mouth—his searching gaze ran the length of each tree that encircled (in his view) the building Brescio, Stefano, the guys delivering the drugs and the police were in.

"What kind of trees are they?" He asked rhetorically, wondering how a branch could support his weight.

"Never mind what type of tree it is! How the hell did he climb the thing! He weighs 300kg's!" Violino stuttered, echoing his voice off the windscreen.

"Some trees can support the weight of a plane . . ."

"What the f-u-c-k you talking about Mario..?" He screeched, firing question marks at him.

His index finger pressed the walky-talky trigger. "What the fuck you mean you're are up a tree . . . !" Each of his words bounced off the surfaces in the car like a ricocheting bullet.

Mario mumbled to himself the resistance needed to arrest a mass like Deli's while Violino sat waiting for a response. His memory took him back to a British movie where all of the characters were gangsters in some way-shape-or-form, muddling all of their dealings in a hilarious ballet of movers and shakers. And then shook his head at the arrival of similarity.

"Don't worry about a thing kid," Deli said, steadying his position on the tree branch.

For extra support, he nestled his back against the trunk, giving him a better weapon sight toward the first target.

"The police have made their move kid. It is chaos in there."

A rock drama of sound broke the evenings' steady breeze. Ordered shouts and frenzied disclaimers muffled their way through the wall of mortar and glass.

The blast of sound brought true the actions, Deli witnessed with his own eyes.

He drew the sight of the police issue to bear on Stefano once more, as his body lie flat on the concrete floor. His ankles were crossed and his hands were cupped to the back of his head.

Shouts of *drop your weapons and lie flat on your stomach* coloured the proceedings.

In a microsecond of calm, he pulled the trigger. Moisture carried by the breeze of night smudged a tracer of dampness through the air into the open part of the window embedding itself into its new home—the skull of Stefano.

A delayed dribble of claret marked difference to the concrete floor, as he adjusted his sight position to Brescio's tortured face.

Twists of white and red marbled his surprise at the evening's events, as again, he pulled the trigger—a shockwave of treble marked a second entry point success, the body fell to the floor as if it had been caught of balance by the desk it found in obstacle.

"It's done kid," he announced.

He slid himself down the tree trunk, shouts and yells still painted the night.

The police continued to secure the inside of the building, uncovering bags of drugs and weaponry and arresting the figures of delivery.

His feet made contact with the ground, the sparkle of two shell-casings at rest by the base of the tree marked an artistic moment that in hind-sight reflected the meaning of nature.

A voice entered his head, like tuning into a radio station broadcast *fuck or be fucked.* His face mimicked relief and concern as he leant over studying the two shell-casings taking one last look into the window at the play of bedlam—caressing the police issue in the palm of his hand, spinning it around like a spin-the-bottle and left.

"Are you out Deli?" Violinos question brought the walky-talky back to life.

His calm demeanour returned; reacting to the communications device more from memory than in the moment. That eerie feeling he left by the scene of the two shell-casings had faded, as he heard his own voice respond to the question asked.

"I'm fuckin' out kid."

A short pause of silence littered the speaker, as he waited for a response.

"It's all done?"

"It's all done. Two queens discarded and the police are like pit bulls sucking peanut butter."

The head-sets fell silent.

Violino and Mario looked at each other in exasperation.

What the fuck!

CHAPTER 10

Tuesday morning was a hive of activity at the station, officers and brass ran from one office to the next, carrying files and plastic pouch pockets containing all types of documents.

Ronato noticed a map of Nudgee hanging from the whiteboard. Blue, red and green marker lines traced different parts and positions highlighting entry and exit points along with addresses.

Their department seemed to be out of the mix and sparse of investigators with only admin noticeable and although they were busy, they weren't frantic like the other departments.

Reaching their desk they placed some personal items into draws and flicked through folders left on them. The relative quiet ran a chill down her spine.

One of the admin girls shuffled passed Ron on her way to another detectives' desk to drop off some files.

Holly greeted her; a good morning asking if she knew what was going on.

"Where is everyone?"

Ron averting his attention from a file greeted her, "Hey Heather."

"Morning Ronnie," she responded with puppy love coyly smiling back, before answering Holly's question.

"Arr . . . there was a shooting at the industrial estate at Nudgee last night. Two guys died."

Ron and Holly looked at each other. A shade of surprise coloured their faces. "You wouldn't know where at the industrial estate?" He asked.

Holly leaned forward upon her chair focusing heavily on Heather.

Heather swang on her hips answering the question. "Buchanan Road."

Holly grabbed her bag while her brother snatched the car keys from his desk, stumbling over his feet to keep up with his sister leaving the mumbled chatter and clicks and clacks of admin and computer keyboards behind.

*   *   *

Seppi sat in his car at the end of Weyba Street Nudgee, balancing a cell phone between the side of his face and shoulder while a digital camera was at work in his hand. His eyes were focused between the view finder and display screen recording movements of blue uniform police officers and crime scene investigators.

A confusion of voices filled the earpiece of the phone after he dialled Violinos number causing a giggle to wobble his sides.

Signalling his attention, Violino responded. "I'm here. What colours do you see?"

"There are different shades here," Seppi replied. "Ultraviolet," (Uniformed, he heard Violino scribble notes.) "And dramatic dark blue:" (Detectives; a shriek of sound from pen on paper culminated behind a drag, as he underlined with an exclamation mark.)

"Any familiar faces Sep?"

"Yeah," Seppi chanted. "Donna is here."

"Donna! That could work out an asset . . ." Violino jived smoothly. "Take heaps of happy snaps for us," he ordered disconnecting the call.

Seppi's earpiece fell silent. Looking down at the camera activated the zoom function recording the action playing out.

*   *   *

Buchanan Road was awash with crime scene activity, as Donna and Eric arrived at the warehouse. Police Crime Scene tape corralled the entire block off, as interested on-lookers scrambled for the best vantage points.

Television crews and reporters under pressure for the big scoop made a nuisance of themselves between the *busy bodies* and investigation units, trying to trick whatever comments they could out of somebody in uniform.

At first glance Donna noted the conditions; weather had started to roll in. The previous nights' breeze had turned into a gale and heavy grey cloud cover was rolling in waves of rips and curls. Then there was the vegetation. The gale interrupted the calm of the trees surrounding the property, showering pine cones and nettles down onto the ground.

Eric headed off into the building to start building their investigation. Donna continued with the outdoor scramble, shutting out the loud murmurs from the crowd instead studying each movement of the investigators doing their jobs.

She pulled a notebook from her pocket, as one of the crime scene investigators came toward her, his eyes focusing immediately on hers.

She read his mind flashing her badge, drawing him toward her.

He stopped by her side and opened his notebook sharing crime scene particulars with her.

"From what we can ascertain at this stage, the shooter was elevated off the ground when the round was discharged."

Donna eyed his features, as his gaze was firmly fixed onto the page he was dictating from.

"What makes you so sure?" She asked, interrupting his flow. (Their bodies moved in sink.)

He turned pointing out fabric fibres found on the trunk of a tree in perfect firing angle to the position of the bodies in the warehouse and then pointed to plaster castings that were being taken of slight shoe impressions they found on closer scrutiny next to two shell casings sitting on orange pine cone nettles.

"From what we can ascertain, he came this way" (pointing to the back of the block through the trees) "and climbed this tree," (highlighting the first branch) "balanced himself on that branch and pulled the trigger, oh . . . and he's a heavy fella. The shoe impressions we found could only have been made by someone weighing" (he pouted his lips thoughtfully, twisting his open right hand side to side) "around 250 to 300kg's:"

Donna took a step back and looked up to the height of the branch. The scientific investigator laughed, as he watched the surprised expression shape her face.

"How..!" She asked, moving closer to the trunk of the tree running her hand carefully over the bark, "did a 300kg man climb this bloody tree? Are there puncture marks in the ground from a ladder?"

The scientific investigator continued to laugh as he shrugged his shoulders.

Donna kneeled down taking a closer look at the ground surrounding.

"We've checked that. No sign of anything to assist him up."

"Is he human?" She asked, laughing herself. "Maybe we are looking for a little green man calling him self Houdini . . ."

"Who ever it was, they were professional. He took," (the investigator looked down at his notebook reading the names of the bodies,) "Brescio Caratella and Stefano Picci out while the address was being raided by plain clothes."

Donna nodded in acknowledgment.

He flipped the top cover over closing the notebook.

She looked up the tree, kicking her mind into problem solving mode.

The other investigator turned away starting off, stopping suddenly.

"Oh. Donna! The shell casings were police issue," he tilted his head returning to his investigations.

Donna looked at the tree and at the police working in the building through the window and then at the chalk figures drawn on the concrete floor.

*   *   *

Looking at Violino with a smile on his face, Mario ended his phone conversation.

"We know who the supplier is and where to find him," he reported.

Violino stood up and instructed him to call Deli telling him to wait at his place for them.

Mario pulled his cell phone from his pocket dialling Deli's number.

Violino slid his car keys off the table and with Mario—headed for his car.

*   *   *

Holly's tummy had started to rumble after Ronato mentioned lunch and the Calabrese Club. It was a place they knew well as children, sharing many Christmas and Easter celebrations with other family members and friends. And it was a place that held many good memories.

They entered the building to find a flood of people sitting at their tables, eating lunch or talking over drinks. The cool air-conditioned atmosphere provided welcomed comfort from the heat of the day.

A waitress carrying a tray of drinks pointed them toward an empty table near the rear of the dinning-room snatching it before it could be taken by anyone else on entering.

To Holly, it was like entering a time capsule. The decor and its presentation hadn't changed a bit. Even the music was the same, although sang by a different artist. Where it would have been Mario Stanza, the vocals had changed to Luciano Pavarotti.

The waitress finding them at their seats greeted them a good afternoon opening her note book to take their orders.

Ronato tapped his fingers on the table to the music playing out of the sound-system. Holly sat smiling watching him, he looked more and more like their father each day matching their habits like two spirits sharing the same skin.

As the waitress came back with their order of drinks, an elderly man had followed, looking Ronato over with great detail.

The gentleman was hunched over with a head of grey hair and a much wrinkled face.

Ronato alerted Holly; they had been spotted describing the man to her, as the waitress placed their drinks to the table.

"Ronato..!" The man called.

Ronato looked at him trying to recognise his face but nothing was registering.

"Ronato, dis is you," the man asked, stopping level with Holly's chair. "You don't remember me?"

Again Ronato looked at him but his face was to foreign due to the passing of time.

As the man saw Ron eye him, he looked at Holly and his eyes filled with an instant pool of tears. "Holly . . . my beautiful little Holly, you're a woman now. Do you remember me?" He asked, placing his old hand gently to her shoulder.

Holly remembered back to when she was a little girl, during a Christmas celebration. A man had picked her up out of her chair and carried her over to the Christmas tree, where a lady waited with a big pink present.

The man swung her from side to side, laughing and chanting her name.

In a second, she felt her feet take the weight of her body and her eyes filled with a reciprocating well of tears, as her arms leaped from her sides to embrace the gentleman who had recognised her and her brother.

"Compare` Cavalini. Oh my God, how are you!?" Sang from her lips, their embrace held their bodies tightly to each others. (Her ears rang with the same chanting she remembered at Christmas time.)

Ronato too stood in his place; his hand extended out and brushed the side of the gentleman's face affectionately.

"I knew it was you. As soon as you walked in, I knew it was my two little ones," the old man said, tears running down his cheeks.

Ron pulled a chair placing him upon it.

Holly sat back down running her hand across the table to rest on his.

"I was only talking about you the other day," he said, watching Ronato slide his chair into the table. "E` now you are here."

"Is Comara here to?" Holly asked. Excitement electrified her voice, as she looked around the room for her.

But his face dipped momentarily to the table. "No. Comara died three years ago, nothing bad . . . just old age."

Ronato's eyes started drizzling tears as well, as his memories took him back to many a Christmas, where Mr. Cavalini would play table football with the boys, telling them who he thought they would marry when they were men.

"And how is Pauli. Still a cheeky boy?" Laughter rang from him, as the question took his aged ears.

"He is going good . . . he is his own boss," (pride streamed from his old face in recognition of his sons efforts.) "And what of you Ronato, what do you do?"

"I work in security."

"A good job..?"

Ronato nodded a positive reply to the question, (their hands met across the table with warmth.)

"And what of my Holly . . . what do you do darling?"

His smile filled her heart with love.

"I am a model," she said, her eyes sparkled; the pride she saw in his.

Their eye contact momentarily broke, as the waitress delivered the lunch orders.

Compare' Cavalini laughed as he looked down at their plates, a nodding action accompanied the laughter. "Ravioli Bolognese for Holly, e`, Chicken Cacciatore for Ronato," applauding his own memory. "See. Love never forgets."

"Where are you sitting Compare`, would you like to join us?" Ronato asked.

But the old man shook his head saying he was with another party.

"Do you remember the house? I still live there. Please give me the pleasure of your visit. Pauli lives there with me and I know he would like to see you again. You come, si?"

They nodded in acceptance. "Soon compare," Holly promised (watching the old man slide his chair away from the table.)

Ronato stood up assisting him to his feet.

"Holly . . . do you remember Violino?"

Yes she replied.

"I think he would be happy to see you again. When you mamma took you away, he was very sad."

He touched their faces again and repeated the invitation leaving the table.

Holly and Ronato took their seats looking at each other.

Ron picked up his fork playing with the Chicken Cacciatore on his plate before chiding *well, if no-one knew we were back before—they will now* a smirk covered his face.

* * *

Late morning had turned into early afternoon, as Violinos Alfa Romeo 156 danced its way over the changing surfaces of road.

The D'Aguilar Highway gave way to the Kilcoy—Beerwah Road. Mario, who sat in the passenger seat (directly in front of Deli in the back,) traced their way with a Brisbane Street Directory.

You've got us lost haven't you chimed out of Violinos mouth, following the apex of each curve in the road.

Mario pointed his finger in a forward direction telling him the next turn was just up the road, reciting Commissioners Road laughing at the correlation.

"It's just up here on the left. We park across the other side of Narrow Bridge, and then walk south following the river for about half a click."

"Fuck me Mario, are we commandos!?" The young Don barked jovially.

Mario slapped him on the shoulder pointing to the road—flicking pages in the Brisbane Road Directory explaining the movements of the drug supplier . . . An unspoken understanding between the men hinted for the young Don to shut up and watch where he was going.

"It's the way this povero moves the shit. He grows it—produces it and loads it into his truck. Then he takes a drive down to Teneriffe where he picks up a container. He re-packs the shit into the cargo being carried in the container; that way, if the contents of the container are checked for any reason, the investigation is directed away from him," shrugging his shoulders mockingly.

The container comes from Asia floated out of Deli's mouth, showing Mario, he understood each movement.

Mario continued. "He then makes scheduled stops moving the shit; from container to tool boxes to cabin depending, until he has emptied the contents of the container to his legit customers, or delivered the container to its drop off point. If he empties the container himself for his clients, he places the stuff back into the empty container and drops it off to Brescios greasy mitts," ending the brief angling a look over to Violino who in turn looked into the rear-view mirror to Deli who was looking at the scenery through the windscreen, as Violinos mouth opened asking his consiglieri a question.

"Shit Mario . . . allot of fucking around no?"

He shrugged his shoulders. "Different strokes . . . The cargo isn't jelly beans. It's fuckin' H."

"Yeah but still . . . It's a lot of fucking around."

The Commissioner Road; sign loomed larger through the windscreen and Mario pointed at it, directing Violino to make the turn. The Narrow Bridge came to view shortly afterwards and they crossed it, parking the car in a small clearing.

Violino looked at Mario with concern and confusion.

"South..? Where the fuck is south?"

"Fuck kid you should have done National Service," Deli advised, frowning at him.

And Mario laughed pointing to the mountains. "The mountains are west. So east is that way," he pointed his pouted face at the young Don slapping his shoulder in the direction they were to go.

"Half a click..?" Violino asked in a comical manner.

"Yeah, just down here." Mario answered him, watching Deli's hefty frame stumble across a lump of dirt.

They found the house. The truck sat parked, framed by blue sky and mountain views. A chemical smell scented the air.

"Smell that kid?" Deli asked.

"H," Mario scoffed elevating his nose toward the house.

Deli slipped on a pair of surgical latex gloves removing the police issue fire-arm from his left pocket, checking its magazine cocking it ready.

As they made their way around the house, a slender man ratty in appearance came into view.

In typical Roman style, Mario flicked his chin at him in question.

"You the owner of this truck..?"

The man nodded in a positive reply asking who wanted to know.

Deli raised the weapon pointing it at him pulling the trigger firing round after round into his chest in a tight cluster until the magazine was empty.

"You think he's dead?" Violinos question found sarcasm, as they walked over to the slumped body which soaked the ground it laid upon red.

Deli wobbled the head with the toe of his shoe. "Well kid, it ain't breathing."

"Why do you think that is Mario?" The young Don asked; sarcasm painting his way.

"Cause there's blood blocking his airways kid."

"Ants won't go hungry," Deli added.

A dumb expression shaped his fatty face.

*   *   *

"Where have you two been..?" Sgt. Sugar yelled, as Holly and Ronato found their way into the office after lunch. His voice resembled a foghorn, as Donna and Eric sat smiling at them, watching them entered and stand at attention by two empty seats.

"Well . . . at least you have remembered your manners. You may sit."

They snugly sat.

"We have been discussing the events that took place last night at Buchanan Road;" Sgt. Sugar continued, shuffling with some pages on his desk.

Donna leaned toward Holly and said, "Brescio Caratella and Stefano Picci were killed last night."

Ronato replied that they knew—that Heather of administration had told them.

Sugar looked over at them asking, "Where the hell have you two been?"

His tone full of worry—sounded each syllable. "I hope you weren't at that bloody crime scene because if you were, it would be curtains for this operation. It was a professional hit that took Caratella and Picci out *and an extremely brazened one*! There must have been twenty police officers there last night," pausing momentarily painting serious looks to the eyes of his sub-ordinates. "And this bastard took them out with surgical precision."

"How do we know it was one person?" Ronato asked.

Donna answered the question. "There was only one set of shoe prints around the perimeter of the building. And he was a big boy. The trees around the complex leave a lot of debris yet there were quite pronounced shoe prints embedded into the ground."

"It wouldn't be too difficult to hide around that property, especially at night because of the trees. With a silencer and scope the difficulty would be greatly reduced." Ronato aired his thoughts.

"With twenty officers around," Sugar reminded them.

"From the angle of the entry wounds—the shooter was off the ground when he pulled the trigger," Eric entered into the chatter, after Sugar's exclamation.

Holly looked over at Eric with a puzzled look on her face. "Wait . . . Donna said he was a heavy man?"

Donna nodded.

"How did a heavy man get off the ground to take a shot at two men..?"

"He climbed a tree," Eric replied.

Donna nodded again.

Ronato and Holly shook their heads in disbelief.

"He climbed a tree." Donna told her.

"That's right, Holly. He climbed a tree." Eric stated.

Then Donna broke in.

"There was clothing fibres found on the bark of a tree metres away from the open louvre, situated on the left side of the building."

"That building is around the height of a two story building . . ." Holly aired, confused.

"That's right Holly," Donna said.

Eric laughed in the background, as Ronato dropped his head backwards to gaze at the office ceiling.

"But that's not the best bit. The shell casings were police issue."

Holly and Ronato looked at Sgt. Sugar's face. Their surprise suggested their discomfort at what Donna had just aired.

"Do we know who's?" She asked—concern evident.

"Forensics' are working on that, and the shoe prints and DNA. We should know more in a couple of days" The sergeant stated, sliding a manila folder containing the case files across the desk at Ronato.

Donna reached into her handbag for her cell phone. Its ring, made Holly jump out of her skin.

Sugar smirked at her surprise. "Edgy?" He asked her.

She threw him a smart aleck turn of her head.

Donna ended her conversation dropping the phone into her bag. The glow of her face stole Sgt. Sugar's attention. Her eyes were ablaze with anticipation.

"You have something to add?" His question brought silence to the room.

"Yes sir. That was Chris of Lights & Lace."

Holly and Ronato instantly averted their attention.

"Apparently there is going to be a re-union," (she looked across at them in turn.) "The old crowd . . . Violino is throwing it . . ."

"That's our in," Sgt. Sugar exclaimed, clapping his hands together. A smile covered his face. "When he sees you, he's going to shit," excitement flavoured his voice.

Donna nodded acknowledgment.

"That's it then," Holly said, a show of revenge tainted her aura.

Ronato looked at his sister with regained worry. A chill ran down his spine. The emptiness he felt when he was told about his fathers' fate returned and hoping Holly wouldn't fall the same way.

*   *   *

The Mediterranean Club was as normal, happy punters enjoyed their dinner soused by its atmosphere.

Violino sat alone in the booth closest to the counter with his eyes fixed on Clara—an erection pushed him passed the pain barrier, as her movements produced a blue movie starring them to play an endless loop in his mind.

He was his usual arrogant self as she passed him with an arm full of plates she'd cleared from a table.

Her skin crawled under his gaze and she hoped he'd keep his mouth shut and not attempt communication but her luck was out, craving the safety and privacy of the kitchen.

How about that drink he asked, prompting her to stop by him.

"Order something from the menu and I will get it," she said with trepidation.

He blew her a kiss and ran his finger up the black fabric of her mini skirt stopping at her hips, mimicking a kiss at her vagina.

"Your menu doesn't have what I'm thirsty for," he said full of lust.

She stepped away from his reach heading for the kitchen, the plates in her hands rattled from anger only to return intent on revenge throwing a laminated list of garbage disposal instructions his way grumbling *maybe this would be more to your liking.*

And leaning into the table folded his arms on its surface; a sarcastic smirk lined his lips under a cold frosted aura.

He said. "No honey, the only stink I want to eat is in your panties, so get over here and steady yourself across the table," patting it, pointing toward her vagina.

Fuck you Violino she spat, trudging toward the counter.

He wrapped his fingers around the half finished drink in front of him feeling a hand push down on his shoulder from behind.

A voice croaked in his ear. "You still up to your old tricks, Violino?"

Flicking his head around to see the time wrinkled face of a man he called Compare for as long as he could remember.

The man smiled at him patting his shoulder thoughtfully, saying *you always were a demanding one* sitting down at the opposite side of the booth.

Violino smiled at him saying while catching a glimpse of Clara trudging passed. "Compare Cavalini, what are you doing here?"

The Compare responded. "Violino I am an old man full of life and you are a young man short on experience. You should be at home tucked into bed."

Violino laughed and said. "Compare can't you see that's what I'm trying to do!"

The old man reached across the table placing his old hand upon his young friends advising. "If her father heard you talk to her like that, he would string you up by the balls for eighteen months and sell you to the Chinese ristorante down the street as prosciutto."

(Laughing Violino replied *he'd have to catch me first.*)

Clara returned to the table toting a plate of pasta Cabonara and a glass of Vino Rosso, cutlery and a bowl of Parmigiano placing it all down in front of the elder.

He laughed at her fussing winking warm heartedness.

Violino sat mesmerised at the state of play asking. "How the hell does she know what you want, you haven't spoken to each other?"

The Compare laughed and said. "Violino, we have a language all of our own."

Clara made a face at the young Don saying. "This man is a kind gentleman who has warmth and respect. You on the other hand are a pig that vomits," spitting her words like an aggressive snake.

Compare Cavalini thanked her and watched as she returned to her duties adding grated cheese to his pasta before hinting at his intention to speak.

"I would have thought you would be in the company of Holly somewhere?"

Violino lifted his stare level with the old man's.

"You've seen her too?" He asked, more like a statement than a question.

"E si, at the Calabrese Club at lunch time; she was there with Ronato. My God she has grown into a beautiful woman, just like Venus and Ronato, a strapping Gladiator like you read in all the best fables. A true Italian . . ." He said, resting his back against the cushioned booth. "I couldn't believe my eyes when I saw them . . . I had a dream the other night I would see them again and like a wish come true, there they were."

Violino leaned into the table. Interest folded the skin of his forehead asking. "Did she tell you where they are staying?"

"No," the old man answered after a mouthful of wine. "Only that she was a model and he was some sort of security person."

"Security . . . We need a decent security guard. I wonder if he would be interested in a job . . ."

"Violino why don't you find where they are and ask for yourself..?"

"I don't know where to look. Chris doesn't know where they are staying and no one else has seen them but you. When she left . . ." (He halted himself.)

Leaning over the table—the Compare placed his hand on the young Dons. "I know boy. I could see in your eyes, you were upset," (their eyes met once more.)

"If you talk to her like you do Clara and I find out about it, it will be my knife that cuts your balls off. Understand?"

Violino smiled understanding sliding out of the booth blowing Clara a kiss saying.

"I understand Compare."

* * *

The scene outside Lights & Lace was like a horror flick, a light summer shower had sprayed the molten tarmac and pavement with water: each droplet fought its own battle with the conditions as a dense cloud of steam hovered; a lonely linger; in company to the entrance of the nightclub.

Holly, Ronato, Donna and Eric thought they had gotten their nights mixed up, for where there would normally have been strapping security guards holding their own among a growing crowd of impatience, there was merely a sign dictating a private party.

The guys closed ranks looking silently at one another.

Ronato ventured toward the door (while his compatriots surveyed the entrances stillness) making contact with its smooth surface finding a pulse vibrating the secured fixture.

He pushed on it finding the door opened with little force. Muffled sound spilled through the gaps of the second doorway leading into the main entertainment area saying *it's on guys* curling a sign of invitation toward the doorway.

Their bodies were met by waves of energy, as a continuous thud from bass speakers found electricity in their throats. Seams of light broke throw thick clouds of disco smoke and an eerie aliveness gave celebration to each of their eyes.

It reminded Donna of Florence during carnival time. Purple and red lights coloured the fog at night, giving it a pretty ambience.

Eric was the last to enter—a memory of a movie reminded him of the experience out front and he shared it with the others.

"What was the name of that movie where a girl leads a guy (who played a fighter pilot of an F-18) into that freezer that led to a secret society nightclub where it was full of Vampires?" He stuttered. "Did that make sense?"

Laughing, the others looked at him thoughtfully.

Ronato scoffed, lost on the memory and movie title. "Hmm . . . I think I like the sounds of that. A room full of shooters and suckers."

Holly and Donna giggled his name giving him a friendly slap on opposite shoulders.

"You are just full of surprises aren't you?" Donna exclaimed, surveying him in a different light.

"Would you like to find out just how much?" He replied; a smirk coloured his glowing face.

She smiled back at him.

Together they fought through the crowd of faces, some they recognised and others were a mystery.

The bar was a welcomed sight, pushing their way into its steadiness.

The layout of the club was still a mystery, as they had only ever seen it at night. The walls were all painted black from top to bottom and who ever designed it in Holly's mind was a genius. Small passage ways opened out onto stage platforms where dancers and other performers would whip up endless explosions of excitement adding to sexy scented disco smoke which floated down from the ceiling cementing incredible lighting effects all of which made you want to find the nearest secluded place and make love.

Yet the atmosphere wasn't of a seedy nature.

Eric brought the first round of drinks and Ronato pointed to the third floor inviting everyone to follow up staircase, the sound system was booming and their ear-drums tickled to each thud.

At the summit of their climb, Donnas' heart skipped a beat as she spotted a familiar face sitting in a booth, grabbing hold of Holly and pulling her toward it when the familiar face looked over and they each squealed each other's names. *Dimity!!!*

Donna!!!

Holly!!!

"Oh my God . . . Holly!" Dimity squealed again in surprise, her pleasure at seeing her was genuine.

She slid across to the edge of the booth getting to her feet grabbing hold of the two ladies giving them a big hug and kiss, laying eyes on Ronato who was standing behind Holly larger than life. Tears of loss, welcome and memory welled in her eyes and she said after holding each in turn. "What happened to you? One day you were here and the next gone!" (Sign language acted each word.)

Holly and Ronato looked at Dimity and then at Donna and then at each other before finally directing their attention back to Dimity with big welcoming smiles.

Dimity laced her arms around them once more kissing their cheeks.

They all slid into the booth and got comfortable. A glow of recognition still lit Dimity's face—sliding her hands across the table to Ronato and Holly's.

"God it's great to see your faces again . . . what brings you back, are you on holiday? She asked, imitating a Southern American accent.

"We," Holly started to reply, "have moved back to the area," glimpsing her brother before bringing her attention back to Dimity.

"Where did you go?"

"After dad died, mamma got a job away. So, we had to move."

"Well it's good you are back. It's funny . . . But it seems everyone is moving back . . . like we're all supposed to be together forever. Do you remember Sarah? She is working for a computer programming company in Sydney. I here she is transferring back to Brisbane too. Pauli *he's here somewhere.* He's a brickie. Lisa," (Dimity tilted her head in question of recognition to them.) "She became an Architect and she's around somewhere . . . you should see her sometime tonight. *Oh* and Violino . . ." (She leaned into the table intentionally.) "Holly when you left . . . he changed, like a part of him died," (she held her breath, while surveying Holly's response.) "Well he's now the head honcho *if you know what I mean . . .*" She gave a thoughtful look of light heartedness to Donna. "Sorry darl. I forgot," she whispered, as she pointed toward her while looking at Holly and Ronato. "Law enforcement," laughter broke out between them.

A foot kicked the Austrella siblings under the table before a body leaned into the flickering light.

"Chrissie . . . you cheeky little shit, should have known you'd be here somewhere. We didn't see you at the bar . . ." Ronato said dryly, their hands clasping in a brotherly handshake across the table.

Holly's foot found his shin. "Not working tonight Chris?" She asked.

"NO . . . what are you joking . . . on reunion night!? I'd have to tender my resignation if Violino and the guys got me to work. I am one of the gang, you know," he stated matter-of-factly.

"As if I would forget that," Holly replied. "Dimity do you know Chris had a huge crush on you, when we were kids?"

"Yes. I know," she replied.

Chris laughed, as he confessed a secret they shared. "We've practised the w i l d thing."

The confession brought surprise around the booth.

"Dimity..! *The bow and the arrow . . .*" Holly laughed.

Donna kicked her under the table.

Holly screeched *OUCH* making everyone laugh.

"How was he?" Donna asked.

Dimity looked at Chris and smiled, her eyes flashed like fireworks. And laughing she said *crushed nuts.*

*   *   *

Seppi surveyed Violino on approach and asked before sipping his drink. "What's up kid?" (A smile curled his lips slapping his side.) "I bet she's here kid—you just haven't seen her yet," he counselled, taking another sip of his drink while looking around. "I didn't realise there were so many of you freckly shits breaking our balls all those years."

Violino slouched upon his bar stool.

"Fuck kid, there are three floors here; you know what I'm saying! Go and look around . . . find Chris!" He suggested, heading for the office.

Violino swivelled on his bar stool and looked around, a sea of familiar faces and mannerisms greeted his every angle.

Strobing light flickered through disco smoke that drifted from ceiling to floor, like a newly formed atmosphere sustaining a new biological species.

Splatters of laughter and chatter periodically broke through the music, adding to the charged atmosphere, the memory of sending out a book of invitations and folding them and placing them into peel and seal envelopes and the enjoyment the guys and himself had doing it, brought a smile to his face like back in the old days when he was a kid playing with the rest of the gang.

He enjoyed the feeling of familiarity and warmth it brought—the memories they relived seemed priceless, especially in the climate they faced in preset tenths.

His search for Chris found interruption. A chorus line of faces stopped him in his tracks, reciting memories and laughs brought on by a by-gone era.

But there was only one face he sought to see, that of an angel with perfect legs and eyes that opened a gateway to eternity.

But even so he let himself go, taking in all of the faces in all of their merit and social pasts. Friends which to his memory were in fact family;

men and women that were once boys and girls he played with kissed and experimented; life's growing pains.

Each level brought new old faces and new memories and sometimes, artefacts. Sporting emblems and matchbox cars shared space with each word and laugh and with each sip of beverages inhabitations fell silent a little more.

The interruption found solace in interaction.

He climbed the staircase to the next floor finding Pauli, splattering a memory he had with an old football friend of his. His hand movements played a tapestry of different field positions and tactics and his friend laughed and joined in on all of their boyish antics.

Pauli pulled him over and introduced him to his friend. A memory raced to Violinos recollection and the laughter around the second floor bar grew louder.

Pauli's friend signalled his need to visit the amenities room, leaving them to wait by the bar.

Positioning himself closer to Violinos ear, he asked him if he had seen Holly yet.

Shaking his head in response—took Pauli under the arm steering his ear to his mouth.

"Have you seen her?"

"Yeah she's up on the third floor with arr, Donna, Ronato, some other guy, arr, Dimity and Chris."

Pulling at his arm—Violino dragged him toward the staircase.

"You are gonna show me where," he said, with excitement and apprehension flavouring his words.

Pauli looked back at the bar for his friend but Violino told him not to worry, they would catch up with him later.

They stumbled up the first few steps unbalanced by Violinos shoving.

"Have you spoken to her tonight?" He asked, halfway up the stairs, pulling on Pauli's shirt.

"No . . . I was up here just before and saw her sitting in the booth with Dimity and the others."

"But you didn't talk with them?"

"No Violino. I didn't talk with them," he stuttered, as he felt Violino push him up the stairs again.

"Pauli! Make out we haven't seen them. Just make out that we've stumbled on them by mistake," the young Don ordered, pulling at his shirt once more.

"OK! Ok Vio," Pauli said, flinging up his hands, part in frustration and part in confusion toward his friends antics. "Leave it to me . . . It'll be a big surprise."

"E` but not an obvious surprise ok..?" Violino pleaded.

They reached the third floor and as Pauli had said he could see Holly just off in the distance sitting in a booth with Dimity and Donna. His thoughts ran back to what Compare` Cavalini said about how beautiful she had become and of Ronato's manly features.

He pulled Pauli close and told him to approach the table and say hello. And then said he would follow up and ask him if he wanted a drink.

Pauli agreed to the plan but couldn't understand why Violino wanted to play games with her.

He approached the booth.

"Arr..!" Donna screamed, as she looked up and saw his shadowy figure approach them. "Pauli! Pull up a pew and join us," she said, her hand tapped the edge of the table. "You know Holly and Ronato don't you? Or do I have to introduce you to our fleet footed ones?" She asked, using a mocking police tone.

He pulled up a chair and sat down, tapping his fingers to the music upon the table.

"Holy ravioli the Austrella kids . . . Dad said he saw you at the Calabrese Club," he confided stretching out his hand to shake Ronato's across the table. "I'll give you a cuddle when these criminals get out of the way," he stated, smiling at Holly. "Dad was right. You are hot."

Holly's face turned bright red hidden by the dim light.

Donna kicked him under the table. "Criminals Pauli..," she asked, more as a statement, as she ran her focus up and down his body jokingly.

"Your police aren't you?"

"E`..!"

"There you go. Ground level of the mob . . ." (A mouth full of pearly white teeth glowed under the fluorescent light.)

Donna lifted taught fingers to her mouth biting down on them.

Pauli ran four fingers under his chin; finding giggles in the comedy act.

Then out of the corner of her eye, Donna saw another shadowy figure approach, carrying two drinks in its hands.

"You move quick Pauli," the man said, as he dropped another glass full of alcohol upon table—finding recognition in Donnas' eyes under recognition the situation brought around the booth.

"Violino you remember Holly and Ronato Austrella," Pauli said, as he looked back over his shoulder.

Violinos eyes lit like fireworks in a candle factory at the sight of Holly. She was as beautiful as compare` Cavalini had said.

Her brown hair cascaded her shoulders and her lips were full and red. He wanted to slide across the table and bite them softly; looking at her chest—strong yet curved and featured.

Hello Violino left Holly's lips but all Violino saw was the sensual movement of future lust.

"Hey Violino," Ronato broke the booths silence, as he outstretched his hand in greeting.

The young Don reciprocated the gesture looking into each other's eyes.

"It's good to see you both again. Where did you go?" Curiosity contorted his face.

"Mamma got a job away. So we left. That's about it really." Holly answered.

His eyes burned holes of emotion into her stare. "Well I see you've found most of the old crew in the criminal element, anyway."

Donna lifted her eyebrows in question.

Pauli laughed, as Violino finished the statement. "Law enforcement... Ground level of the mob..," laughing, slapping Pauli across the back of his shoulders.

Donna looked up at him. "Grab a chair Violino and sit down," she said, pointing to a vacant seat just off to one side of the booth.

He grabbed it and sat down taking a sip of his drink to help steady nerves—critiquing himself at his movements reminding himself that he was the head of a family correcting his mood accordingly, melding himself into the atmosphere of his friends.

Small pockets of conversation broke off from the main group, yet mixed and mingled at the same time.

A heady scent of Myrtle which floated down amongst the disco smoke, combined with the alcohol and music to create a charge of familiarity that the group hadn't felt since their childhood.

Ronato and Violino found themselves embroiled in a heady conversation of discovery, as they asked each other questions of what they have been up to and what they were doing now.

Violino shook his head fully impressed by the news that Holly was a fashion model and that she had modelled for some house-hold names in the industry. A fact that didn't seem overstated from what he saw through his eyes.

She was a woman in every sense of the word and he was equally impressed to hear Ronato tell him about his security career, although the details were less than forthcoming. But he understood that, considering the vocation.

Then Ronato shook his head in acknowledgment of Violinos responsibilities, as part owner of the nightclub, and the other businesses and interests he had.

The theme of the music changed from good old contemporary stuff to modern and the girls wanted to dance. Donna and Dimity slid out of the booth, holding Holly's hands firmly to drag her off to the dance floor. Pauli and Ronato followed their way close behind. Eric flashed passed, only stopping to shake Violinos hand in introduction, as he was sitting next to Holly where the music was to loud to really understand anything.

Chris was last to move.

Violino join them on the dance floor showing what he could do.

The smile on Chris's face opened a new chapter in the story life-and-times of Holly Austrella and Violino Bruglioni.

The feeling of familiarity felt good, the old crew were nearly back together and the atmosphere was like it had never changed.

On the dance floor, the girls swirled and twirled seductively. The guys took on characters of matadors and emperors. Violinos eyes danced from Donna to Dimity to Holly as they presented a smorgasbord of different arousals with suggestive hip and leg movements. His penis grew full and charged hoping for the slightest touch to be granted to his finger tips while the lighting and scented smoke added to the erotica.

*   *   *

Upstairs in the office, Seppi and Salvatore sat sipping whisky watching the celebrations down below through the office window.

Mario sat at the table counting the nights' takings from the evening before.

"Mario! Come have a look at this," Seppi said, like a father out of pride for one of his own. "There is history on that dance floor," he swooned.

Salvatore placed a hand on his shoulder thoughtfully.

"Sal, Seppi come over here and leave them alone. Things will work themselves out. Come. Count," Mario instructed, throwing fifty and hundred dollar bills around the table.

"If this doesn't fix him up, nothing will," Salvatore aired in a stately manner, waving his hand in the air, heading for the table.

CHAPTER 11

The Mediterranean club was busy and vibrant much to Violinos dismay, as the reunion had challenged the face of the clock. Chatter and noise seemed to bounce off each inner surface into his head as a sickening orchestra of jack hammers and constructions crews worked off the night's festivities.

With each glance Mario and Seppi laughed at him while Salvatore took pity calling over a waitress to order him a coffee and soda water.

"What time did the reunion finish?" Mario asked; his laughter broke through each word like a musical score.

Violino looked at his watch and grimaced *half an hour ago* responding shakily.

Laughter broke again and he rested his head in his hands as his coffee and soda water arrived sending his stomach into a churn with a sorrowful sigh escaping his lips.

"What time did Holly leave?" Mario asked a second question, chuffed at his discomfort. (Violino took a sip of the soda water answering while holding his stomach.)

"Just then," he sighed, briefly pausing to grab the coffee with shaking hands. "She has a stubborn streak that one . . . she's too independent." (Another volley of laughter broke amongst the booth,) his head found solace in his hands while Salvatore aired *that's women kid.*

Mario pointed at him from across the table *you wait till you marry one!*

And then Seppi jumped in spilling his thoughts *or one marries you.*

Violino dropped his chin shaking his head saying *fuck the lot of you* as he gingerly got to his feet starting for the entrance.

"Where you goin' kid..? Father Option's is comin' for breakfast!" Seppi called.

The young Don turned, attentively focusing his gaze on the guys responding *you have breakfast with him . . . I'm goin' home to die . . .*

*   *   *

"We've got him coming out of the Mediterranean club and he is alone." Eric reported while watching Violino appear from the building. (Ronato typed the data into a laptop computer.) "He looks like shit," he added, as he turned the ignition key, flicking the indicator signalling intentions to oncoming traffic.

Ronato reported. "He looks like the human version of a rain forest. Basically the same as I feel." (Eric gave him a; *I don't get that* look.) And Ronato explained *green with steam.*

Watching him hale a taxi they followed it.

Ronato busied himself with the laptop, recording information step by step, as they snaked down busy streets to a private address.

"Oh we're at El Duce Street, New Farm arr . . . number 1860," he called down the wire to the waiting ears of Sergeant Sugar, tapping the data into the laptop. "It's his place."

Eric pulled up across the street adjacent steadying himself for another long wait.

*   *   *

"Holly are, you good to go?" Sergeant Sugar asked while watching the entrance of the Mediterranean club from the air-conditioned comfort of his car.

"Lights & Lace looks clear and I am good to go," she replied; sitting in an unmarked police car in the underground car park of the nightclub with a suitcase full of surveillance equipment sat ready by her side.

Sergeant Sugar said. "You are good to go Holly. Be careful. In and out as quickly as possible," he ordered, full of concern.

"Donna, are you good to go?" He asked once more. The chill in his voice found Donnas' ears and she responded.

"Yes the Calabrese club is steady and I am good to go."

"Be careful Donna and be quick."

"Yes sir," she replied.

Opening the back door with briefcase in hand, she entered the premises. A steady flow of chatter emanated from the kitchen, making her way to the office situated near the back door, close to where she had entered. She was grateful in her surprise to find the office unlocked.

The layout was simplistic, a desk sat in the middle of the room with paintings of Calabria decorating the walls with a wall unit of shelves and filing cabinet set against the back wall.

Sitting at the desk she opened the brief case grabbing a listening devise sliding open the third draw placing the bug on the underside, left hand corner of the second draw.

She then grabbed the nanny-cam packed neatly in black foam and stood up, positioning a chair under the air conditioning duct placing the camera securely on the slot furthermost away from the closest corner of the desk.

With the camera placed and listening device well hidden, she returned the room the way she found it, closing the brief case and leaving closing the door behind her on her way to the exit. Once there she again checked there was no one loitering in the car park or staff turning up for work exiting the building.

She got to the car hopping in, setting the case onto the passenger side seat, under deep breaths to steady herself as adrenalin ran her heart rate high and a cold sweat frosted her forehead.

"It's done," she said, winding down the driver's side window.

Sugar dropped a deep breath and sighed *one down one to go* staring intently at the entrance of the Mediterranean club happy there had been no movements from the other family members.

"Did you have any problems?" He asked.

No sir, no problems. I'm in the car leaving the site," she transmitted.

*   *   *

A sigh of relief left Holly's lips at the sound of Donnas' voice; she had run around placing bugs in the bar areas, rest rooms, cellar and ticketing office with her sights well and truly set on the office.

She pushed the door open feeling a shiver creep up and down her spine from the creak of its hinges.

A comfortable setting met her eyes on entry—leather recliners, flat screen television set and a polished cedar table took her first site and then the bay window which gave such a superb vantage point to all three levels of the club quickly acknowledging nothing would break the laser beam of a parabolic microphone aimed at it from an elevated position.

She quickly planted small cameras and listening devises in the ceiling and chairs, leaving as quickly as she entered.

A strong curiosity grew toward a doorway situated behind the bar, climbing down the stairs, taking stock of the inventory she had left.

One camera and bug remained.

Approaching the door gaining entry, her eyes widened giggling at the discovery of a shower cubicle thinking *what a funny place to put a shower.*

The stark contrast between white tiled walls, floor and ceiling and a single black bench bolted to the floor opposite the shower aired an unconscious difference from her ideas of décor.

With no visible place to plant the remaining equipment, she left locking the cubicle, a dizzy spell from palpitations tightened her chest and she felt the need to exit the premises as soon as possible.

Giving the place one last sweep she left; making her way to the car. A cold sweat insulted her body and an intense feeling of fear sickened her to the stomach before a chill ran the length of her spine and an atmosphere of death shook her to the bone.

She jumped into the car hoping to leave without being seen transmitting her exit from the premises.

Another sigh of relief found audience in her ears as Sugar gave her a verbal pat on the back sensing a return of security and confidence the furtherer she travelled away from the premises along with a craving for something sweet heading for a gelataria for gelato to go.

*   *   *

The Mediterranean Club had half emptied, as Mario watched Father Option's enter the cafe`, his black robe flapped, as an appreciative breeze jostled the hemline.

Getting to his feet from the booth, greeted the pontiff before catching Clara's attention for service.

"Ciao` papa come stai?" He extended his hand in welcome.

"I am very good Mario and yourself, are you well?" The priest responded.

His Irish accent set a smile on Mario's face nodding in response.

Seppi and Salvatore greeted the priest, as Mario slid back into the booth next to the wall, signalling the father to take his place.

After a short wait, Clara took their breakfast orders retreating to the kitchen to have them filled. A spring in her step highlighted good humour after the guys exchanged funnies with her.

The atmosphere between the men was comfortable. Light heartedness settled their chatter, as their breakfast orders were promptly filled, settling each mans famished appetite.

Salvatore reached across to the centre of the table grabbing the salt shaker; the pace at which he commenced the order of business rang bells in Mario's head.

"How's construction coming along?" His eggs and grilled tomato socked up a shower of salt.

Father Options' laughed and tapping his expensive gold replying.

"Good. It's finished; something to do with Italian construction I believe?" (A chorus line of nodding heads added to the chimes of cutlery chanting on china.)

Mario's forefingers and thumps found couple hood waving appreciation of accomplishment.

Seppi's smile gave full focus to his wording. "Those boys work fast."

"Yeah and they are skilled. At no time did I hear anyone ask about what I was having done at the church. I heard nothing. I saw nothing. And nor did anyone else," the pontiff celebrated, his smile glittered brighter than the sparkle of his watch.

Seppi asked; *the church was built by Italians wasn't it?*

"Yes it was back in the war years."

"Well father, like anything touched by Italian hands, it will have a long life. Look at the colosseum," Salvatore aired.

Pride streamed from his eyes and his voice was strong with confidence.

Father Options' smiled at him nodding. "I have no doubt Salvatore. No doubts what-so-ever."

Mario suggested, resting his knife and fork onto the empty breakfast plate.

"Now that the renovations are done, we can start to arrange charity events and fit the entertainment area out with other small luxuries."

Sal said. "We've got the tables and bar waiting for delivery. Fridges, flooring, wall decorations and boat have been ordered. We should be up for business in about two weeks."

Mario nodded in full ore of Salvatore's organisational skills. His mind went back to Violino's thoughts—the day they went to meet with Don Cavalieri.

Money—*booze and boodie* smelling the success where he sat.

*   *   *

The midmorning rush on the cafe` had trickled to a stop. Sugar sat in his car, as the surveillance of Mario and the others brought an unexpected surprise.

As they walked out of the premises a priest seemed to be nestled in their company, a willing party member tied to their hips.

Pointing his cell phone camera at the cluster of bodies he took stock of the acquaintance for future prosperity. He thought maybe the failed raid on the church in Christie Lane, South Brisbane was a prospect for future attention. Maybe it was sheerly coincidental on the part of the pontiff to be leaving a cafe` at the same time as known mob figures but, as a professional investigator, he felt compelled to put every offering of information under investigations on the file.

Priest or not: Coincidence or not, the pontiff seemed very friendly with Mario, Salvatore and Seppi and he needed to prod his gut feeling.

*   *   *

Violino unlocked his apartment door, a whirlwind of self pity and alcoholic poisoning unsettled his demeanour. He staggered in kicking the door shut with the $300 Kangaroo skin boots on his feet feeling worst-for-wear.

His hands reached to loosen the knot in his neck tie pulling it off, suit jacket and shirt were; the next to go on his way toward the bedroom.

Stumbling through the doorway he found a body at rest atop the bed. A beautiful blond figure with bronzed skin was wrapped in a black bra and panties.

He gently sat down next to the woman, eyeing her face.

The bed sunk and resettled, as his hand traced her outer thighs. The swirl in his head started to settle feeling colour return to his cheeks.

He freed himself from the rest of his clothing and lay; beside Tammin on the bed, her mouth watering lines and shape fixed itself perfectly to his memory as he started for her bra strap. The roughness of its material ran indifference to the cup and its contents and his fingers lingered over her soft peaks before sliding the morsels from their bounds inch by inch.

She remained in slumber as her strong jaw sat in contrast to her soft face and lips.

He kissed her legs sliding lips and tongue along the path to her feet looking up at her from the level of the bedcover steadying his eyes to take in the detail of her legs and thighs which glowed creamily while her vagina notified presents through panties.

His manhood stood pride of place breaking the patient stand of his mouth and tongue running the gauntlet of her thighs toward her lust.

He pulled at the black fabric, slowly and softly unveiling a misty moist grotto of fantasy.

He kissed her, lingering over her clit bringing it to rise, the blood flow turned it a deeper shade of pink, scenting the air with love.

His fingers penetrated her in company with his tongue. Her stomach rose and fell with deeper insertion, as she came too swirling her fingers in circles of content through his hair.

Time slowed down but their patient movements found tempo in each minute.

She chanted his name under swoons of pleasure passing her lips while his thoughts painted Holly voice over her opening gratefully accepting her ejaculation.

CHAPTER 12

Muggy conditions flooded the stations car park—squad cars and plain clothes units sat in waiting for officers of all rank to settle into them under pockets of laughter filtering thought the maze of cars by night shift officers rolling over rosters about funny things they'd seen and heard over graveyard shift.

Holly and Ronato arrived at the station to find Donna and Eric sitting at their desk, discussing the events of the reunion party and the Mediterranean cafe`. Sergeant Sugar sat with them on the corner of Eric's desk and photo's lay over opened files and data taken in contents with the case.

After a brief meeting in Sugar's office the four officers left heading for the car park.

Impatience and gut feelings formed a crust around Holly's heart and her face shrouded in thought as her feet found rest in the centre carriageway, with the others following suit to her movements.

She looked at them and asked. "How are we going to do this?"

"I think we should go in separate cars. Just in case," Eric advised, dangling a set of car keys around his index finger for extra leverage. "Violino might be there and, Donna is a police officer you know..?" He suggested, tilting his head.

Donna nodded. "He's right. We maybe friends, but . . ." Her tone was matter-of-factly.

Ron shook his head in disagreement, an arm rested around Holly's waist focusing on Donna.

He commented. "We are friends, we grew up together, especially us—you—Donna—me—Holly and Violino we were the closest of all the guys. Where there was one the others were always close by—I don't think if we are seen together regularly it will raise suspicion. They already know Donnas a police officer, so what! I saw Violino like the rest of you did, cuddling and kissing her on the dance floor at the nightclub. She is family to him, I think.

If we go together," (he pointed to Eric and Holly,) "and Donna changes into police uniform and bumps into us there, it will seem more natural."

Looking at him the others gave their full attention.

"Donna should dress in police uniform. She is on duty, so if any unexpected questions come from whomever—they will get natural answers. And if Violino is there, Donna is free to slip away. Shit me and Eric will be able to do the same because his whole hearted attention will be on Holly," (he stated relaxing his shoulders.) "Let's just keep everything as natural as possible. No scripts or screen plays."

The others nodded in agreement.

Holly's arm found comfort around her brothers' waist after his eyes rested on her gaze nodding understanding of his feelings.

Donna entered into the idea by telling the others about a visit Violino made to the station, after he had the park in his name and the buildings well underway.

She said. "After he purchased the sports ground he came here and asked for regular police visits and patrols around the premises" *laughing shaking her head,* as a calmness settled over her body. "He came here because it's headquarters and because he has a head for hierarchy and because I am stationed here. He asked for me, and then asked my advice.

If the family are there and see me in uniform, it will be natural—nothing will seem out of place. Just in case," she laughed weaving her hand in

Ron's playfully. "You may make a good other half . . ." She giggled. "Shall we give it a go in the back seat of number five over there?" (Flicking her head toward the squad car and twitching her eyebrows.) "I'm a woman in uniform . . ."

Holly laughed, as Ronato went red.

And then looking at Eric asked *have you got your gun on ya* conspicuously looking around to see if anyone else was around before opening his hand saying, "quick . . . give us your gun and I'll whack them. You get the car and pop the boot before someone comes . . . We get rid of the bodies . . . Who's the wiser..?"

The girls laughed.

Holly playfully punched him in the stomach, as Donna told him it would never work—they would be found out.

"We are hot, young, single women with vacancy written on our foreheads."

Smirking Ronato added *oh is that what is says.*

Laughing, Eric started for the car flicking his head at Ronato and Holly to follow him while Donna made her way back into the station to get changed.

*   *   *

The atmosphere at *La Societa Sportiva* was carnival like; end of season league games in football and hockey dominated passions between mums and dads there to support their children.

Club colours, flags and balloons flew in a slight breeze and the club mascots *two German Sheppard's* ran around vying for attention by anyone bidding their welcome while uniformed police patrolled the grounds, partaking in the events and social activities like a sponsor fulfilling their role.

Seppi laughed, as he watched Violinos eye for detail toward the occasion. He'd set up extra sun shades over the seating stands to help block the sun's rays and sunscreen bottles were placed around the park with signs to alert everyone to them warning of the importance of drinking lots of fluid to stop dehydration.

"Fuck kid settle down destiny will sing her story," Seppi advised in full smile mode, as little children ran around his legs playing with one of the dogs pulling the big kid out to laugh and play along with them. "They've gotten this far by the some of their talents and grit. Let the play continue . . ."

Violino acknowledged the comment swirling his hand along an imaginary line. "Yeah yeah yeah," he stuttered. "It's a special occasion for them.

This is their first time fighting for the league title and I want them to know there are people behind them to do well. Fuck Seppi, they're kid's not fucking degenerate gamblers and junkies! They're our girls sitting third on their football classification. We have our football boys in equal fourth and our hockey players are fourth with four games to go and they are all here playing fucking home games!"

He cried before covering his mouth, swivelling 360 degrees in search for little ones.

He watched the snack bar guy carry extra drinks cases and ice creams out of the golf cart and into the snack bar patting his shoulder considerately pointing at the club, letting him know where he would be.

The snack bar guy nodded acknowledgment accepting the keys to the golf buggy watching Violino slide his hand across Seppi's back, as they started on foot toward the club.

"What time are the others getting here?" He asked, finding Seppi laughing at him—his questioning frown needed no interpreter.

"Fuck me kid you should have done national service. Time management and the ability to operate under pressure . . ."

"Cut the shit Sep . . ."

Seppi Pointed in the direction of the club's bar. "They've been here for two hours, sipping coffee waiting for you."

The young Don consulted his wrist watch and then Seppi chanting *two fucking hours* before covering his mouth in search for little ones.

The show pulled at Seppi's heart strings.

"Father Option's?"

Seppi nodded as their pace toward the club increased. "Yeah kid. He was the first, other than me to arrive."

Seated around the bar were Mario, Salvatore and father Option's, they stood to greet the young Don. Mario and Salvatore gave him a kiss on both cheeks and father Option's a warm handshake.

He pointed toward the office heading the line of men into it.

Standing just inside the doorway gesturing for the men to sit around the desk, he closed the door behind him finding station upon his leather chair.

Their seemed to be a glow above everybody's head running a sense of optimism the length of his spine. "Well! How goes the renovations?"

"Renovations are finished." Father Option's replied.

"They're finished?" Violino questioned.

He sat forward folding his hands on the desk top. "Fuck me those boys work fast. Remind me to give them a bonus for Christmas this year Mario."

Mario smiled back at him.

Violinos eyes brimmed with delight and forward planning. "Is the floor plan underway?"

"The floor plan is done." Salvatore stated, tilting his head to one side starting to resite inventory. "One fridge, tables, gambling chips, chairs, carpeting, glasses, linens, safe, wall decorations, sound system and general entertainment package. Might I say you have a great eye for details kid," he laughed, finding movement across the desk to shake the young Dons hand.

Smiling Violino asked another question.

"The entrance..?"

"All taken care of . . . We have a platform at the tunnel entrance, nothing that will take the eye of passersby but enough to give confidence. And steel gate that can be locked so nobody can stumble in."

Salvatore's smile grew brighter.

Getting to his feet Violino rested against the back wall, the smell of money hung sweet on his nose while playing with change and keys in his pockets.

"The booze guy..?"

"The place is ready for grand opening," Mario responded. "Everything you could possibly expect is there, waiting for the touch of human hand and consumption. We will have show girls carrying trays of drinks and nibbles. And we have charity nights already planned to soak up the filtration of noise."

Leaving the comfort of the wall and making his way to the back of Father Option's seat, Violino confidently rested his hands on the holy mans shoulders.

"Father you are going to be one very rich pontiff."

The father swivelled his head to meet the young Dons gaze. "I know my son. Praise be; the Lord."

"Praise be; the Lord," Violino replied, clasping his hands together rolling his eyes to the ceiling.

*   *   *

Eric pulled off the road into a cobble stone driveway which to Holly's delight was aligned with Christmas trees spanning a flood of childhood memories to flutter her heart.

The driveway stopped at a large blue sign which read *La Societa Sportiva; the Social Sporting Club of Kedron* the blue letters on white background reminded her of the police insignia.

She sat to attention between the gap separating the front seats asking if they were at Violinos sports ground, her sweet voice tickling Eric and Ronato.

"It sure is," Eric replied, as the car wobbled over the cattle grate and into the park.

Her eyes busied themselves by rolling all over the parks features, small grandstands, snack bar, sporting fields and an endless sea of children decorated everything her eyes could see. Gardens and flowers brought depth and character to the lawns and a huge club house with Roman columns dominated the skyline to the back of the property.

They parked beside a police car and disembarked; Ronato fumbled with wallet and cell phone while his sister collected her hand bag preening her looks.

"This place is amazing," she squealed, yielding a better look around.

Ronato nodded in recognition of the effort rhetorically asking *he did this in three short years? Impressive..!*

Eric agreed and then asked if they felt like a cone of gelato.

Holly nodded excitedly, her response reminded him of his little sister at carnival time, the way her eyes would light up at all choice of sweets and delicacies.

They stopped at the snack bar and Eric grabbed the flavours menu reciting each intoxicating flavour with Shakespearian drama while Holly jumped up and down applauding each suggestion like a little girl given a pet pony for Christmas, her song and dance tickled Ronato's memories of childhood.

And then Eric asked after reciting the final flavour. "Ok what are you up for?" (The snack bar guy stood waiting for their orders with scoop and cones at the ready.)

Holly responded. "I'll have a Della Donna please," her eyes fixed firmly on Eric's, as she performed a little dance on the spot.

He laughed and copied her before looking over at Ronato who shook his head at the both of them—joining in on the performance.

He responded. "I'll have cioccolato con pistaccio please."

The snack bar guy filled Holly's order first and her tongue lavishly lapped up each morsel of the silky substance while her curiosity found focus on the club house.

"Hey hey hey..!" Ronato called after her, "take the treat and run . . . don't worry about the hired help,' he joked performing a fake limp to his walk.

"Oh Ronnie . . . I'm a woman. I need to discover things," she laughed back at him.

"It must be a family trait then . . . I'm paying for the cones and you two waddle off," Eric puffed, as he caught up with them, a run of gelato ran down his cone over his fingers, lovingly licking at the full flavoured trickle.

"So this isn't just a football club like the Gladiators but a combined sporting interest?" She enquired. (Eric's nod answered the question.) "Do these teams play in a league or is it just a place where others contact Violino to rent the necessary field?" She questioned.

Eric processed the question for a second or two before answering.

"Yeah—no, this is Kedron Social Sporting Club or as the sign says *La Societa Sportiva*. I do believe from what Donna says, Violino did try to amalgamate his idea of a junior sporting programme with a sporting club interested in multiple sports but nobody was interested. Then I believe he approached the two big football clubs and football and handball entities but no one could afford to do anymore then what they were already committed to, so Violino and the others decided to go it alone. He arranged for the police to patrol the grounds and that is done every day. He went to the council and planned every aspect of the lawns, gardens, irrigation system and buildings," (his eyes washed over the Austrella's as a confused look washed over his face.) "It's hard to understand why he would want to participate in the activities he does, when he can build and run a successful story like this. The kids love him, the community loves him and he loves the kids. It's strange," he reported, scooping up a mouthful of gelato.

And then Holly asked, using a royal English accent. "Shall we visit the club darling," looking at her brother taking the lead.

Roman columns stole her imagination, as a streak of Italian pride washed over her body at the foot of the entrance. Chandeliers, marble flooring and gold trimmings dropped her bottom lip, as a query wobbled like a locomotive upon a rickety track.

This is a juniors club . . .

Eric led them into the trophy room. Rows of trophies stood amidst a forest of glitter under the lights waiting to be engraved while banners and trays of all kinds sat upright in glass cabinets.

"My God this place builds champions!" She sang; her eyes travelled from one accolade to the next.

"Future champions," Eric corrected. "The club is only new. The banners and trays belong to Violino and his henchmen from their younger days while the trophies are waiting for success which apparently could come this year as their football and hockey teams are doing well but this said, Violino and his band of thieves do spend a fortune on their training. If the write name is in the country, they book them and he also purchases DVD's and training aids and as a special encouragement, throws a huge party at the end of the year to celebrate their accomplishments whether they win something or not," unscrambling another line of thought *with all this, why does he* stopping abruptly, as a group of children entered the room.

Ronato stood in the doorway looking at the floor plan.

"Is that a licensed bar?" He asked.

Eric confirmed and then pointed to the opposite direction saying, "Eatery slash restaurant . . . the best provincial pizza you will find outside of Italy," (lifting his thumbs up.) "Shall we order?"

Holly sang *Pizza, hell yes!* (While dancing; on the spot.)

The group of children laughed as they watched her.

Turning red with embarrassment, Ronato headed for the ristorante hiding his face behind his hands, while Eric followed in kind.

Holly watched them take off over her shoulder turning to follow but was surrounded by the children who clapped and applauded her performance. She curtsied and then elevated her voice so that Ronato and Eric could hear her and saying *those two ghastly guys are with me, the one in the lead is my brother and the other, a friend* pointing toward them.

The children laughed, as the tallest of the group complemented her on her beauty, taking her hand and kissing it.

She said *thank you* feeling her face blush.

Eric's cell phone rang, just as he and Ronato sat at a table. (The Godfather ring tone tickled Ronato's funny-bone, as he swivelled a menu around reading from it.)

Eric kicked him under the table saying *it's Donna.*

(Holly pulled a chair and sat down.) "What's on offer?" She asked, giggling girlishly to herself.

"What's so funny?" Ronato queried.

And she responded. "That little boy propositioned me."

Ronato pouted and said. "Must be an Italian . . . We are the kings of romance . . ."

Holly gushed *Hmm . . . must be* and then reached for the menu from her brother.

"So what's on offer here?" She asked.

Ronato answered full of chuff. "You have to read it to believe, they have everything!"

Oh really . . . ! She chimed, as Eric spoke in the background.

He said goodbye to Donna placing the cell phone onto the table.

"She's here and on her way," he advised, as a waitress arrived to take their orders.

Eric asked the others if they were ready to order before reciting his.

"I'll have a small Siciliana and Napolitana," and then pointed to Ronato who said *I'll have a small Calabrese* while Holly ordered a Basilicata. "And a bottle of Cecchi Chianti and jug of Chinotto Cola please," he finished.

The waitress finished writing down each particular asking if they'd be paying together or separately erupting a fight around the table as they fort over who was going to pay until Holly said it was together.

The waitress acknowledged and Eric thanked her as Donna reached them, pulling a chair and sitting down asking *have you ordered yet?*

*			*			*

Violino lead the guys into the bar wearing a resolute smile, a sense of accomplishment sent a chill down his spine from the news about the church.

The only thing to do now he thought to himself *is to arrange a charity night and get a game going.*

Swivelling on his feet he headed for the bar signalling the attention of the bartender. "A round of drinks if you will," he ordered, calling the others over cheering. "Whisky all around I do believe."

The bartender lined a row of short glasses up filling them with a shot of whisky, dropping a scoop of ice into each.

"There you go, salute`," he cheered before placing a fifty dollar note onto the bar.

Each man in turn raised his glass saluting achievement.

And then the young Don added. "Now all we have to do is bring a resolution to the other matters, and glide on easy street."

Mario, who was standing next to him, patted his shoulder nodding in full agreement saying *not long kid. Not long now* tracing circling through the condensation, covering the whisky glass.

And then Violino looked down at his watch emptying the contents of his glass in one gulp before tapping the bar to get the others' attention saying *the games about to start*!

Salvatore and Seppi copied him and proceeded out through the doorway in close company and then Mario and Father Option's, when the sight of a police uniform caught the fathers' eye.

"You have lots of police here," he commented.

Mario looked in the direction of the fathers' attention.

"There's allot of scum who prey on kids' father. We are just trying to protect them," he replied.

Father Option's gaze stayed on Donna.

Mario laughed resting his hand on the pontiffs' shoulder.

"No need to worry, we know that one." (The fathers' eyebrows lifted in question.) "No papa, she is good friends with Violino and I used to bounce her on my knee when she was a little girl. She calls me compare` like she does with Seppi and Sal and the other two sitting directly beside her. Here look," he pointed to Ronato and Holly. "Ronato Austrella, the man with his back to us and his sister Holly."

Father Option's looked at Mario in recognition of her name.

"That's the girl Violino likes?"

Mario nodded.

Then father Option's leaned sideways to get a better look at her face. And in an instant, his expression changed—his smile at Violinos choice in woman turned dark and his breathing went from comfortable to a sudden gasp.

Mario took the fathers' hand into his own steadying his stance.

"Are you ok papa? Come—we will get you a drink." (The father looked at him.)

Placing his arm around the pontiffs' waist, he led him to a table in the bar area before fetching a glass of water.

"Here you go, sip it down slowly. What happened?" He asked; the concern on his face mirrored that of the fathers.

"That girl," the father said—pointing toward the restaurant, taking another sip of the water. "The girl Violino likes. Holly. She is the police officer that raided the church," (his face turned grey glazing his eyes over.)

Pulling the chair next to him, Mario slumped onto it, disbelief and shock knocked the air out of his lungs like he had been punched in the solar plexus.

He looked at father Options with real concern shaking his head from side to side.

"Are you sure father? That's fucking Holly Austrella you are talking about not some fucking chippie or slut. Violino wants to marry her one day, pledge her with his seaman . . . Create new life," he spluttered.

Father Options nodded his confidence stating. "I could not forget that face or those eyes. That is her. No mistake," he dipped his eyes to the table after charting the different colours in Mario's.

"Arr fuck me, how the fuck am I gonna tell the kid. It's the woman he wants," he spat, looking across at the father before finding recognition of the moment.

"If you can make her, then she can make you too."

The Father looked at him with real concern.

"If she sees you here, fuck . . ." Mario slurred.

He got to his feet pulling the father off his chair.

"Come on, we've got to get you out of here before she sees you, or we are all fucked," (he confided, covering the fathers' right profile.) "Now don't say a fucking thing to Violino. I want to make sure what you say is true. I'm not calling you a liar but she is one of the family and always has been!"

Father Option's agreed that he would not tell Violino or the others anything but made it clear that Holly was the officer in charge of the raid on the church.

They marched out of the building heading toward the fathers' car.

The father opened his door sliding in, winding down the window listening to instructions.

"Remember father. Not a word."

Father Option's agreed, starting the car driving off.

Mario stood still and dipped his head toward the ground sliding his fingers through his hair.

What the fuck fell out of his mouth before lifting his chin looking toward the club.

*   *   *

Donna took a sip of her Chinotto Cola looking around at the others. "Have you seen anywhere creepy-crawlies might find roost?" She asked.

Eric looked around the restaurant to see if anybody was seated at tables close by shaking his head (his eyes met hers.) "We will have to treat this area the same as the others."

The waitress delivered the first orders of pizza smiling at Donna asking *on duty again today?*

Donna nodded and responded. "Yeah, some people have to work," pointing at her.

Nodding the waitress said *I'll just get the other orders. Is there anything else I can get for you . . . more drinks, bread?* (Looking at each of them) but all said they were fine.

"Well?" Donna continued. "I think; this place needs a bit of everything. Office, bar, in here . . . And the grounds . . ." (She took hold of Eric's stare.) "What company patrols this place at night?" She asked, sliding her hand across the table to steal an olive off his pizza.

"I'll have to look into that. But I agree the security angle would be the best way to go," slapping her hand, as she tried to take another from his craving.

Holly looked at them and laughed. (The waitress served the rest of the order disappearing back into the kitchen area.)

"This looks and smells great . . ." She panted; her eyes were a rainbow of surprise and anticipation.

Ronato separated a piece from his Calabrese to cool down entering into the discussion.

"I think we should concentrate more on the office," looking at Donna, and then around the room for any sign of it. (Donna caught on to his search telling him it was behind the bar pointing toward the doorway, passed the trophy room to his right.) "I think the important stuff' will be discussed in their. With what you've told us already, there is no way he would risk airing this stuff in front of children."

The others agreed falling silent to the sound of munching.

*   *   *

No sooner had Mario jumped into his car at the sporting fields, he found himself parked across the street from the pizzeria. His mood was out of sorts and his mind travelled in opposite directions at the same time, as a cold sweat filled his brows.

Looking down both sides of the street, he crossed the road. A frenzied confusion of words jumbled around his mind, trying to make sense of the task he was going to asked Deli to perform.

Reaching the entrance, he entered the premises.

Vito was serving people at the counter, when he saw Mario's frame step into the restaurant. A broad smile covered his face and an instant order of coffee sounded from his mouth to the waitress on duty with him.

Then Mario saw Deli's bulk enter the room from behind the counter, his large arms already outstretched to welcome him speaking bucket loads through his smile of the respect he had for him and the friendship they'd built over the years.

"Mario..! Ciao`." Deli swooned.

Stepping out from around the counter, Vito took Mario's hand, as he led him and Deli to the closest table.

Other patrons in the restaurant smiled and nodded their welcome and appreciation of the closeness of the men.

"What do we owe this pleasure Mario?" Vito asked; his hand found the back of the waitress's buttocks, as she placed a round of short black espresso's around the table. A smile parted her lips.

Nodding her presence, he flicked a glance at her saying. "She's a good girl. She's studying vulcanology, arr . . . What do you call . . . ? Err . . ." He stumbled.

Mario shook his head and Deli looked at her with an impressed look upon his face.

Laughing, the waitress said. "It's the study of Volcano's. What causes them, eruptions . . . that kind of thing," smiling, heading back to work.

Vito nodded and waved his hand above the table in recognition of the study, as he looked at the others. "Yeah that," he said, before adding. "Go and get yourself a big scoop of gelato sweetheart."

Her giggle was heard at the table.

Mario let a smile escape his face before focusing on Vito and Deli's grimly painting his mood.

"I have been given some shocking news today. But I want to have it looked into before any decisions are made about how to handle it."

Placing his coffee upon the table, Vito steadied himself.

What have you been told? He slapped the table saying *fucking Sunday's . . . Nothing good happens on a Sunday.*

"Father Option's told me at the fields, that Holly was the girl who raided the church . . ." Mario confided, (suddenly halted by Deli's voice.)

"That sounds like bullshit. How well do we know this father? He's seen the good life. Maybe we've shown him too much," he scolded.

A hot streak of colour and disdain covered his face.

Mario rested his hand on Deli's knowing that all the kids had a place in his heart with memories of laughter and play fresh in his mind.

"Deli I want you to follow Holly. I want you to do it because of the relationship you have with all of the kids and because, we have to protect Violino. He has hopes of one day marrying this girl. You can see how, if this is true, things can go pear shaped for the rest of us."

Vito showed his understanding while Deli's face changed shades of red to grey to white. He sat bolt upright resting his frame against the table—looking at Mario telling him he felt very uncomfortable with her surveillance but he would do it. That he wouldn't trust anyone else with the detail.

Mario nodded and preached. "Oh and Deli—Violino, Salvatore and Seppi, they are not to know anything. Only us here, understood? This is an Omerta."

Deli nodded.

Vito followed suit, his face showed the same concerns as the others lifting Mario's attention with a question.

"If Holly is a police officer and Donna is a police officer, then maybe they are working together because since the news of the Austrella kids return, they have been virtually inseparable . . . What do we do? What happens if..?" He trailed off; a feeling of sickness filled the pit of his stomach, stirred up by his own confusion.

"We have to do what's right for the family," Mario ordered.

A tone of steely determination shook his voice but his eyes told of a different story. A small welling of tears sat in the corner of them, painting the same look at the others.

"I'll start tomorrow," Deli advised, resting his back against the chair, taking a sip of coffee before looking around the table. "I'll start by tailing Donna. If they are working together, I'll see them together at the station," he planned, as he lifted his eyebrows intellectually. "But if this is proved wrong we have to find a new father cause I'll be cutting up this one. Father Glynn will become Shark Fin Soup," he announced.

A cold presence chilled the table.

Fair enough Mario stated, shaking on their code of silence.

CHAPTER 13

By morning a sense of calm settle over Holly—the old faces of the area started to see her and her brother around familiar haunts again with old friends from school and the playground reacquainting their friendships, while Violino was very attentive to her every whim. A matter that didn't escape her feminine wears, as moist patches formed in her panties whenever he made his presences felt.

She nestled herself into the car seat turning the radio up while checking her mirrors under red light conditions at a set of traffic lights waiting for green watching the car in front, wondering what her brother was thinking about and whether he was at piece with what they were working toward and whether or not he would one day settle down and have little Ronato's and who he would choose to have these little one's with.

She smiled and the lights turned green and in unison their cars eased forward in a snaking flow matching others on the road.

She wondered what her brother was listening to, if he had the radio on or whether a CD or cassette was playing. It was a game she often played when on her way to work.

The city rim turned into the city centre and then the police station, following her brother the whole way copying his entry into the bowels of the car park from the dark concrete platform.

In unison they exited their cars like a choreographed dance, shutting their doors and heading for the lift together.

"What were you thinking about on your way here?' She asked.

A wide smile covered his face. "You've been playing your little game again haven't you," he laughed. "I was thinking about a long legged brunette, chanting my name in an erotic game of sexual bliss closely followed by tremendous explosions of hot liquid gushing out of our genitals."

She punched him under a reddening face, not expecting the answer.

The lift door opened and they found themselves in their department. Donna and Eric were richly engrossed in paperwork. The administration crews were running around desks and personnel—and telephones were ringing hot.

The siblings looked at each other with question, and then at Donna and Eric, who had noticed their arrival.

Donna waved for their company while Eric placed files at the edge of his desk for them to read.

"What you got," Ronato asked, taking hold of one of the files.

"Have a guess whose gun was used at the industrial estate?" Donna mused, looking up at them matter-of-factly.

Eric's phone rang, as Holly and Ron ran their eyes over the file Ron had in his hands while Donna answered the question for them *Senior Constable Station's.*

"Senior Constable Station's firearm was the gun used at the industrial estate. The slugs' forensics pulled from the skulls of Brescio Caratella and Stefano Picci, and the shell casings they found outside the window on the ground, were from Senior Constable Station's gun."

Holly and Ronato looked at each other with fright.

"But didn't you say that it must have been a heavy man that did it, because of the shoe impressions found around the investigation scene?" Holly asked.

Her eyes momentarily left the page she was perusing to focus on Donnas gaze.

Donna nodded. "That's why we think Senior Constables Station and Best have met with foul play. Their police unit was found outside of a gentleman's club in Nudgee. Remember the investigation on the finger-prints found on the car? Well now, we think we know where the bodies disappeared to."

(Eric slammed down the telephone looking at the others. His voice spilled what he had found out.)

"That was Sugar. He's with the forensics crew at Mt: Glorious. A small boy, who was playing with his dog within' the forestry, came across it digging a hole and biting at an arm that it had dug up. Sugar wants us all there, yesterday," grabbing his weapons holster and car keys.

The others followed him out of the department to the lifts.

Holly's body shuddered. "Jesus Christ . . . That's close to home. They raided the church with me!" She exclaimed, focusing on the lift doors.

The raid flickered from her memory onto the stainless steel, like a motion picture.

Donna's arms found her shoulders steadying her.

"Holly. Station and Best were tailing Salvatore. You know what that means?"

Her motion picture flickered to an end looking at Donna.

Donna continued. "Salvatore would be our best point of initial investigation . . . With you and Violino in close quarters, keeping an eye on him—and Ronato and myself tailing you, Eric is free to watch Salvatore. We are going to get these bastards. We are going to win!" (She held her tight in her arms.) "They were tailing Salvatore! That's our in..!"

Ronato, Donna and Eric smiled at her.

Holly began to laugh.

*   *   *

Deli sat in his car at the entrance of the police station. He'd followed Donna in the early hours of the morning—memorising her licence plate. Clouds of fog and due hovered over the streets and rowers performed their early morning training schedules on the Brisbane River.

He had watched many cars drive in and out of the car park, unable to identify any faces. Glare from the morning sun's rays flashed across windscreens, making identification impossible. But found that, as the sun raised higher in the sky, so did the problem of glare disappear.

A flicker of light caught his eyes, focusing on the body of movement. A grey Ford Falcon appeared from within' the Bowles of the station with Donna in the passenger side seat and to his dismay, Holly appeared in the back seat immediately behind with another person sitting behind the driver. And waiting for the car to enter the street, started the engine following them onto Roma Street, heading in a westerly direction.

His thoughts took him back to a time when, as children, Holly, Ronato and Donna would bounce on his knee and run around their backyards with him. Or he would push the girls on their swing-sets or play tea-party remembering the Christmas's and Easter's and all of the football finals when their team had made it all the way to the Holy Grail.

From Roma Street they travelled briefly across Coronation Drive onto Hale Street and the inner City Bypass, shooting through Bowen Hills onto Horace Street and then right into Lutwyche Road. The area brought yet more memories of their childhoods and the times they had spent together, as that part of Brisbane was a big Italian area.

From three cars back he noticed them making a right hand turn onto Gympie Road, Strathpine catching the familiarity of their path, as Mt: Glorious filled his memory with the bodies they had left up there, as a smirk covered his face at the memory of Salvatore's reaction to decapitation.

He found himself wiping a cold sweat from his brow—the left and right hemisphere's; of his brain fought semantics between themselves and his hand—eye coordination deciding to follow the leader all the way to their destination.

*   *   *

Donna pointed Eric into the laneway he asked her to look for—police cars, forensics units and unmarked cars filled the parking area. Onlookers were kept out by police perimeter tape.

Eric flashed his badge through the window at a uniformed officer who then pointed him toward a pathway lined by forensics tape, down to the crime scene.

"Do you feel that?" Ronato asked, as they got out of the car. His stomach started doing somersaults. (Eric looked at him nodding.) "How big were your breakfasts? I think we are about to lose them," he stated.

A stench of rotting flesh lingered the air.

They started down the path toward the crime scene, the sound of their footsteps were smothered by grass, as out of the trees came a regiment of bodies. Yellow forensics tape surrounded an entire area. Police dogs ran trails of other scents and body bags lay opened and ready for victims on the ground.

Sergeant Sugar was the first officer to approach; his face tortured by what was uncovered.

He said. "I'd offer you good greetings but after what I've seen here today, I'm not in the mood for it. Four bodies; Senior Constables Station and Best along with two others, forensics is running DNA now. But it was the way the bodies were found. The genitalia were decapitated and used as plugs for each other," (his face showed total confusion.) "I've never seen anything like that before," he stated, looking down at his notebook to continue. "However I can tell you that these men were not killed here. Soil samples found on their clothing is not consistent with soil samples found in this area," (he noticed Holly's discomfort and asked.) "Are you ok with this scene Senior Constable Austrella?"

She nodded, covering her mouth and nose, proceeding with the others toward the bodies.

Donna, on arriving at the victims identified the two John Doh's.

"Sir, body one is Hector Islomavic and his buddy, body two, Thomas Flokovic compatriots of Brescio Caratella."

Her face was a portrait of the Sergeant confusion. "Why would the family incarcerate these two? They were good earners and workers for the family. I don't get it sir?"

Sugar placed his hand thoughtfully on her shoulder pointing toward ground markings found around the bodies.

"Forensics also found shoe impressions that match the crime scene at Nudgee. It seems the same heavy-set-man, found his way here."

Donna shook her head while looking around the crime scene.

Holly and Ronato started their own perusal of evidence making notes on what they found while Eric found himself locked in deep discussions with the same forensics guy he spoke to at Nudgee.

"Sir, it makes no sense. No Mafia entity I know of—makes this type of statement." Donna suggested, shaking her head. "It's just like in the movies, depending on who the rat is. Either they kill them and leave them somewhere to be found, or they kill them and get rid of the bodies. This is sloppy. Nothing like a Mafia hit. There are no records in the data saying, this is a Mafia hit. And yet, there are similarities."

Sugar nodded.

Holly and Ronato closed the circle of brainstormers.

"Sir," Holly broke in. "I think this is a family hit . . . but, they've made it look like another cell of some sort. Something must be happening within' the family itself sir. Maybe it is the Gold Coast connection. Remember Donna?" (She took Donnas' hand.) "There was always friction between Brisbane and the Gold Coast. We," (she pointed to her brother,) "used to hear dad talk about it all of the time . . . Maybe this is a Gold Coast action."

"What would make that strange is its connection to Brescio. Brescio was the Don's nephew or something wasn't he?" Donna asked, peering at Holly.

"That's right. He was immediate family with the Don. Rumour had it, that the Don was going to bump Brescio up a rank to match Violino. *Why would he knock him off?*"

Her answer turned into a statement shaking her head in confusion.

Sugar stepped into her suggesting it was about time she got chummy with Violino again.

"The cookie is hot. Let's blow him out, ok?"

Holly agreed nodding starting back for the car.

Donna, Ronato and Eric followed her, they felt they were close to busting the entire family strangle hold; and as soon as forensics released their findings, they could start working on warrants and arrests.

*   *   *

Deli wiped his eyes with a handkerchief. The information Father Option's had given Mario, turned out to be true.

He drove past the laneway himself and Vito had pulled into the night they disposed of the officers that were tailing Salvatore, and the two young troublemakers they whacked at the waste substation, continuing along the road he was on. His mind felt numb, as he knew what had to be done. But he didn't want to be the one that did it.

He reached the summit of Mt: Glorious pulling off the road into a rest area phoning Mario.

"It's true," he said before hanging up. A dead silence filled the cabin of the car.

*   *   *

Violino pulled into the drugs lab set up by Brescio and Alessio Nuarmina. It was a secluded building hidden amongst tall trees conspicuously placed near a police station.

Apart from the rustling of leaves caused by a gentle breeze, everything was quiet. There were two cars parked in the driveway and he walked the premises to make sure there was no one else there while checking his firearm for rounds—finding the magazine full proceeding toward the building's entrance (a smell of disinfectants found his nose and a smile lit his face.)

He opened the door to find two of Brescio's flunkeys; Kalem Tomasina and Ross Dentrow standing at a portable stove, stirring something in a wok.

Ciao` Kalem come stai? He asked.

Kalem nodded in response.

"What's in the wok?"

He looked at Violino and answered *about 5 kilos of unprocessed H* before looking across to Ross who shared a smile with him.

Violino headed toward them asking if anyone else was in the building. (Ross shook his head and Kalem said no,) as he looked down into the wok, the foul stench of H made him feel sick to the stomach.

Looking up at the two men and pulling the firearm out of his trouser pocket, he aimed it at Kalem blowing his brain matter all over the wall behind him before pointing the sight at Ross.

Ross in a fit of shock begged Violino not to but he pulled the trigger. The slug found accommodation between his eyes and his body fell to the carpet—a spray of blood exploded from his forehead like a high pressure sprinkler system.

Walking the rest of the building checking the rooms were as Kalem and Ross had stated; Violino wiped his finger prints from the gun noticing a rubbish-bin under a bundle of heroin packets placing the weapon under it before smearing blood caught by his shoe prints into the carpet, leaving making a mental note to *burn the shoes and drivers side car mat.*

Jumping into his car idling down the driveway and onto the road where another smile lit his face, making a mental note *nobody saw me enter the premises and nobody saw me leave.*

Turning the sound system up, he drove down the street hoping it wouldn't take too long for the bodies to start smelling up the place, as he knew the police would find it puzzling to uncover Don Cavalieri's prized souvenir, amongst crime scene evidence.

CHAPTER 14

Mario found the nightclub seasoned under a light mood with Chris and Violino seated around a table sharing conversation on this and that and Seppi with Salvatore watching on at the bar under a compilation of easy listening music playing mid volume.

He signalled his greetings to everyone under the barmaids gaze on his way to the office while waiting for Deli and Vito to arrive, hoping they wouldn't be too long, as his stomach churned under the stress of knowledge he carried, wondering how they were going to break the news to Violino and the others.

He entered the office a teary mess of gloom, the mood of family he felt on entrance stabbed a knife into his heart fighting to gain control over his emotions standing central to the plate glass window watching Seppi play fight Chris as was normal behaviour 'the old days.' But he knew the old days were about to change forever in Violinos eyes, as his cell phone signalled a SMS message.

Straightening his appearance he started for the door knowing it was Deli and Vito letting him know they had arrived.

Vito's voice carried over the sound system like the coach of a sporting team, giving Chris instructions on how to sow up Seppi.

A full barrage of laughter broke around the bar forming another tear in his eye.

Violino said. "Fuck me Mario I think you're turning into my mother!"

Suddenly twisting and turning uncontrollably, as Vito found his ticklish spot making good use of it.

Deli in the moment looked at Mario understanding his feelings.

The young Don retreated from Vito, reddened from laughing straightening his suit looking at Chris saying *come on, doesn't anybody fucking work in this place* as other staff started turning up for their shifts, watching Chris gather them around the bar for pre work drinks, smiling in a leadership way.

Chris caught the look and returned it appreciatively.

Looking at the others, the young Don laughed challenging them to a race up the stairs. Vito and Deli cheated, taking off before Violino said go—under fits of laughter.

Salvatore chuckled at their boisterous behaviour.

Calling them a bunch of geriatrics midway up, the young Don pushed passed them, saying he'd call them an ambulance for exhaustion and accelerated heart rates.

He staggered through the office door heading straight for the bar laughing and suffocating, fighting for breath and balance as the noise and vibration of competition grew louder from the approaching hilarity, pouring six drinks of whisky before sitting at the table in waiting, heaving heavily.

Mario was the first through closely followed by Salvatore and Seppi. Vito and Deli finished a dead-heat fighting each other for the upper hand. The look on their faces was priceless.

Mario gave Violino a curious look and said. "Fuck me kid . . . do you have any idea how much stress the staircase just went through with these two racing up them side by side? I'm surprised they are still there!"

Violino laughed, cementing himself to the backrest of his chair saying sarcastically . . . *national service hah?*

"When do you think we should have our first gambling night," he asked, looking around the table at the others.

But Mario took control over proceedings saying they had more important things to discuss.

Deli slurped on his drink after getting his breath under control looking first at Violino and then Mario.

Violino slumped on his chair, wrapping fingers around the cold glass of whisky in front of him starting to say *we have* but was interrupted by Mario halfway through his thought.

"V, you are not going to like this," Mario cringed.

Violinos shoulders shrugged in question.

Sucking in full lungs of air, the consiglieri continued. "Donna, Holly and Ronato are not what they appear to be," stopping again, watching Violino squint in confusion.

Readjusting his seated position, the young Don tilted his head looking at Mario. "What do you mean they are not what they seem? Donnas like a sister to me and a police officer. Holly is a model, who if I have my way will wear my wedding ring and Ronato is in security. What the fuck are you talking about?"

The young Don asked.

Mario shook his head; he didn't want to be the one who broke this news, as he was the one who told him of his fathers' death. The one who told him Holly and all of her family had moved, and now he was facing the same fears of seeing his eyes in turmoil again.

"Violino, Donna is a police officer, but she is not family. She, Holly and Ronato are in the police force and they are trying to build a case against the family," he emptied his lungs in a huge discharge of air.

Violino took a sip of his drink replacing the glass to the table. His expression showed a palate of questions like a puzzle created by razor blades slicing through a Leonardo de Vinci before asking. "What do you mean building a case against the family? Donnas' a police officer but Holly and Ronato, I don't understand *who the fuck told you this shit Mario!?*"

Deli shifted in his chair under a heavy breath finding new focus, entering into the crisis.

"Listen kid. I saw it with my own eyes. Mario got me to follow Holly and after some detailed surveillance I saw Donna, Holly, Ronato and some other guy at the Mt: Glorious sight, where we—me and Vito dumped the bodies of those two other police officers that were tailing Sal. I was sitting at the entrance of Police Headquarters when I saw them together. I followed them from there," he stuttered under a glazing of eyes—at the sight of Violinos.

Mario's voice carried over the heaviness of the room once more.

"I told Deli to follow Holly because father Option's recognised her at the club on Sunday. Remember when we were heading out of the building. You Sal and Seppi got out first. Well that's what took us so long to catch up because as we were walking out, he stopped and saw Donna sitting in uniform. I told him that it was only Donna and that she was considered family but then he asked about the other girl. I told him that the three sitting closest to us were all considered family and that's when he told me that Holly was the police officer in charge of the raid. I asked him if he was sure, that it wasn't a mistake in identity but he looked at her one last time and said that was definitely her . . ." welling up in tears as he had done so many times before as the family Consiglieri.

Violinos head sank into his hands. A shake entered into the demeanour of his shoulders and his breath grew more rapid.

Mario's voice filled his ear drums once more.

"They've been here. They've been at La Societa Sportiva. They've been seen at the Calabrese club and at Night Spot Italia. I think we should sweep the places for bugs."

The others nodded in agreement.

Violino sat silently unmoved with his head in his hands.

The room fell quiet from the shock and Mario moved to the back of the young Dons slumped body placing his hands on his shoulders, breaking the silence with condolences for his young friend. The same friend he had watched, grow into a man.

"Violino . . ."

"It's ok Mario," Violino said, resting his hands on the table while shaking his head. "It's ok. Papa used to say that life was full of shocks. Some slide by the wayside and others shake your very foundations. This is one of those," his voice faded away like hot air swirling into ice.

He looked around the table and witnessed each mans grief. The office felt more like a morgue than the business end of a circus.

I'm sorry kid filtered through the air from Deli's mouth.

He reacted to it with a shake of his head denoting respect for his friend and then looked around at Mario (whose hands still sat atop his shoulders, steadying the rugged waves of a sea in turmoil.)

"It's ok compare`, I'm ok and I agree with you. We should sweep everything, starting with this place . . ."

Getting to his feet, he steadied everyone in the room with sign language before settling himself by the window, placing a finger on it—facing the others. "If they've been talking," he stated using code. "Then it would take a little time to get up and running. When you plant a seed it doesn't grow straightaway. It needs time to process," gazing around the office and out the office window. "But we are lucky men because we have things in our hands that prove growth," he looked at Mario with a smile.

Walking over to the desk, Mario pulled out an object that looked something like a cell phone.

Violino pointed to the apparatus and continued. "That little thing can trace the seeds of growth. And it will point us in the direction of every seed planted."

"Violino how long does a seed take to get going?" Vito asked tilting his head in full interest like a child asking a teacher an important question.

"If done straightaway—a day depending on when and of course who planted the seed," he advised.

He walked over to the office door opening it, signalling each of the men to follow.

"Let's go outside so I can show you where I want to plant," he said, drawing a circle in the air to signal Mario where to point the device.

Mario pushed the start button focusing on the screen and instantly, multiple traces showed up, lifting his head to Violino, turning the screen to face him, placing a finger to his mouth.

Violino looked at the screen alerting the others to follow him outside.

On arriving in the alley, Mario and the young Don peered down at the apparatus.

"All traces are gone?" The young Don queried, more as a question then a statement.

"No V. It means we are out of range of the devices," Mario corrected him.

"So they're bugging us . . ." Violino asked, looking back at him, his question was more rhetorical. "Ok. Well, I think if we move them, they will know we are on to them. But I know one thing though—there can't be that many working on the case."

Mario smiled, as he looked at the young Don shaking his head. "You are right Deli. This kid is fucking bright."

Deli lifted his index finger to the comment in positive response.

Violino stared into space out of grip from their reality speaking distantly when he did speak. "I know one thing; we can't afford to fuck up. Maybe I should get closer to Holly. Feed her a few misdirections. *Among other things*," he uttered.

His tongue traced the outer rim of his lips and his eyebrows danced a merry jig.

Mario nodded along with Salvatore and Seppi putting an arm around the young Don saying *maybe you should. But I think we should talk about it somewhere other than here.*

Agreeing, Violino asked. "Where can we go?"

"The German club in Mt: Gravatt. I feel like a beer," Deli suggested, placing his arm around Vito's mid-drift starting for the nightclub door.

Mario tilted his head to Deli saying. "Looks like we're going to the German club: Everyone ok for a lift?"

*   *   *

The departments' office was a welcome relief from the outside temperatures the sun spewed upon the streets. Holly and Ronato sat at their desks flicking through reams of documented evidence from the forensics' lab which concerned small arms calibres, fabric fibres, hair fibres and other DNA information about the victims at both the Industrial Estate and Mt: Glorious crime scenes.

From the crime scene in the mountains, the forensics' crew had ascertained that the Industrial Estate at Nudgee and the Mt: Glorious crime scenes were linked but they didn't know by who or what crime body. The fact that body parts were cut off and inserted into different personalities didn't smell of a mob hit.

Donna headed over to Holly's desk sitting at its corner; an open file lay in her hand finding her voice while her eyes stayed glued to the page she was reading.

"This has just come in from scientific. The footprints we found at Mt: Glorious are the same as the Industrial Estate but . . . there are still no more clues as to the organisation that committed the murders. Who would cut a penis off only to shove it into another person's rectum?" Holly questioned.

Confusion and disdain covered her face as she looked up at Donna.

Donna was no closer to answering the question then anybody but shared Holly's look answering *it's a sick world we live girl.*

Leaning her back against the chair, Holly picked up a blue biro asking Donna a question.

"Are we sure Senior Constables Station and Best weren't on the take? Why else would they be killed and placed alongside two of the Cavalieri's family members?"

Donna took her eyes off the page she was skimming refocusing on Holly.

"How do you know they were Cavalieri family members?"

"Donna; come off it, you knew Brescio—he was a bit of a wanker. You must remember him?" She said, sarcastically.

Sergeant Sugar picking up on the atmospheric change around the two women, closed in on them to chase their ideas.

"You have a thought Holly?" He asked her.

"Sir I cannot speak Senior Constables Station and Best, I didn't know them well enough but I can talk about Brescio Caratella who always let everyone know who he was related too—to buy some recognition. Sir, it just seems strange that two highly regarded officers would be found dead in strange circumstances.

They were assigned to the church raid and did their job but it was like they weren't there . . . in the moment," (she looked at him.) "Sir looking through this police report and scientific lab report there was drug residue found on the bodies. The Bruglioni family has never had an association with drugs. That has been the domain of the Cavalieri family and families under their association. Violinos father didn't like the drug trade because he knew he couldn't trust anyone that used it and whoever sells it has to use it to check it for quality. These two men found with 'Station and Best' were friends of Brescio," Holly exclaimed.

Donna looked down at her, her lips were pursed together not willing to agree with what she stated, but not willing to disconfirm it either.

Ronato shifted in his chair entering into the discussion. "I have to agree with Holly sir. If it's drugs then it's the Cavalieri family. The Bruglioni's were only interested in racketeering, black market and the odd killing and by the evidence coming in; I'd definitely say that this was a drugs thing. Maybe Brescio stepped on the wrong toes. It seems to be stemming from him. Maybe there was a sit down with another entity, which didn't go the way of this other body and the shit hit the fan. It wouldn't be the first instance Brescio pissed somebody off. The difference in this case being, it got him killed."

"Could that be possible with what you know Donna?" Sugar asked her. "Your original investigation lay within' the Cavalieri family," tracing the outline of her face.

A blank expression showed the deep level of concentration she had for investigating her beliefs.

"It is very possible and as I told you in our first meeting—it was the Cavalieri family that our investigations started with," pointing toward Eric Nadalle. "But that kept on closing in our faces. I still believe, if we keep a close eye on Violino and his family, something will come out of all this effort. We'll get both sides of the river sir," she stated, as determination glowed resolute on her face.

Sugar tapped the surface of Holly's desk with his closed fist, looking at both ladies, dipping his head in respect before saying they will continue on with the Bruglioni family investigations.

He then looked at Holly and asked. "Have you gotten close to Violino yet?"

She responded to the affirmative but said it was proving difficult to spend a lot of time with him.

"He's attentive sir but it seems there is something else on his mind which gives what Donna is saying validity, but, not," she stated puzzled.

"Make it happen, Holly. It's very important." Sugar instructed, heading back toward his office.

*   *   *

The German club was nicely quiet, as the men entered the place from the premises car park. Only a small group of patrons sat playing poker machines, the rest of the club was empty.

Deli was the first person to the bar buying the first round of drinks.

Mario found a table and gestured for the others to sit while Deli and a waitress walked over carrying the refreshments.

The waitress placed the tray of drinks to the table, her face glowed and she smiled brightly.

Will that be all gentlemen she asked?

Her thick German accent caught Violinos attention and she felt something crawl up the back of her leg heading toward her spiritual place, looking down witnessing Violinos eyes tracing his hands progress.

She adjusted her hips forward and backed away from the table in one action, her eyes beamed and her face turned bright red, leaving the table while looking back at him on her way to the bar.

Mario dipped his head and laughed; consoling the young Don's shoulder like a father trying to catch the attention of a way wood son saying *your brain is constantly on pussy.*

Deli laughed shaking his head in recognition of what was going on.

"Fuck me kid."

Violino shook his head in response. "No Deli, not you. Her," he chuckled.

Seppi joined in on the banter saying *nice looker the fraulein, I'd let her tongue my balls.*

Then Salvatore said. "It's nice to see you in such good spirits kid," watching him closely. "After what you've been told today, you should feel like shit but look at you. It's almost like water off a ducks back," he aired, as his fingers found the coolness around his frosty glass of beer. The amber colour reminded him of sap jewellery.

Violino shrugged his shoulders to the stares that followed his every movement.

"Yeah I've been thinking about that and fuck it," he stated.

"Fuck it. That's it. Fuck it!?" Seppi asked—his hand reached across the table taking Violinos. "Fuck—its ok kid, you can let out some emotion. We are all men he—made men. We know what it's like to be hurt by someone you loved."

Love . . . I didn't love her Seppi well maybe once but not now. I didn't know her anymore. But I wanted too . . . her legs, her mouth, her tongue, her mound looking deeply into his eyes.

Seppi lifted his hands saying. "We get it kid. Fuck. If you keep talking, I won't be able to walk out of here without causing a scene," pointing both of his index fingers toward his groin before sipping his beer, nodding.

"So you won't have a problem when someone clips the bitch?" Salvatore asked curiously.

Violino shifted his weight relaxing his hands around his stein. "No. No I won't feel too bad. It's not as if she's trust worthy or anything. But I can tell you this. It will be me that clips the bitch . . . doggie style. Missionary, spoons . . ." (Making circles in the air.) "But whatever we do from here, it has to be done smart."

Mario took over the reins of conversation.

"That's right this entire fucking problem started because of the drugs thing. Fucking Brescio and his fucia brutti, the Cavalieri family have to be made responsible for this shit."

"Yes but how do we pull off clipping federal and state government and family members; up the tree? It's not as if there's a tribunal for mobsters," Seppi added.

Vito aired. "I for one don't want fucking federal apparel sitting pretty in my place," anger painting his voice.

Violino glanced around the room to make sure there were no extra sets of ears listening and stated. "And there're won't be for too much longer. We have to leave the listening devices and surveillance equipment where they lie for the meantime but business can be done outside party lines. I for one think we should start doing all of our business in the Gold Coast. That way, prying eyes will follow . . ."

"Very smart kid," Deli aired saluting his beer.

Reaching across the table, Violino patted his hand with a steady look on his face.

"Like my father used to say, you take out the leader. We find out who is leading the investigations against us and take that person out. It will buy us some time to set things up."

"Fuck me kid . . . Take out a high official in federal law . . . just like that?" Vito scoffed under his breath.

"No Vito not just like that. Look we'll do all of our business at the Coast. The casino, and other places we know the Don and his associates go. The government can only follow can't they? So we place things where they can be found. We'll frame the Cavalieri family and clip a couple of figures along the way. Simple," he stated.

His throat welcomely accepted a cold flow of beer and his heart started to settle its beat.

"Look . . . we have to do this thing quickly," he stated after concealing a burp. "If we are still talking about how we are going to do certain things in two weeks, we are all going to find ourselves dead or in prison." (The others looked at each other.) "I think we should take out the lead of investigations first—that way, it will rock their walkway and destabilize them. We then frame Don Cavalieri and clip his closest associates and family hammers," (rolling his eyes.) "All the little guys can do time, their fucking heads are so full of the shit; it makes no difference whether they live on the inside or out. *It shouldn't be too difficult for us.* We don't have anything to do with that side of things," he stated.

His eyes picked up on the German waitress; her long legs sent a quiver to his groin.

"Things might work out better for us. The Don already knows about the fate of his favourite nephew. He thinks Brescio fucked up with the drug thing, especially since more of his men have been found dead." Mario informed them.

"Fucking drug labs," Deli stated.

"Yeah terrible shit," Salvatore scoffed, patting the back of his shoulder.

Violino sat bolt upright in his chair. "We have the advantage. We've done the ground work properly and things are starting to run. All we have to do is follow both sides of the fence; lay our cards on the table when the time is right and take all of the money to the bank. No fuck the bank, we'll take all of their monies and share it around between ourselves," airing with confidence.

"I have a funny feeling we'll be seeing the Don sooner than later anyway. He seems to be losing a lot of his own," Mario stated, clicking his fingers at the waitress for service.

The young Don got out of his chair prompting Mario to ask *where you going kid?*

He pointed to his groin and said. "I need a leak" and then grabbed the waitress leading her toward the kitchen door before looking back at the others sitting, watching him at the table. He dropped his hand to the curvatures of her derriere squeezing the cheeks hard.

Salvatore shook his head in disbelief stuttering *this fucking kid with pussy.*

"Leave him alone. I remember you with that girl in the freezer truck," Mario shared with the table.

Seppi sat reliving the little indiscretion with hand gestures.

Salvatore's face created a new shade of red while Mario, Vito and Deli laughed.

"Yeah fuck you Mario. Fuck the lot of you . . ." He wheezed.

"It's funny," Mario stated. "You sound just like the kid," erupting table in cheers.

*   *   *

"Well brother here we are again, just the two of us," Holly laughed.

Her cell phone had no messages stored on it and neither did the answering machine when they got home.

"I can't believe this! We are two young attractive, interesting, passionate Latin's. Yet," she opened her arms in question.

Ronato responded by sipping his drink while eyeing two attractive 20 something's who'd walked passed their table at the licensed cafe`.

"Maybe it's because we are too conscientious in our responsibilities toward keeping the streets safe and sound," he uttered in depression, watching one of the 20 something's bent over to adjust her shoe strap up the street, flashing the blueprint of her gift to his hungry eyes.

Sighing he took a long deep sip of his drink uttering. "I'd be happy to just get laid. It's been awhile for me," looking up to find Holly laughing at him.

Her face was a deep shade of red.

He uttered. "What? Aren't we all family here—and adults..?"

"Oh Ronnie, maybe you should ring Donna. She might like to polish your pencil. Fire your pistol—blow your . . ."

"OK, ok dear sister dear sister," he chided lifting his palm in a surrender gesture. "But maybe..," he laughed.

Their table went quiet for a moment, as thoughts trailed off to individual dreams and needs with periodical thoughts of the case.

Ronato had a burning question dying to be set free within' the hustle and bustle of turbulent air. His memories trailed back to when the local streets were childhood haunts. He never told Holly that once he caught her and Violino fooling around at the Italian club, or the sounds of her sighs, as his fingers searched and played with her body and needs.

Now his thoughts were teetering around her feelings for the young Don, remembering the look on her face when she found out it was his father that killed theirs. But in that, each person has one other person that fits into their hearts and spirits perfectly and to his mind and memory, no one else had fit like Violino did with Holly, despite the history. There was water under the bridge.

His body shivered, as a breeze found his mood. It was hot but cool at the same time, like summer had decided to yield a night of pleasant reprieve.

His drink was a comfortable colour of sunset orange at the bottom of the glass and sky blue at the top, he didn't know what it was called and didn't care, it tasted good and that's all that mattered, as his mind went back to the car and sitting in the back seat with Donna. Their hands mistakenly brushed up against each others and their legs touched through the material of their clothes—smiling at the tingle that shivered its way to his penis, liking the way it made him feel wondering if Donna felt the same thing.

Then his eyes found his sister and without making it obvious to her, looked at her, shifting his viewing position. Her long brunette hair and brown eyes could set the atmosphere to tantalize the most stubborn of men. She looked more like a Goddess, Venere—Venus, than some bloody police officer risking her wellbeing for the sake of others *who probably wouldn't return the favour.*

He could hear voices from their recent past, voicing opinions about her looks and about their wants and needs. Men of all shapes and sizes would comment about her legs, her eyes, her lips while others would say in a more gentlemanly setting, that she reminded them of Cleopatra. Her long lean Mediterranean lines and curves didn't belong in a country where respect came second best. She was a medieval sculpture. She was his sister. And he worried for her future and his own.

"Well dear brother, what shall we do?" She asked him.

He shrugged his shoulders re-introducing his drink to his lips.

"We could always call Violino. Maybe he's doing something with the other mafia members he associates himself with," she laughed, re-hatching her thoughts. "Well. Shall I call him?"

She reached into her handbag pulling out her cell phone, waving it in front of his eyes.

Her smile was bright and captivating.

Again Ronato shrugged his shoulders, taking another obliging sip of his drink enjoying the caress of the breeze across his body.

"Yeah why not, who knows? Maybe he knows of a young girl for me, while you two are dancing in the meadows," he suggested smiling at her.

"Ronnie! Dancing through the meadows?" She asked him.

A Slight hint of titillation met his ears.

"Holly. Do you think we would have made good mobsters?" He asked, lifting his palms to her in a *wait a minute and listen way.* "Look at it—we grew up in the business. We know all of the main characters. We studied

and partied with them; knowing full well, what they were. Shit what we
were! Do you think that if we were in the mob, we could run it better
then the professionals?" Sitting against his seat watching his sister look
at him with more than one question rattling her mind.

"What brought this on? Are you thinking about changing loyalties?"
She asked, with a sarcastic look on her face.

"No not at all, it's just that, as you stated, we are two young attractive
people in uniform. We are the epitome of every sleazy dream about
people in uniform and yet I haven't had sex in bloody ages. I may not
even remember how to have sex, or even what sex really is—I'm like a
blonde who hasn't had fun..!"

"I'll call Violino, that way you can rub shoulders with the old and
maybe pick up some skills for the new—you." She laughed, (pushing the
cell phones directory key finding Violinos number.) "Shall he meet us
here?" She asked; smiling deeply, as her building excitement left a wet
patch between her thighs.

"See Holly you prove my point. Maybe we are in the wrong business.
Maybe Violino needs to be police and we need to be the mobsters."

"Yeah whatever my brother . . ."

Suddenly she opened her palms to the air squawking. *Violino! High,
have a guess who; this is . . .* (Giggling) *I and my desperate for love brother
Ronato were wondering if you would like to come to the cafe` we are at and have
a drink or three, or more with us. Oh and do you have a lady friend. I'm starting
to worry about my brother.* (Her face shone, as she listened to Violinos
response while watching her brothers.)

Ronato picked up on just how much his voice had an effect on her.
He could see the tell tale signs of flattery showing up on her cheeks and
her chest and around her ear lobes. Her lips were growing redder and
fuller hearing her say goodbye watching her place the cell phone back
into her handbag before her eyes met with his once more.

"He's bringing someone. He said he won't be long," taking her drink.

He watched her sip from its rim noticing a smudging of red lipstick stain the glass, looking at her again saying *ok* reassigning his gaze sharply into hers stating *that she better be a looker, or you two won't be getting any either.*

Silence crept up on them once more and he thought back to the question he had just asked about the mobsters' life answering it himself for himself.

He was a police officer and a bloody good one.

"Holly. Do you think we should call the others and tell them we're having drinks with Violino?"

She shook her head.

"Anything we find out or discover can wait for report tomorrow," she stated, pulling out her make-up compact tidying her face with foundation, lipstick, eye shadow and blusher. "Do I look nice?" She asked, pouting her lips and blowing fake kisses.

"Yeah not bad, I've seen nicer though . . ." He laughed.

She shook her fist at him.

"You're lucky you are my brother or . . ." She stopped suddenly looking at two girls who were dressed up to the nines in nearly nothing stating. "Yes that's right girls, he is my brother. He's young and very single and going for a song. Step right up . . ." (The girls looked at him. One laughed but the other stopped and had a good look.) Ronato offered her a seat but her friend pulled her away.

"Thanks for that," he laughed, finding cold comfort in his drink.

*   *   *

The office was quiet and quite eerie. Donna switched off her computer terminal, grabbing her jacket starting for the elevator, when she heard her voice being called. Turning, she found Sergeant Sugar approaching her at a slow jog.

"Sorry to disturb you on your way out but I have a question. Do you think Holly is comfortable in her role on this case?"

His eyes focused on hers thoughtfully, as his hand found his chin, tilting his head ready to take in everything she said.

"Sir; Holly and Violino have a lot of water under the bridge and in a strange way—and I know it will sound strange to you but Holly is completely at ease in his company. She has no fear for her safety because Violino will not hurt her. He loves her and he always has. She will be fine."

Sugar nodded acknowledgement.

"Ok then. Let me ask you this. Do you think it possible for their relationship to rekindle, and if so, could she be turned into the dark force?" A subtle smile curled his lips. But his eyes shone the intensity of seriousness.

Donna laughed in appreciation of his sense of humour. "Sir I honestly believe that they will probably share relations but that's it. Holly won't be turned. She lives by the code. She always has."

"Have a nice night," Sugar offered his greetings.

She replied with respect leaving the office.

*   *   *

Holly combed fingers through her hair, as background noise of chatter covering all descriptions became more noticeable.

A black Alfa Romeo 156 pulled up to the curb reflecting the cafe's neon lights. The passenger side door opened taking Ronato's attention at once.

Two athletic legs stretched from within' onto the walkway supporting a very beautiful woman sporting a classical hourglass figure and well shaped derriere.

His eyes bulged at her beauty, as she turned to face the cafe` revealing a stunning mouth and lips—hair danced in the breeze like silk and her eyes coloured the deepest bedroom brown.

"Are you ok Ron?" Holly asked, patting his arm. "It's ok big boy . . . Breathe—breathe . . ." She instructed, watching his childhood fantasy turn to reality.

Another figure filled her peripheral vision as a voice tickled her ears across the breeze.

Ciao bella, come` sta?

Violino filled her eyes from the drivers' side to the pavement s*to bene?* He uttered under question, taking her breath as her eyes focused on his athletic body. A silken shirt flapped in the breeze uncovering sparkles of light defining shadows of rippling muscle hidden beneath.

He slid his arm around the woman's waist, gracefully gliding toward the table.

"What are you drinking; can I get the next round?" He asked under a thick Italian accent melting any defences she had away, feeling her muscles contract under each of his words.

Ronato stood in welcome before introducing himself to the woman on the young Don's arm, saying.

"I'm not sure what this stuff is but Holly got them and they seem nice. I believe the bartender will know what they are; he's found it difficult to take his gaze off her all night," (transfixed on Tammin the whole time.)

Violino removed his hand from around Tammin's waist introducing her to Holly, as a smile of recognition fell upon witnessing the thirsty lust bite into his old friends' desire—laughing as he watched Ronato play the gentleman in seating her. (The static of her stockinged legs held his eyes to ransom.)

Violino uttered. "I'll go and get the drinks then. Tammin what would you like?"

She responded. "I'll have what your friends are having. It looks nice," watching him disappear into the cafe`.

Holly swivelled in her seat breaking the silence around the table by asking Tammin what she did for a living and had she lived in the area long.

Tammin filled Holly's curiosities under a hot flush of recollection, as the memory of Violino chanting her name during sex filled her with nausea asking, if they knew him long.

Holly replied stunting the hum of background chatter.

"Yes we grew up here. We all went to school together. I can tell you some stories about Violino. He was a cheeky little shit when he wanted to be . . ."

"Nothings changed then," Tammin replied rolling her eyes.

Violino returned, saying *here we all go. You were right Ron—that; bartender has a thing for Holly and like you; I've got no idea what the hell we are drinking* placing a tray full of drinks upon the table. "Have we all introduced ourselves," he enquired jokingly. (The looks he received were of a friendly nature, apart from Tammin.) "Great. Let's go clubbing. There's this great place down by the river. It's just opened! Don't know what the bloody place is called, but it's supposed to be hot and I wouldn't mind checking out the competition. Interested?" He asked.

"That sounds great," Holly replied, grabbing a drink from the tray.

The car ride to the nightclub was short and to Ronato's surprise, Tammin slid her arm around his waist—thumbing his shirt, backwards and forwards almost cuddling him.

And Violino took Holly by the hand meshing their fingers together.

Ronato asked full of query. "Where is this place you are talking about?"

Violino answered with a smile. "I know this looks a bit suss but the entrance is around the back of the building along the pathway, just down there," (he pointed between a small break between warehouses that sat on the banks of the Brisbane River.) "See just down there," he pointed again wrapping his spare arm around Holly's waist to steady her path along the uneven ground to the walkway on the riverbank.

Tammin cuddled up to Ronato

Feeling his groin grow, he realised his hand was moving in an up and down motion around her upper thigh, buttocks region. But she didn't seem to mind.

"What kinds of people come here?" Holly asked Violino.

His eyes found hers and she felt herself melt, her wet spot turning into a torrent.

"Oh you know, bankers, politicians, coppers, models, that sort of cross-section. A good mix . . . You should fit right in being a model yourself. Maybe you'll bump into someone you know. Maybe they'll ask you to do a display here tonight. What a buzz that would be!"

He chimed—a genuine interest seemed to sound on his voice.

She definitely found interest in his hands, as his fingers found the curvature of her backside.

"Yeah maybe . . ." She replied, trying not to sound overawed by his attentions looking back at her brother and Tammin. "Come on you two, plenty of time for that later!" She called.

They got to the entrance; the guys on the door let the ladies and Ronato in straight away and then waved Violino in with little more than a handshake. Meanwhile a line of desperate people pleaded for entry like junkies starving for another hit.

The club reminded Holly of Lights & Lace once inside with dark paint covering the walls giving the premises a sense of depth even though it was a single level and smaller space. But the music was great and they danced together for hours, as surprise found her witnessing Ronato let himself go with Tammin, even catching them kissing.

Violino had started the night in great spirits but seemed to get agitated as the night progressed but the mood swing didn't stop his hands playing discovery channel around her sensitive area from time to time.

"Shall we go Holly?" He leaned over and asked; sweat ran down his chiselled face dripping with consistency from his hair. "Would you like to go and," his question halted as his lips found hers.

She collapsed at his touch kissing him as he was her; their water started flowing beneath their bridges working familiarity over her.

Pulling away from him, she said yes to his invitations and suggestions looking around for her brother but was pulled away by Violino in the direction of the door.

They kissed on the path, this time more sensually. Her hands found his time piece and his, her opening lingering for a little while locked in arms before leading her back to the car.

"What about Ronnie and Tammin?" She sighed; her breath was flushed and hot.

"It's ok; they are big boys and girls now. Tammin will probably take him home, or him her," he suggested.

But again, Holly sensed his response was more an outburst than a reply.

*   *   *

Tammin backed Ronato into a dark corner of the dance floor running her leg up his outer thigh; her mouth found his entering her tongue into the equation, slowly dancing his desires into a plea.

"Ronato would you like to?" Her question stopped abruptly focusing on him.

He nodded trying to speak but the music was too loud.

He felt hers hand trace the outer part of his crotch loosening tooth by tooth the pressure around his penis until human flesh insulated his manhood.

He looked around at the surroundings in surprise struggling to keep control of his functions under the persuasion of her touch, concealing him against the fabric of her dress so that no-one could see it and then took his hand running it up her dress under the fabric to her panties.

She instructed him to pull them down around her upper thighs, the pounding of his erection against her naked flesh sent shivers along the shaft, as her fingers nearly took him to the edge of out of control guiding him inside her before pushing against his torso.

Her tongue left his mouth and traced a path to his ear where she whispered *fuck me . . . no one will notice.*

In a wave of unexpected pleasure, he fired a salvo of seed deep inside her. Moans and growls were hidden by loud music and the fear of getting caught combined with the pushing and shoving of the surrounding crowd against their bodies.

Sweat ran down their faces in the same manner it ran down their thighs.

Pulling out of her—she tucked him back into his trousers before finding the sodden fabric of her panties, repositioning them neatly around her waist, finding his hand and leading him out of the building.

"Come home with me Ron. I like you and I want to spend a night with you," stepping up to him again kissing him taking his hand—leading him toward a cab rank.

*   *   *

Soft music played in the Alfa, Violinos free hand found the naked flesh of Holly's thigh.

Flickers of traffic lights sent her mind into a fantasy she once dreamed off where a dark stranger and an Alfa Romeo whizzed her through city streets toward unbridled sex, lust and rock n roll. So far, all of the pieces fit the puzzle growing sodden with anticipation.

"Do you want to come back to my place or shall we find a park and go for it?" He asked, a smirk filled his face reminding him of something she had told him in their past. "Do you still have that dream? You know the one, where you are driving in an Alfa with a tall, dark and handsome man?"

Holly felt her face flush, the sensation burned like the need between her legs and looking over at him she answered his question, placing her hand on his crotch and pulling at his zipper.

Violino let out an unexpected sigh, which took her completely by surprise. She stopped and looked at him taking in all of his features asking if he was still in love with her.

The car fell silent of words, taking the right hand turn which lead to Mt: Coot-tha and the secluded yet popular lovers' lane parking area, overlooking the cities lights.

"Well are you?" She asked him again, focusing on his, not sure exactly what she was looking for but feeling completely at ease in his company.

He looked over at her; his hand had stopped searching her opening and legs. His mood changed but in the moment, he focused all of his energies to keep her sense of security un-breeched.

"I did love you once but that was a long time ago. I don't know who you are anymore or what makes you tick. I'd like to rediscover the soul inside the person again but that takes time and in my world, time is something I don't have a lot of," he confided.

The car found forward motion again. Violinos foot pushed against the accelerator pedal to help the engine push the running gear up the steep incline of the mountain retreat.

"When we left, you were working in the family. Are you now?" She asked but his response was sometime coming.

Feeling the mood of the car change, she tried to re-establish the atmosphere by placing her head on his shoulder.

Instantly there was a reaction and his answer found voice. "I am in the family. I try to keep people from getting into trouble and I mediate difficulties between rival parties," he said.

His chest tightened as his nose took in the full scent of her body.

The orange indicator light flashed across the road and through the gaps between the trees, blending with the colour of green grass.

It was cooler up the mountain road than she had expected shivering as she pushed the button to wind down her window. "I haven't been here in years. I have forgotten how beautiful it is," (her hand found the door lever getting out.)

He watched her as the gentle night breeze took hold of her dress wrapping it all so sensually around her body. His groin was virtually talking to him, begging him to jump out and take her on the bonnet in full view of curious eyes—and before he knew it, he was next to her, standing at the left hand corner of the car.

His lips were at dance with hers and his fingers travelled over her body like hers were over him pushing her back to the bonnet where his lips found her neck and ear lobes.

Holly's sighs found the night air feeling the straps of her dress slide down her arms. The cool breeze surrounded her bare breasts; nipples standing pride of place.

Then a giggle escaped her lips as she thought about how his penis would be reacting to the action knowing it wouldn't take to long to find out, as his teeth and tongue played with her breasts above handed raids pulling at sodden material thrusting inside her.

The Alfa's suspension soaked and matched the rhythmic movements of their bodies in time to each thrust. Her lust found extra lubricant mixing with the scents of their bodies, enchanting her fantasy deeper and deeper into a reality.

He repeatedly chanted her name, as she caressed each of his whispers leading him to the plateaux nobody else could get her to.

She came, ejaculating pent up emotions and frustrations over his groin. Her voice grew deeper and her belling shook and recoiled aching her back atop the panel work of the Alfa's bonnet, ejaculating again and again under symphonies of her own sounds.

In pleading for Violino to follow suit she tightened her muscles around his probing shaft—but he held off, instead concentrating on her breasts, sucking and biting them, teasing her nipples and exploring her body with his fingers, manipulating her arousals and erogenous zones, thrusting harder as he reached for extra penetration under waling groans and heavy breaths—contracting her lust tighter and tighter, playing with his manhood until he came, filling her pocket with gushing fluid spurts, voicing voice with her but thinking of Tammin—mind, body and soul.

He grabbed her hips thrusting inside her harder, feeling his penis throb wildly, as the acid of his lust looked for escape.

Please for his attentions grew louder and her hands and fingers found his back and shoulders under spasms of satisfaction, prompting her back to arch off the bonnet, positioning a higher angle of attack. Her buttocks pressed hard against the bonnet and her legs spread wide apart, straddling his powerful thrusts. And again her world confused reality with fantasy as the plateaux found her eyes and her tears ran the length of her cheeks in the embrace of gravity.

Thirst quenching spurts of his efforts filled her belly and together they fell silent and still to the paintwork under them.

The car suspension lost its spring and their bodies steamed the coolness of the night breeze.

She kissed his cheek and whispered. "I'd forgotten how good we are together."

The weight of his body eased off hers settling his eyes on the deep brown openings to her soul.

"I hadn't," he replied.

The thought of Seppi and Loretta in the shower, played like a Hollywood scene.

CHAPTER 15

"Have you heard from the kid today?" Mario asked, as he and Deli crossed the street from the pizzeria to his car.

They jumped in and settled themselves for a trip. Mario fired the engine and checked his mirrors signalling oncoming traffic of his intentions asking *have you talked to your friend yet* while entering the flow of traffic.

Deli responded. "Yeah the kid was right, there is only a small number working on the case. My friend has a friend working in that department—administration," (watching passing scenery through the window.) "Our administration girl confirms two women and two men as working investigators."

Administration girl..? Mario Questioned. "Is she on our books?"

"No she probably doesn't know she's let anything slip, our friend is friends with her." Deli aired gabbling *quirky nature.*

Mario shared the same thoughts and then added. "Fucking police force today, what do they teach their subordinates—how to blab shit? It goes to show you Deli, if you want to keep a secret don't tell a cop, hah and they're supposed to keep people safe. I sure as fuck don't feel safe around them . . ."

Laughing Deli embellished a little more. *She confirms bugs and cameras' have been placed and says they are up and running—intelligence officers are now listening. This started last night and video surveillance started two days ago.*

Looking at Deli with some concern, Mario uttered. "That means when we discovered we had been tapped, they were watching us!"

238

"Probably," Deli responded. "The intelligence officers are Donna," (they looked at each other nodding suspicions . . .) "Another guy by the name of Eric Nadalle who is Donnas working partner and Holly and Ronnie," adjusting his gaze to the steering wheel. "Apparently they moved back here from Melbourne. Holly asked to be placed on the investigations team," he said disdainfully. "The officer they are reporting to is one Sergeant Nelson Sugar."

Mario turned onto the Pacific Motorway heading for the Gold Coast.

Deli checked his mirror for a tail, as Mario mirrored his actions on the drivers' side.

"What would it take to take out this Sugar character?" Mario asked in a steely tone clasping the steering wheel in agitation.

"Not much. Our official friend has given me an address. It's a very plain looking place on the North side, not far from his work." Deli offered.

Checking his mirrors once more, he asked Deli for the exact address. "So where does this fucker live?"

"Allenby Street, Spring Hill—just off Boundary Road . . ." Deli answered.

Mario nodded. "Yeah, I know where that is. I think we should create misdirection . . ." A smile painted his face.

Deli agreed rubbing his hands together.

Mario laughed. "It seems we think the same things Deli . . ."

Deli nodded settling them into their seats for the rest of the journey.

*   *   *

It seemed all eyes were looking at him, as Ronato entered the Station. Officers of all description, administration staff, felonies and visitors types seemed attentive to him unsettling him to the point, he felt down for his fly questioning *had I zipped up when getting dressed?*

Finding his desk he opened the top drawer throwing in his wallet and other personal affects.

Other investigation Officers working on other cases greeted him, offering identification to his mood and look.

One administration girl said he looked like a *big walking light bulb* as he entered the office. She wrote down her phone number on a yellow sticky note pad telling him to call her saying she'd like to play in the sand box with him.

His face instantly turned red but lifting the yellow sticky note off the desk and placing it in his top shirt pocket.

Somebody's upper thigh made contact with his shoulder and his body abruptly shook forward.

A feminine hand traced the desk's top and her voice filled his ears.

"Well look at you. Did you get up to things last night dear brother?" Holly asked. A cheeky tone coloured her question, as she focused on his blushing face.

"Maybe . . . What about you—did you get up to anything last night—oops I mean this morning," he corrected, placing a finger upon his mouth at the blimp.

Turning on her heel slid out her chair. "Maybe . . ." She answered. "We are seeing each other again tonight. What about you and what's her name?" She laughed.

"Tammin," he answered, his fingers ran the length of his pocket. "No I don't think so. She said it was just a one night thing but it was very good, well for me anyway," looking at her shrugging his shoulders. "It's been awhile for me you know?"

He looked away laughing.

She laughed back saying *I know* and that the whole office and possibly the world knew.

Lifting a closed file he left on his desk from the previous day, he opened it, skimming its content.

"What are we doing today?" He asked.

Her answer washed over him with enthusiasm.

"I, dear brother, get to tail Violino. Something I've been looking forward to for some time now and you being the lucky thing you are get to come with me," she looked down at him with a smile.

She slid her chair into the desk, taking her handbag flinging the strap over her shoulder pointing to him, inching her finger for him to follow her while divulging a set of car keys with her free hand.

Watching him place weight on his legs, she laughed like she was responding to a private joke.

"Come on popular boy," she sang, starting for the car park.

Ronato looked at her, as his puzzlement returned looking around at everyone in the office, grabbing his wallet from the draw saying in bewilderment *popular. Everyone in this office is popular. Not just me.*

*   *   *

Deli focused firmly on the canals, as sun light flickered sparks of colour against the water. Small fibreglass craft mixed for space with larger cruiser type boats, as Mario's car glided over the road surface with a ballerina's ease.

Naples Avenue; started to wind to an end. The parking area at its conclusion prompted Deli to check his pockets for the usual things, wallet, car keys and handkerchief.

Laughing Mario said. "Look at that! We are just in time for the next ferry," pointing to a small covered boat mooring itself to the small dock at the very perimeter of the car park overlooking the water.

Both men leaped from the car, as Mario secured his baby with its alarm, checking his own pockets for wallet and the like heading for the boat with Deli.

"Great place to come if you're being tailed," Deli patted his shoulder. "I know where the kid gets his intelligence."

"Believe me Deli the kid gets his intelligence from his parents, his father in-particular. But his concentration is based from us," the consiglieri stated, drawing a circle in the air conveying everybody in the family. "He has as much of these nuts as those nuts," grabbing his groin conveying Violinos mentality. "A good general he is but supreme commander and overseer of everything? Not yet. That's what we're all here for—to show him the way."

The buoyancy of gangway and boat were tested and re-adjusted to Deli's weight.

"Ahoy-their-yee-land-lovers," bellowed out of a man wearing a fine Italian suit, finding a patch of sunlight, reaching to assist the men onboard in full welcome.

"I haven't seen you to desperado's for some time. Are you coming aboard for business or pleasure?"

Deli slung his arms around the man kissing both sides of his face while Mario patted the man's back, after shaking his hand and settling himself onto a seat, watching Deli re-acquaint an old friendship saying *business my old friend.*

"The pleasure is seeing your fucking old face again," Deli said with glee. "One day I'll have to tell you about this fucking guy and the day he saved my arse from a kingdom of cut junkies," chuckling.

Mario could see the history between the two men only imagining the time they had together and the things they had witness as Officers in the Italian secret service.

The man in the suit, Giacamino, asked if they were heading for the humble abode. Mario and Deli nodded asking if the old man was there.

Giacamino nodded igniting the engine.

Standing closer to the back of the boat watching white foamy water shoot out from the outboard motors listening to the pleasant hum replace the expected roar, Deli smiled to himself heading undercover away from the biting suns rays.

A past event shot to memory finding sound through his voice dangling a question at Giacamino.

"Do you remember the motherfucker you tied to the back end of that cruiser in America . . . that drug fucker?"

Giacamino tilted his head searching through a past corridor of time and with a flick of his hand, looked at Deli. "Si, the water ran red with Bolognese. Good burly for fishing," he quoted while looking at Mario.

The boats floor shuddered, as Deli laughed.

Giacamino showcased his dark humour, as he did actions in memory of the event.

Girung Island lay peacefully amongst its watery surroundings. The Don had purchased it to build a house for himself and his wife to settle, live and die in.

It was perfect for seclusion. An island totally surrounded by water in the middle of a high prised, fashionable city. But with all the attention his dealings attracted from the government, he decided to build a gentleman's club on the site instead. (The Capofamiglia would often be heard saying to his family associates *it was the best investment in security I ever fuckin' made.*)

Giacamino moored the boat against the islands fixed concrete dock, placing the gangway down inviting the two men to the island.

The Tuscan building with its classical archways, gardens and atmosphere drew many a-mans' imagination back to times where gallantry raised the tip of a sword. (Mario giggled to himself the modern similarity.)

Don Cavalieri sang out their names approaching them with open arms, giving them his warmest welcome.

"You two come to get blown—si o` no?" Asking jokingly, as his left hand playfully tapped the crotch of Mario's trousers.

Mario jumped away and said *no business..!*

The Don's smile turned to a frown and then back to a smile while his hand gestures invited them into the building and a more comfortable setting.

The sight of women dressed in very little met their eyes on entering the building. (Mario asked if they could talk in the office, saying the sight of attractive women dressed in a classy next to nothing would sway his focus away from business.) The Don laughed directing them into the office, closing the door behind them before taking his seat.

Mario headed for the scotch decanter and Deli, to a seat overlooking the Dons' desk pouring himself a drink, offering one to each of the men in turn, taking his place in a seat next to Deli.

"What is the meaning of the visit gentlemen?" The Capofamiglia asked, arrogantly.

"We have a friend in the government sending us a jpeg on the officer in charge of the investigations into our families and his sub-ordinates." Mario stated.

The Don looked at him stating to Deli, that Mario should have been a law man because he spoke like one.

Deli agreed punching Mario's shoulder playfully.

The Don curled his fist playfully waving it in front of his guess' faces gritting his teeth, resting his hand over the computer mouse double clicking into each program to his in box and sure enough, over the speakers, the computer voice said he had mail.

He doubled clicked on the envelope on screen and a face appeared seconds later of an older looking man with blonde hair and an official look with a high ranking police uniform and decoration pins on his blazer.

"Is this the piece of shit?" The Capofamiglia asked, swivelling the flat screen around to face the Bruglioni family Consiglieri and head hammer.

Mario read the name of the man that sat under his photo.

"Si, Sergeant Nelson Sugar. That's the povereto."

Deli looked at the screen focusing the image to memory; his eyes traced every outline and facial feature. *Who gets to clip this prick* rang from his lips.

The Capofamiglia roared with laughter sliding a hand across the table to Deli's singing *that's what I love about you my friend—you haven't lost the thirst for this job. You are my favourite Bruglioni in the business.*

Deli smiled back at him.

Re-acquainting Mario's attention, the Capofamiglia said.

"I want to know more about this poofter on the screen, you two come with me. We'll eh, talk about things. E . . ."

He moved the curser across the monitor clicking on the print function, printing the photo file before escaping from each program, leaning toward the printer grabbing the print out—the full aroma of his aftershave entered Mario and Deli's noses, adding to his atmosphere of respect.

Getting to his feet, opening the office door, he turned to face his Bruglioni family guests for a brief second before asking with a hint of boyish charm.

"You two sure you don't want to work up an appetite with a girl. Good exercise," eyeing Deli's frame before laughing. "Deli, you let the girl climb you. I don't need any accidents here."

Deli looked at him and laughed filling the air with a smart comment of his own. "Yeah they say I'm heaviest down below," grabbing his balls, sprouting laughter.

The Capofamiglia closed and locked the door, following the men down the short hallway saying to one of the women standing by the front desk *we go to the casino* lightly tapping her bottom.

Mario's eyes squinted from the suns glare.

*   *   *

Violino stomped through the front door of Tammin's apartment. His heart thudded under adrenalin with anger edging his demeanour.

"Well?" He asked. "Is he or isn't he?"

Tammin got to her feet looking at him; a sick feeling entered her stomach, as she felt uncertainty under his presence answering the question with a timid voice.

"Yes, Ronato is a police officer. I looked through his wallet and clothes and saw his badge and felt his gun," she blemished.

He walked around the sofa that separated them—strength filled his arms and a freight train roared in his chest, grabbing her shoulders shaking her delicate body—his breath was hot on her face and eyes dark and angry.

"You felt his gun. I bet that's not all you felt," he suggested, angrily.

She stood her ground throwing back an angry stare spitting. "Holly . . . Is that the girl you've been whispering when we've been together? She's very pretty."

"Did you plant it?" He asked, relaxing his hold, gazing over her body—tracing every line and curve before cupping her chest softly and delicately and then forcefully, pushing her down into the sofa.

Nodding, too frightened to spill a word, her eyes glazed over under his intent stare.

And then he said. "You ever look at another man again; I'll kill you on the spot. You are my woman *understand*," slapping her face, pushing away from her body leaving the apartment.

She sat still on the sofa. Her heart pounded like a thousand land mines setting off their charges.

A cold sweat filled her brows and a tingle electrified her spirituality.

*   *   *

A rush of atmosphere quickly met Deli and Mario as they followed Don Cavalieri into the casino salivating at the sight of people from all walks of life gamble in the hope of meeting their impossible dreams.

The Don opened his arms like a religious prophet turning to face his compatriots, the look in eyes brought full meaning, as he said *the human spirit in definition is a hungry need to fulfil their dreams of greed and sleaze. These people want to fuck and be fucked, just like anybody else.* (His fingers pointed at the punters running from one table and poker machine to the next.) "But it's this lot who are the most desperate and who never succeed in their life endeavours. But that's good because their failures find my pockets," he smirked, pulling his pockets inside out pointing toward a door which read *staff only* leading them toward it.

They entered into a white corridor where uniforms covering bodies of all types hustled and bustled behind the scenes.

"My worker bees," he said. "These people hold my respect because they work and as such control the paths of their own destinies. They fuck when they want to and when they want to. I respect that."

He pushed open another door which housed security staff pulling the printed image of Sergeant Sugar out of his pocket handing it to one of the security men, saying. "If you see this person in the casino, I want to know about it. Ok?"

The security guy took the photo saying he would have copies made and sent to the CCTV office.

Don Cavalieri looked at Mario and Deli saying *my Gestapo* pushing open another door that lead into an office stretching his arms out like a world leader, asking. "What do you think of my home away from home?"

Mario and Deli looked at each other pouting their response while watching the Don opened a desk draw pulling out a wad of one hundred dollar bills.

"See what success can bring," he uttered stuffing them into his inside suit pocket, before relocking the draw. "Come—now we eat," he said, rubbing his stomach.

They made their way down the white corridor, slaps echoed off the walls and ceiling as the Don slapped female and some male buttocks on their way to the casino's restaurant.

Turning as they reached the last exit entering into general population, he asked *what you feel like. The chef's menu is governed by the flavours of our Spanish brothers. I can recommend the seafood pieia, it is Magnifico* pinching his lips before pushing open, the door.

*   *   *

Gets around this guy of yours Ronato implied, typing data into the unit laptop.

She mumbled her brothers' wise-crack mimicking his typing on the steering wheel, as she told him to find out who lived at the address they found themselves stationed at.

He finished typing in data and clicked into an online telephone directory entering the address into the search engine.

Holly leaned over to glimpse the computer screen but was blinded by glare witnessing her brothers face light up with a pinkish blemish.

"Who is it?" *Who lives here!* She cried, trying to turn the laptop her way.

"You will never believe it in a million years," he chimed, looking at his sister. "It's Tammin."

"Your Tammin..!" She screeched—her eyes lit like a torch powered by 100 candles before saying in a voice of cheek *you won't have to go out of your way to find her now, will you?*

He smiled and tapper her leg and then the computer.

"It just so happens dear sister, one of the office girls gave me her phone number this morning and encouraged me to cal her. And do you know what, I think I might," he pondered.

She giggled uttering. "That would be Julia. She's been wet for you since we arrived." (He drowned her with a; *you don't know everything* face) as she teased him with giggles.

Violino appeared from the premises and Holly fired the engine, watching the Alfa Romeo pull away from the curb abruptly.

Ronato watched the events as Holly teased him further with her laughs as she scoffed *men, all you focus on is women—women—women while women focus on 100 things at once. Where would men be without us?*

"I don't know," he responded. "A Barbie house begging Ken for a latex one perhaps, you tell me," he chuckled, waiting for a response.

But none was forthcoming, as Holly drove silently in a daze of thought.

They followed for another few turns. Ronato recorded each new piece of information, as it came to mind and fruition while Holly pondered repeatedly to herself *where are you heading?*

Chuckling to himself; Ronato said *stumped you haven't I?*

Holly leaned toward him utilising the cars in cabin forces thumping him before saying *shut it.*

*   *   *

Three plates of Seafood Pieia arrived at the table impressing Mario and Deli with its presentation and aroma, the Spanish theme was a nice change tucking in with delight.

The restaurant had a nice feel to it Mario thought, as it didn't feel like you were sitting in a casino watching people desperately try to make their dreams come true. Instead, it had a serene feel like a cruise ship gliding on ocean waves, or a first class flight travel.

The Don dropped his fork on his plate and asked, deflating Mario's serene thoughts.

"Mario tell me more about this piece of shit, this fucking arr police officer," wiping his mouth with a serviette.

"We don't know allot about him apart from he is one of the Brisbane side and the lead officer in investigations being conducted on family business in Queensland," his gaze took in Dons.

"This fucking guy is the Commander of Queensland?!" The Don slurred.

Mario leaned into the table, grabbing the salt shaker sprinkling a light dusting over his plate saying *you want to play with drugs. You play in a bigger sand pit.*

Composing his posture, the Capofamiglia leaned his belly against the table, lifting his fork at rest next to his plate.

Mario sensed another question would come before he filled his mouth with food.

"This is this Brescio shit?"

Mario nodded questioningly. "We have heard; Brescio held talks with other people about increasing his hand in the drug trade. People in the Sunshine Coast, up north, Townsville and Cairns but these people were not Italians they were mainly Asian's and Africa's, Australians—those types," he disclosed, pleadingly drooling for more Pieia while Deli sat happy to play the silent third party.

"Who do you think killed the little prick Mario?" The Don asked, drawing another fork full of food to his mouth, happy to steer away from eye contact.

"We think it was the Asian's, or somebody in his own crew," he put his fork down wiping his mouth before finding the coolness of his beverage adding *who the fuck knows with that shit. It could have been Stefano Picci; people who deal in the shit, play with the shit. To be honest with you, we may never find out. Shit, it could have been a police hit, a dirty cop who clipped him. Who knows?* Taking a sip of his drink, he quickly eyed the room. "The problem we face now is that his body and a few others that have been turning up unannounced, sparking interest within' the coffers of the government. They want to know what the fuck is going on here. The police and investigators are putting their fucking noses into everything. None of us can relax," he stated.

Agitated with the news the Don grabbed his knife.

"Well we have to make this problem go away," stabbing at the air before decapitating a piece of fish. *The sooner the better* he stated, as a person caught his eye.

Smiling, invited the person over.

A security guard approached the table with a printout in his hands.

Mario and Deli averted their gazes to the print-out as the security guard pointed a finger toward the lobby of the casino.

"This guy is out there," the security guard said, his forehead drew lines above his eyebrows.

The Don took the printout perusing it looking passed the doorway toward the lobby. "This fucking guy is out there, you say?" He looked back at the security guard and then at Mario and Deli.

The security guard nodded.

Meshing his hands together, the Don said to the security guard. "Don't let this person leave the building. Take him down to the offices below so I can have a little word with him and if anybody asks questions about this guy in future, you have never seen him ok?"

The security guard gave acknowledgement.

The Don found delight with the cutlery and the taste of the cuisine.

Mario and Deli watched the security guard leave the restaurant on his way to find the police sergeant.

The Capofamiglia finished his lunch and the contents of wine in his glass uttering *la bella Mafia* before standing up throwing the napkin onto the table.

Mario and Deli followed suit finding the Don slide his hand across Deli's shoulder asking. "Do you know how to use power tools?" (Deli looked at him responding with a dip of his head.) "Good. I have an idea," he sniggered.

*   *   *

Violino drove around the streets of Brisbane content on listing to the banter between Holly and Ronato. The listening devise he gave Tammin was placed well as he could hear every noise within' the police unit, while watching it tail him through his mirrors.

His hands cupped the steering wheel like a sculpture would hold a chisel, as revenge mustered a calling for arms in his heart. Images of Ronato lying in a pool of his own bloody excited him but no more than the ideas he had for his sister Holly listening to them talk about him and his family.

The laughter they shared while recording each idea and snippet of thought toward their investigations infuriated him more.

He watched as their ride imitated each of his turns likening the tick-tock sound of their car indicator to a nail gun firing each of its pointed rounds through a human skull.

He was going to square the ledger but not before a bit of fun. He had plans for Holly and after their last encounter, his mouth watered for her while knowing within' himself, the novelties he held for her were over. She proved herself to be quite foreign from a family background. She was a traitor and she would be treated as such.

*   *   *

Mario and Deli took station on a couple of chairs in a downstairs storage room which was dark and dingy, as the Don searched around the walls looking for the main light switch. Sweat formed on their eyebrows rolling down their faces as their noses picked up a musty smell left by days on end of closed doors lacking air circulation.

The Don found the switch and the room became ablaze with light. Power tools and work benches shared space with replacement lounges, restaurant and gaming room chairs and other apparel of all descriptions. Dust lay visibly on the concrete floor and stain marks hinted toward activities other then carpentry, as a roller door hinted another access point for deliveries.

Mario and Deli looked toward the door, voices could be heard coming from its opposite side and then at the Don who opened his arms like a performing opera singer saying *my office away from the office* smiling dangerously.

He picked up a power saw from the work station noticing a chair and gaffer tape by Deli saying.

"Deli, grab that tape and swivel that chair around. Mario, when this prick enters push him into the chair and help Deli secure this bastard onto it. We are going for a little drive."

Deli did as he was ordered while Mario got into position, as the Don plugged the power saw into an electrical socket.

The door opened and as planned, Mario pushed the officer into the chair while Deli harnessed his body with a few good wraps of tape before he knew what hit him. Again and again the role of gaffer tape screamed, as Deli secured the Sergeant to the chair.

The Capofamiglia laughed at the industry before his eyes pulsing; the trigger of the power tool for extra affect before raising his hand to Deli to stop.

Mario sat in the chair he found against the wall while Deli leaned against the closed door next to the security guard.

The Don approached Sergeant Sugar with the power tool in hand pulsing; its trigger to menacing affect staring deeply into his eyes before slapping his face. A loud crack of flesh on flesh bounced off the walls, as an instant red mark appeared on the officers' cheek. (The security guard laughed.)

"Why are you following me you blue piece of shit?" The Don asked, again slapping the sergeants' face.

Sergeant Sugar grimaced but did not answer as he watched the power tool get closer and closer.

Pulsing; the trigger, the Don pointed to the security guard to open the roller door unplugging the power tool from the wall, loading it and himself into the driver's side of the courier van while inviting Deli and Mario to join him in the front.

The security guard loaded the sergeant and himself into the back.

*   *   *

"Jesus Christ, where is he going?" Ronato squealed, frustrated from the constant travel. His eyes and mood were sick of the black car three cars up. "Do you think he's made us?" He asked Holly.

Her hair danced from side to side, as she shook her head in response.

Looking down at the laptop, he clicked into the satellite surveillance program the police used to track their units.

"Where the hell are we?" He asked himself, a red circle flashed along a snaking line on the screen. "Jesus Christ. Mt: Mee!"

Holly looked across and said *no thanks.*

Ronato shot a look at her. "Not me . . . That's where we are; fucking Mt: Mee!"

Holly looked across settling him with her calming voice.

"We're only 45 minutes or so away from the city. He's going for a drive, or maybe he has a meeting, whatever he's doing, there are eyes watching so don't worry."

He shook his head as her smile caught his eye and said *just like mamma.*

She giggled and agreed *yep just like mamma.*

*   *   *

Violino laughed, as he looked into the rear-view mirror listening to Ronato wine and whinge. Memories served him well of family excursions where Ronato would complain for days about each long drive into the country applauding himself for driving the full distance around the Peachester Range putting his foot down to enjoy the windy roads of the mountain.

*   *   *

"What is this place?" Mario asked, as a rusted out shell of a building sat vacant amongst cracked concrete and flowery weeds. Every window in the premises had long been shattered and a scent of rust filled the air around it.

The Don pointed toward an industrial sized door replying *this place used to be a fish market, now it's a friend's storage dock for nets and fishing stuff* parking under the buildings cover.

Deli and Mario slid out on Deli's side under a depressing sight of dust, dirt and crap filling their view in all angles before an old meat saw stole their attention, rusted and seized in its original place.

Old rusty hand saws and ice picks hung on nails up and along hardwood posts and framing whilst bricks and broken glass covered parts of the cracked and shattered ground.

The courier vans roller door slid open and sergeant Sugar fell out, the sound of the chair sliding on metal created an aerie squeal, replaced by the thud of his body rolling across concrete—the chair gave little cover or cushion.

Don Cavalieri laughed patting the security guards shoulder, his appreciation of the act greatly amused him looking around at the others saying *that type of thing is against the Geneva accords* and then applauded adding. "So is this . . ." (His shoe found the police officers mouth, like a football player kicking a ball.)

The power of the kick dazed the sergeant as his body skidded 180 degrees atop the concrete ground. Blood ran from of his mouth while his jaw bruised and swelled.

Mario looked down at him and at the blood before surveying with greater detail the old concrete floor, as blood stains from another time marked like patchwork the surface, looking over at Deli sending him a message of sign language.

(Deli approached leaning his ear toward his mouth to listen.) "Whatever the Don does, try to get some physical evidence we can use elsewhere against him," he whispered.

And then Deli added *and enjoy; the show* as the security guard handed the Capofamiglia the power tool.

Grabbing the Sergeant with his free hand, the Don dragged him by the shoe to a power point set against a wall, righting the chair with the help of the guard and after plugging the tool in pressed the trigger repeatedly before asking again and again *why the fuck are you following me?* (Looking at Mario and Deli, restated the question.) "Us..?"

But Sugar didn't answer, as the question bounced into his ears like fragmented sound.

In a fit of rage, the Don took hold of Sugars left hand placing it atop a plank of wood the guard sat across Sugar's lap cutting his fingers off. (The sound of metal dissecting bone horrified Mario's ears.)

Deli squinted as blood sprayed from the blade down Sugar's leg, across the security guards shoes and up the Dons suit.

Sugar shook in fits of pain and shock, as spurts of blood rained out of his fingers in second intervals, under the Dons' repeated questioning.

Why the fuck are you following me and my friends?

With little response coming from the police sergeant, Don Cavalieri ordered the security guard to rally up some plastic bags and a change of clothes.

Tears of pain and blood ran down Sugars reddened face, as the power tool cut and severed body parts until the pain and sound went away numbed by shock.

He felt torture—coldness—lifelessness and then nothing.

Shards of skin, fat, tissue and flesh found permanent rest upon the ceiling, corrugated metal scraps and the closest wall, as the Don decapitated the sergeants body. Grinds of sound squealed out of the saw blade as each tooth cut throw bone, flesh and cartilage.

The smell reminded Mario of a meat works, as blood exploded from the cavity like a water sprinkler on full flow, dripping from everything it landed on, leaving its smell thick on the air until the grind of substance had deteriorated leaving nothing big enough to cut.

Facing Mario and Deli, the Don pointed at the corpse saying *burly, sharks love Burley.*

A short time passed when another van entered the shed. Guards dressed in raincoats got out wearing gloves and carrying buckets and plastic bags.

The Don handed Mario and Deli a raincoat instructing them to help scoop up remains.

Mario nodded at Deli watching him confiscate the fingers scattered across the concrete inconspicuously while the others scooped blood and body parts into big white industrial buckets with the head, arms and legs going into plastic bags.

The buckets were taken and placed in a fishing boat docked at the harbour. The Don's suit and plastic bags were taken away for incineration.

Deli concealed Sugar's fingers in a plastic bag placing them into his trouser pocket, under his raincoat before being mustered back to the courier van they'd arrived in by the Don, leaving the site.

The polished grey suit the Capofamiglia changed into matched the life emitting from his eyes and the excitement of his words, as he said. "Today you have brought me an unexpected pleasure. But life can be sweet no?"

Mario agreed, looking into the future. He saw the Don's arms on a chopping block, as he followed the Don's eyesight into oncoming traffic.

A smile covered his face when Deli echoed the words *unexpected pleasures.*

CHAPTER 16

Donna rubbed a headache out of her forehead trying to decipher each order of events from the Indooroopilly crime scene while matching its particulars to other crime scenes associated with their investigations, pondering the last set of discussions she had with Holly and Sugar. The investigation checks she'd run on Bruglioni family interests yielded nothing but it didn't stop the alarm bells ringing between headache thumps in relation to the Cavalieri family, as all of their interests had inconsistent idiosyncrasies not to mention drugs seized from a warehouse known to be a drugs laboratory and a hand gun which through testing was found to belong to one Mr. Eduardo Cavalieri.

A hand brushed against her shoulder feeling company encroach her personal space and the reflexion of a face peer from the computer screen closely followed by a familiar voice posing a question.

"What conclusions do you draw detective?"

She looked at Ronato—the scent of his aftershave was pleasant, subconsciously crossing her legs responding.

"I think you and Holly are right," her eyes ran across the shaving line of his face before falling into his eyes. "I have squeezed the Bruglioni family angle through the eye of a needle and come up with nothing. All of their business interests are legit. I can't find anything that can tie them to anything illegal! Yet I know they practice across the other side of the line," she said, shaking her head in disbelief.

He straightened his posture placing a hand in a trouser pocket, chimes of sound rattled, as his fingers found loose change and car keys to play with.

"What does Sugar say?" He asked, eyeing her between the neckline and shoulders before shaking his head and darting attention back to the monitor.

She looked over her left shoulder, blushing, finding his crotch, before answering, she hadn't seen him (turning back for the screen feeling her chest burn the same colour as her face) while her low cut sweater suddenly felt tighter under the swelling of her breasts and gooey sensation between her legs.

Ronato peered at sergeant Sugars door pondering a session of advice on what and where to probe but found the office to be unusually dormant and mumbled *that's strange. He's always here . . .*

"Yeah," Donna shrugged, thinking nothing of it before asking. "Why are you here? Shouldn't you be out and about keeping that sister of yours in sight?"

He met her gaze stirring in lust. "Yeah well I would be but your partner is covering her."

An administration girl teetered passed asking if they knew where Sugar was. They both looked at her shaking their heads and the girl continued on her way mumbling something too herself.

*   *   *

Mario typed Violino a message on his cell phone, as Vito served plates and sauces of espresso coffee and biscotti. The dining room was strangely cold considering the air conditioning hadn't been turned on, as a constant beat of Morse code tapped from Deli's fingers under repeated glances at his watch.

Placing a hand on Deli's, Mario consoled him. "It's ok—have your coffee, he will get here soon," and then asked under sudden query. "What did you do with the fingers?"

Deli pointed toward the kitchen saying *they're in the freezer.* (Vito confirmed by flicking his head toward the kitchen while pouring himself a coffee; saying he would have loved to see the show.) Deli's grimace turned to smiles as he nodded pleasure.

Vito joined the table dunking a biscuit into his break stating. "You know this thing has to happen now and fast . . . but you haven't got anything to really cement the blame onto the Gold Coast."

Shaking his head in disagreement, Mario said *we have a lot that points to the Cavalieri family—Violino took out the Indooroopilly operation leaving Cavalieri's pistol under a mountain of snow along with two bodies.*

Interrupting with apology, Vito said. "I was wrong, please continue," glowing at the eventuality, as the Consiglieri continued the briefing.

"We have the police sergeants fingers in cryogenics where they will find eventual rest on Cavalieri soil and we have a rundown fish market full of blood stains," (his eyes lit up like a 14 year old boy who'd had his first sexual experience.) "I'd say that's a good start," taking a satisfying sip of espresso, looking into his eyes.

Eyeing them with pride written over his face, Vito said. "That's fucking beautiful."

Mario's cell phone rang reaching into his trouser pocket, saying it was probably Violino, toggling through menu reading *be there soon. Busy,* as a smile lit his face. "He's probably with Holly."

Vito laughed, saying *yeah he's probably getting some use out of her.*

Mario and Deli laughed along with him.

*   *   *

Holly entered the apartment watching Violino drop his car keys and cell phone onto the living room table under glimpses of its décor. The place seemed tidy and in order with a nice aroma of aftershave and the previous night's dinner.

He turned facing her, pressing her body between his and the living room wall. Warm breath cascaded down her neck and chest as a feeling of wetness from his tongue traced lines across her flesh—the experience swelling her upper body tightening the bra and blouse she wore while feeling her face and chest blemish a colour of pink roses.

Tilting her neck to one side, she allowed his lips and tongue full rein over their domain feeling her lust moisten and part like the Nile while warm breath flushed her lobes in a whisper *tell me a secret.* (Hands explored in daring raids her chest and hips, buttocks and thighs, navel and vagina, clothing rippled and creased, expanded and dropped.) Another whisper found her ears as her bra gave way under determined persuasion breaking her breasts free surrendering to the forces of gravity *come on Holly, tell me a secret.*

Her knees buckled to the suction of his lips atop her swollen nipples while her upper body burned with want and lower basted under a thick atmosphere, poked and stoked by hands and fingers, as another whisper softened what was left of her senses.

"Whisper to me a secret and I'll give you a reward."

Pressing her back harder against the wall, she summoned a whisper, struggling to stutter *I'm wet and wanting.* (A heady smell of lust filled their space.)

Skirt, stockings and panties tore from her body under strategic imputes while confused echoes of sound ruffled belt and trouser fastenings.

Tearing open his shirt she gasped at a torn masculine torso showing off a magnificent olive complexion before a strong bulge centred her focus beneath the weave of his jock strap.

He lifted her off her feet carrying her to the dining room table laying her body across its surface. His eyes scanned every inch of her heaving torso under rippling witness of his muscles and muscle, trailing fingers and hands over her thighs and hips before pulling her toward him salivating at the fine delicateness of her wet vagina.

Moaning, she arched her back pushing her breasts skyward—(his hands and mouth, teeth and tongue explored her body in romantic memory and fascination biting and sucking her nipples, breasts, stomach, inner thighs and vagina) before again whispering for a secret.

Her thoughts found turmoil fighting each while she arched and squirmed, forming villages of Goosebumps under every touch, kiss and penetration.

Her lust stretched and retracted lubricated and squelched, feeling friction and power from hip tonic trusting, legs parting wider and wanting pleading with her heart and head that this was the one, the man she wanted and needed and yearned for but for flash backs crippling the fluidity of each memory and satisfying travel (the memory of her father's passing and how she felt when she learned it was Bruno Bruglioni who ordered the hit; and the look in his eyes when she took revenge serving justice via revolver pulling the trigger against him, emptying round after round into him: The feelings of satisfaction watching his pride and joy entomb his body in black leather and Ferrari badges and the sounds of twisting carbon fibre and breaking glass, judged and sentenced to ride the back of his lame horse forever.

She felt the raid turn its last corner for home, as waves of pleasure convulsed her body sending; a-turmoil of sweat and tears down her face. Her breasts and nipples begged for attention under cramping spasms of her own ejaculation—sending a sea of emotion against his groin shortly followed by his, replenishing her parched innards with sown seed.

Her pulse rate started to slow running her hands over her flat stomach; each city containing droplets of sweat started drying evaporating away, as again Violino asked for a secret between kissing and touching her thighs and legs, navel and chest.

His tongue on her sweat spot arched her back readying her for a second raid when his whispers found new lyrics.

"I have a secret," closing his eyes, finding her lips with his. A longing kiss softened her again before the warmth of his breath tickled her face. "I have a secret that I want to share."

(She focused meaningfully into his eyes, lovingly combing the back of his neck and hair.)

"I know you're not a model," entering her again, this time uncomfortably. "I know you work with Donna. And I know you're WORKING AGAINST ME!!" He growled, thrusting his hips violently, bouncing echoes of noise against the table and walls.

Sharp stabs of nauseous pain grappled with her panic, trying to release words. She tried to scream, remembering Eric was outside, watching the apartment from the cabin of a squad car but no sound would come out. And then realised, his hands were around her neck. His penis was inside her and pain triggered a fear for her life.

She felt his tension release inside her feeling him pull out (the look in his eyes spelt death) breath angry and rapid and hands powerful and hard against her face. Painful burns replaced earlier sensuality as her head jolted upward under the pulling of her hair, leading the rest of her body atop the living room carpet—opening her mouth to scream but failing.

He sat on her waist, pinning her to the floor, looking, forcing her to look into his eyes. (Questions ran connection between them.)

"Why come back to do this?" He asked her, slapping her face again.

(A squeal of pain left her mouth, as a small gash opened her bottom lip.) "Why did you think you could beat me? I don't understand?" He demanded.

She wriggled from side to side but his hold was to strong.

"We were going to be together forever," he said, watching her bid for freedom. "You tried to beat me and lost. I've just fucked you like a dog. Your worth has plummeted to bankruptcy," he spat, slapping her face again and again.

Holly lay helpless on the floor, she knew Eric would not hear her screams realising she would have to ride out the situation and see where it led.

Her body wracked with pain and her face burned from continuous slaps bruising her spirit.

Feeling the same turmoil while making love, she focused her eyes on his looking back at the decision of becoming a police officer and on the decision to work on Donna's case, weighing it up against the order against her fathers' death, as the sickness of revenge stirred her stomach again, only this time it was against the man pinning her to the floor—her first love.

She had never realised how similar Violinos eyes were to his fathers. They both had the same sense of charity. Both had kind hearts, if you were in their circle. And both concealed their feelings from outside surroundings.

Dryness lined the back of her throat like she was going to through up, as his words *I fucked you like a dog* sank in.

She rolled her head from side to side in an attempt to gain focus when she noticed him smiling down at her realising her state of thoughts slapping her again, only harder.

Fight stirred within' her wanting to hurt him more than anyone had before, feeling that this was the final stand, the fight for survival.

Her wits were kicking in—police training found its voice and her dagger found voice through the air.

"I have defeated you Violino . . . I took away the one thing you loved most in this world—your father," she croaked, in a low dry voice. "I killed that piece of shit in the line of duty. **And it was poetic**. I found myself in a position of great luck during an investigation into the Cavalieri family. He was in the right place at the right time and got what he deserved, a neat family of taps in the head until the clip was empty. And then for good measure and to throw off the dogs, I entombed his limp, smelly body into his car driving the fucking thing off the mining quarries.

You can't know the satisfaction I got from hearing the body panels crumple and the glass shatter. It was sweet revenge after your father ordered the murder of mine. Oh. And you didn't fuck me bitch. I fucked you little man," as a tiny trail of blood ran from her opened lip.

Violino sat atop her silently, focusing into the colour of her eyes walking a temperamental line of no return, softly touching her reddened face, falling into memory of the family Consiglieri breaking the news of his father's death and in the manner he was found, finding the same cold contraction of stomach and brain.

Holly had it right, he worshiped his father. His world started and ended with the jeans of which gave him life. And he felt sick but not defeated.

He looked down at her naked body. Her breasts were perfect mounds and her stomach slim and shapely showing off a beautiful rich face framed by hair of silk laughing at her.

Her eyes betrayed her—giving away defeat starting to sob.

Running his fingers along her soft lips and face, he whispered he was going to kill her—kissing her while tightening the hold over her—mumbling to himself *it's a shame to let this go to waste.*

He manoeuvred their bodies into the missionary position asking looking into her eyes *who's fucking who?* Raping her viciously, torturing her every sense of humanity, love and justice.

Her body rolled and lapped, squelched and discoloured under an array to hatred and disgust, payback and revenge until spent he placed his hands around her neck pushing against her cruelly.

Waves of flesh convulsed her sides through shear force and thrust, wanting her to feel broken—wanting her to feel the last acidic dregs of seamen hand her life to death.

Her throat convulsed and mouth drooled. Foaming saliva dribbled from each corner, ending his pelvic thrusts.

He pulled out of her lifeless body; tears of sorrow ran down his face looking at her with sadness spilling *the woman I would have killed for.* And then like a smack over the wrists for day dreaming, consciousness returned to present tenths running around the living room, searching for his clothes, stepping into trousers in one leap. His shirt lay flung over a coffee table ripped.

Searching for his cell phone, he turned and looked down at her body once more—its healthy pink turned grey.

*   *   *

Mario answered his cell phone seated around a table with Deli who was sipping on coffee and Vito looking at his wrist watch.

"Si pronto . . ." (He listened for a few short seconds before firing.) "Where you been? We've been waiting for you here for hours!"

Vito and Deli watched, as he listened to the person on the other end of the connection before saying he understood closing the link.

Vito questioned him, Roman style.

Placing the phone on the table sculling the rest of his coffee, he pointed to Deli to follow him.

"That was the kid. He's got Holly at his place. She's dead. He wants us to get around there and take out the motherless fuck sitting in an unmarked car across the street," (watching Deli stand up.) "Vito, can you plant the fingers back at the old fish market for us? We are going to send in an anonymous call to the police. Add that to the Dons gun and *arrivederci* Capofamiglia Cavalieri and his family," Mario smiled, kissing his middle finger into the air.

Deli strode out of the restaurant with Mario.

Vito finished his coffee. Retrieved the fingers from the freezer, writing a note to his staff saying he'd be gone for most of the day—and started for the Gold Coast.

*   *   *

Violino lifted Holly's limp body from the floor carrying it into the bathroom where he placed it into the tub, focusing on her perfection kissing her breasts and whispering that he was sorry.

He ran into the bedroom flinging open the sliding door which concealed his clothes throwing on a shirt, recollecting the incident in his mind making mental notes of what needed cleaning and what could be tidied up.

The living room was a story book of events, as cloths and body fluids hung draped and dripping from furniture—sprawled over flooring and carpet.

Bundling the clothing off the floor, he burnt them in his fireplace cleaning the table where they made love before turning attention to the carpet and the splashes of her ejaculation splotched with the pile, salting and bleaching each splotch before salting and bleaching the murder scene in all of its stages—making his way back to the front room where he sat on a chair eyeing intensely the unmarked car and its occupant.

*   *   *

Mario and Deli pulled up alongside the curb, the unmarked police car had their undivided attention noticing the interior mirror was angled toward Violinos apartment.

Mario swore under his breath and Deli prepared a small arms piston he retrieved from his inside suit holster.

Watching him arm it adoringly, Mario turned the engine off. Sliding clicks from the weapon and the odd passing car were the only noises to disrupt the eerie silent premeditation.

Unclipping his seatbelt, Deli opened the car door fielding the question *what are you thinking of doing* responding he was going to ask the guy for directions then clip him in the side of the head.

But just as they were discussing the act, Mario's cell phone rang.

Answering it, he looked at Violinos apartment falling silent.

Ok fell from his mouth looking at Deli while placing the phone in the centre console relaying not to shoot the detective sitting in the car ahead of them.

"Violino doesn't want the police to find bullet wounds on the bodies but instead, fractured skulls."

Deli nodded and reiterated his belief in Violinos shrewdness.

"He's fucking smart that kid."

Sliding out, the car suspension gratefully decompressed, as he closed the door heading for the detective.

Mario sat mesmerised by the calmness shown; the skill was above reproach, as he tapped on the detectives' car window swing his arms around depicting a question.

The detective did the obvious and wound the window down.

In a split second, Deli struck his forehead with the piston before entering the cabin striking the officer repeatedly until he was satisfied the detective was dead.

Sitting in ore, Mario shook his head at the presents of mind, skill and luck, since the first car passed them on arrival no other had gone by until the detective slumped upon the seat.

"Miraculous," he uttered while watching Violino appear from the apartment crossing the road toward him, turning the ignition key to open the electric window.

"What do you want to do kid?" He asked.

Violino leaned into the window steadying his stance against the cars roof. "Just follow me and Deli," he uttered, heading for the detectives car opening the passenger side door leaning into the cabin, dragging the dead detectives' body out of the drivers' side and into the passenger side seat.

Deli jumped in the drivers' side under the young Dons instruction starting the car, reversing into his driveway where he got out and popped the boot.

Violino ran inside the apartment soon re-appearing with Holly's limp naked body, throwing it into the boot.

Deli matched the action with the other detective.

The young Don jumped into the drivers' side and Deli into the passenger and the car pulled away.

Mario followed, as he was told, shaking his head at their luck. No traffic had passed, and no one had walked by. "Miraculous," he uttered again.

After a short stint amongst Brisbane's traffic they pulled up outside a single story apartment block, where the young Don jumped out of the detectives' car entering the building, soon to re-appear holding clothes, throwing them in threw Deli's window, heading for Mario's car.

"We are heading for the Coast. I want Holly's body to be found near one of the Dons places," he advised—pulled up by Mario offering a query.

"Violino did you use protection!"

He stuttered at the question and then turned facing the consiglieri before answering. "No. No I didn't," a strained look forged his young face. "What are we going to do with her?" (He leaned on Mario's door before adding.) "Whatever it is, it will have to be fucking soon . . . forensics!"

"We can stage an accident and incinerate the car." Mario brainstormed.

Violino clapped his hands together pointing at the family adviser rubbing his thumb and index finger together chiming. "That's why you get the big bucks Mario," slapping the open window heading back for the detectives' car.

* * *

Ronato dropped a closed file down onto Donna's desk looking at her computer screen. The text curser danced across it jumping from box to box along a pro-forma template typing in the full name and address of Don Cavalieri. 'Arrest Warrant,' titled the computer saved form.

"I agree. To get at the Bruglioni family, we'll need more time. Violino and his crew don't deal in drugs. They don't really seem to deal in anything high risk but the Cavalieri lot . . . we have enough on them now to process a case," he shared, darting from box to box following the text curser.

Donna stopped tapping on the keyboard asking him to pull his chair—and sit it beside hers (and as he did,) asked a question he didn't expect.

"If Holly wasn't full of revenge, do you think, or more to the point, do you believe—she and Violino would have become a couple?" Squinting—the choice of wording.

Eying her thoughtfully, he replied *yes*. "You know what they were like growing up. They stuck together like glue. You could say she was constantly sticky for Violino . . ."

Donna interrupted his answer. "And he was sticky for her."

"Exactly," he replied.

"Ok. Do you believe, even though she knows what she knows and the feelings that she has in this matter, that love will conquer all?"

Ronato fell quiet.

And Donna took the silence as a statement for the positive. *So in other words you think love could overcome the odds?* She re-iterated.

"What are you really asking Donna? You want me to tell you if I think Holly will cross the line?" His eyes questioned her. "No. No I do not believe Holly would cross the line. She is not a criminal!" He stated harshly.

A hot streak of anger shook his voice.

Donna's hand rested on his leg tapping his knee in a settling way.

"You know I don't think Holly is a criminal. But sex is a powerful tool, especially when it turns into love. And I've seen love conquer a lot of adversity." (She looked at him apologetically. Her hand stay rested on his knee.) "I've seen love do some pretty strange things."

Ronato placed his hand over hers, finding the colours in her eyes nodding understandingly before putting her straight. "Holly would not turn against the investigation in favour of Violino . . . **whether they have sex or not**."

Nodding, she returned to the arrest warrant, filling the computer screen.

Ronato sat next to her, his eyes watched the text curser dance from box to box under a tingling sensation of her touch.

And then another question parted her lips. "Have you tried to contact Eric and Holly about their movements?"

"Yes. No answer. I keep getting an operators message. *The phone you are trying to contact has been turned off or is out of range. Please check the number and try again,*" he mimicked.

Laughing, she said; he did that well.

*   *   *

Violino mounted the curb around the swerve of Salerno Street leaving a black mark upon the concrete outside Don Cavalieri's home.

Deli sat in the passenger side seat impressed with the forward thinking barnstorming the young Don but hoped the presents of mind wasn't lost on the police saying *remember what I said about you doing national service? Well you can fuck that kid—you got it all!*

A tear of pride welled in his eyes.

Violino patted him on the knee saying; he'd watched and learned from a master.

Deli muttered *your father.*

And then he corrected him. "No Deli . . . you..! I watched and learned from you."

Deli dipped his head with respect looking forward as the seat belt became heavy on his chest, a police car sat on the road in front of them stopped at a set of traffic lights *fucking boys in blue.*

Laughing, Violino said *no shit* in a low murmur looking into the interior mirror witnessing Mario shake his finger at him in an authoritative manner with a smile on his face.

"Fuck me, you fucking wise guys," he mumbled shaking his head.

Deli looked at him in a confused state.

Violino turned the car in an easterly direction from the traffic lights.

Deli watched the squad car disappear in the distance asking where they were headed.

The young Don responded they were headed for Mount Tamborine.

"There's a big cliff up there. We can sit these two in the front seats and idle the car over the fucking cliff. Then ignite the car because the bodies have to burn," he advised checking to make sure Mario was still in sight behind them.

Deli turned up the air-conditioning.

They reached the mountain lookout—cars from all states and territories seemed to be in the parking area.

Thinking it would be too suss to drive the car off the lookout, Violino reversed out pointing Mario down to a dirt track he saw on their climb to the lookout following while Deli readied the clothes the young Don took from her apartment.

"We've got to be quick Deli. We have to dress her like she would for work," he instructed.

He brought the car to a stop placing it in park, leaving the engine running—getting out.

Deli popped the boot from the glove-box feeling the rear shock absorbers pump, as Violino struggled with lifting Eric's body out.

He hopped out placing Holly's cloths onto the roof, trying desperately not to drop them on the ground knowing from his military experience that dirt was difficult to shake from clothing fibres.

Violino placed Eric's body back in the front seat violently. The car wobbled under forces of the bodies' weight and his strength while Deli with clothes in hand, dressed Holly in the boot waiting for him to help carry her to the passenger side.

They placed her clipping the seatbelt around her.

Witnessing all of this, Mario filled a bottle with petrol from the tank handing it to Deli who started pouring the contents half over Holly and half over the other detective whom Deli confirmed was the detective driving the car he followed to Mt: Glorious the day he followed Donna and Holly.

Violino stopped around the front of the car looking into the windscreen confirming he saw that same guy at Lights & Lace the night of the reunion.

Mario leaned over Holly taking the car out of park while Violino turned the ignition key as Deli ignited a wad of paper lighting the detectives on fire—throwing the wad in through the front window, as the car idled toward the edge.

In a great woof the flames the car disappeared over the cliff.

Mario and Deli stood both sides of the young Don, wrapping their arms around his waist leading him back toward the car—sounds of twisting metal and shattering glass filled their ears while the smell of burning upholstery filled their noses.

Hopping in starting for the road—a muffled explosion drew a smile to Mario's face, as he celebrated the notion of an eye for an eye to himself.

CHAPTER 17

Donna hated travelling along the Pacific Motorway, the endless corridor of prime movers rib boning tarmac slipped her into familiar day dreams of sitting at home in front of the television set watching the 6 o'clock news finding out she'd been killed in a traffic accident confirming her as part of the national road toll.

A hand slid across hers resting on her leg—looking finding Ronato wear a concerned look upon his face.

"Are you ok?" He asked.

She looked at him appreciatively nodding re-adjusting focus to the two personalities sitting in front.

The air conditioning was steep contrast to the chief inspectors office and the liquid questions being asked; questions on their investigations into organised crime and the families within' the file, as an icy chill numbed her face realising she was sitting in the back of the chief inspectors car with Ronato heading toward an unknown destination.

Looking into the interior mirror, she asked. "Sir, can I ask where we are going?" (His eyes found hers picking up on the inklings of thought glazing them) and then looked across to his aid mumbling something while in command of the car and its snaking journey.

The aid swivelled in his seat opening a file which sat on his lap sharing what they knew.

"This morning we received an email from the Gold Coast precinct. We are heading to a crime scene," he advised, handing over emailed printouts of a warehouse. "It's an old fish market . . . after an anonymous phone call, officers were sent to this place to investigate a claim. On entering the premises, they found several severed fingers and blood" (the aid looked down at the printouts sitting on Donnas lap.) "We have reason to believe the remains and blood belong to Sergeant Sugar."

Stillness filled the cabin. Donna and Ronato looked at each other, their faces fell; white and green, as misunderstanding, confusion and shock chiselled their features.

The aid, reacting to their reactions added. "He stepped into the precinct yesterday morning asking some of the local branch about the area and the Cavalieri family. Now he's missing."

Ronato reached for the printouts.

"What makes you think Sergeant Sugar has met with foul play?" Donna asked, lurching forward between the front seats, resting a hand on the centre console to steady her comfort.

Ronato continued flicking through the printouts while looking up periodically listening to the chief inspectors reply.

"His car is parked across the road from a casino managed by the Cavalieri family."

Donna sat briefly silent before airing another question.

"What would he be doing asking questions within' the field? It was agreed by all at a dinner meeting that myself, Senior Constables Austrella and Detective Senior Constable Nadalle would do all the outward investigations . . . *what was he thinking?!*"

Road noise filled the cabin momentarily before Ronato asked. "Then I take it sir, we think Sergeant Sugar is deceased?"

The aid tipped his head toward the backseat.

And Donna focused her eyes to the chief inspectors reflexion on the windscreen.

The Chief Inspector said they would know more soon.

*   *   *

Violino made his way down the stairs into the churches underbelly. Sounds of chatter filled his ears and a smell of new carpet permeated the air stepping through the dividing curtain finding to his surprise a mini casino with gambling tables, roulette wheel, cash-out counter, poker tables, a stocked bar and fridges which doubled as entertainment centres grinning under the delivery of a sly comment *what; no topless women and screwing booths?*

He ordered drinks up starting for the bar but was halted by Salvatore who pointed toward the new deck access.

Laughing openly, he clapped in celebration running his eyes over the circumference of the new doorway, its construction was neat and tidy looking behind at his guardians walking through.

Salvatore was behind him saying *just walk into the light my son* voicing a ghostly mimic resting his hands on the young Dons shoulders.

"Sal, you have to give those fucking guys a raise or something. This is fucking great! What does it look like from the water?" He celebrated.

"From the river you would never know this lead to the basement of a fucking church . . . shit kid; you wouldn't know it lead anywhere!" Salvatore chimed.

Violino patted his shoulder, pride running through the men.

"So, when is opening night?" He asked, sparkling like a child in a gelataria.

Mario and Seppi joined them.

Salvatore looked at them answering *three nights.*

Rubbing his hands together, Violino mimicked Dastardly the anime character chirping *you have Chianti in that bar of yours? Mario—call Vito and Deli! This calls for a celebration!* (Spreading his arms around the men and leading them toward the basement.)

Mario pulled his cell phone and called Vito.

Salvatore laughed and nodded saying *fuck kid, not just Chianti but the finest grape juice ever to come out from Italy!*

"Where the fuck did you get that from?" Violino squealed, entering the gambling chamber.

Salvatore playfully grabbed a fist full of his hair saying. "Some things need to stay a secret kid," (bending over behind the bar grabbing a wooden case containing Barolo, presenting it to him.)

Violino reached for it noticing the absence of father Options saying *I bet the padres happy.*

Seppi responded full of chuff. "He's so happy, he's gone shopping!"

Salvatore placed four wine flutes on the bar watching Violino do the honours with the Barolo bottle—sweet aromatics touched each of their noses as the red silk was poured.

In little more than a breath and with each flute accommodated, Violino toasted.

"To Salvatore, Mario and Seppi for your guidance, friendship and efforts I toast you—Vito and Deli for their inspiration and colour—and to father Options and his grocery shopping."

*   *   *

The Chief Inspector pulled into a premises littered with uniformed police vehicles, under cover, special armoured vehicles, fire, ambulance and forensics—the building resembled an industrial workplace while a sign leaning against the steel mesh fence surrounding its borders read '*Fish Market.*'

An icy atmosphere like that of a morgue chilled Donna's bones, as pins and needles attacked her fingers. The Inspector and his aid swivelled in their seats to face her and Ronato in the back—a sick gush filled her throat from the very pit of her stomach.

He offered with a tone of softened authority.

"Donna, Ronato . . . I want you both to take your time. It is very important and will be very important to future investigations if you can tie this incident in with the local crime families.

What you will find in that building will probably shock you but you need to be strong."

His aid looked directly into Donnas' eyes settling a red glaze over his pupils.

They mingled amongst the investigation scene; forensics taped cordoned off areas all around the property.

Donna caught sight of a familiar face making her way toward a huddle of forensics personnel.

"What have you got?" She asked.

He looked at her opening his notebook.

"Detective Senior Constable Donna Fiorella," he said. "We will have to stop meeting like this," (dipping his head in acknowledgement.) "This is a gruesome one . . . inside the market there are multiple blood stains *and well let's just say—this place has been very profitable in its retirement,*" (showing all the signs of shock and disgust.) "In all my years in this business I have never seen anything like this. I don't think I could even stomach lunch," he complained, taking in the features of the two undercover officers and their own reactions. "We think it might be your commander and chief. If it is, he didn't die peacefully. His fingers and head were severed before his whole body was decapitated, placing most of the remains into two industrial type buckets which were placed onboard a small boat at the end of a wharf," (he pointed toward the back of the premises—colour draining from his already pale face.) "We think the implement of choice was a power saw or angle grinder. The coroner seems pretty confident on it being the saw, mainly because of the way the blood splattered over the concrete floor and other features inside the building . . . oh and there are bone shavings littered around the premises as well."

The forensics guy flipped his notebook closed placing it back into his top pocket.

Ronato asked a question. "What do you mean his remains were placed in an industrial bucket?"

Responding, the forensics guy said. "We found two white industrial buckets sitting in the floor of a small outboard boat . . . the officers who discovered the buckets thought it strange that blood seemed to be breaking the seal of the lids, so one of the officers boarded the vessel opening a bucket finding human—or what he believed to be human remains," (pausing, as Ronato turned his back on him whilst Donna covered her mouth under convulsions of sickness of the findings.) "We think the remains were placed there purposefully as burley to get rid of the evidence." (Colour drew from their faces and the Chief Inspectors voice called for the forensics officer.)

Donna and Ronato entered the building and were stunned by a strong stench of decay. Blood pools and splatters not only lay on concrete floors like the forensics officer suggested but also up the walls, support beams and old work benches.

In the middle of the old market sat two industrial type buckets which a uniformed officer told them had been found outside on a fishing boat and then Ronato pulled on Donnas sleeve shifting her attention away from the buckets and towards a work bench next to a power point, where a row of exhibits sat in a line. Envelopes containing photographs taken of the crime scene and boxes containing samples, packed in sealable plastic bags weighed heavily on their need to look.

Ronato opened a box and found one of the packs had human fingers and hair fibres labelled exhibits one and two. A science lab officer investigated who was poking around with the findings flashing their badges asking a couple of questions, while watching the evidence being packed into undercover carry-cases.

The Chief Inspectors aid found them and walked them back to the car.

"We've gotten another call. There's another crime scene at the Mount Tamborine complex. I think you will want to see it."

The Chief Inspector sat in the drivers' seat, his eyes kept forward station, like a private in the army at attention when a superior entered the room.

Donna looked at Ronato, as bile stirred her stomach again.

*   *   *

The crime scene at Mount Tamborine was just off the main complex. Forensics crews walked up and down a narrow dirt track looking for anything that could help with the placement of facts leading up to the event and passed it.

The track; lead down to a small clearing through trees, fresh tyre tracks lay lush green grass over a sharp drop which lingered a strong stench of smoke.

Donna and Ronato climbed out of the car—forensic crews which placed the yellow tape and flags and plaster mouldings, were standing around a tow truck, winching up a burnt out wreck. (Interested on lookers corralled around the outside of the police crime scene tape looking for the best vantage points and a rescue helicopter hovered above, keeping an eye on the progress of the wreckage.)

Donna kept station beside the Chief Inspector. She sensed that the wreck held great importance but hadn't countered on what she and Ronato would witness.

(Ronato was down at the tow truck in deep conversation with the forensics captain they were briefed by at the fish market.)

The Chief Inspectors aid made his way down to the Chief Inspector nodding his head, confirming information the Inspector had asked for before the Inspector placed his hands around her shoulders telling her to brace herself.

"The vehicle being winched up is your partners. Detective Senior Constable Eric Nadalle," his tone was morbid.

Donna's eyes targeted the tow truck and the cable that wound its way around the winch while looking at Ronato, trying to imagine his reaction when he found out.

The aid showed Donna satellite telemetry printouts and then the car's rear-end came into view. Most of the paint had been burnt off and she immediately thought it must have been a mistake but then saw the licence plate; it was definitely a police unit.

A tear started running down her cheek meeting a look of shock from Ronato. But what came next was completely unexpected.

Ronato collapsed to the turf. Yells and screams passed his lips and blurred echoes of Holly—Holly, found her ears. She ran toward him crouching down beside him. Shock from the event blurred her reasoning and she couldn't understand why he was yelling the name of his sister, until, she looked in the direction of his pointing fingers. Two bodies sat chard under an unmistakable scent of cooked flesh.

Ronato fell silent after a sharp crack of sound split the air, looking at him once more, as the grass around him turned a purple colour. And then she looked at the Chief Inspector, and his aid that were lying on their stomachs on the ground, their faces looking in the opposite direction to her position.

A hand settled over her shoulders and she turned to find the forensics guy before another crack of sound split the air.

CHAPTER 18

The church was a hive of activity; Monopoly, Scrabble and Pictionary game boards decorated tables along with bowls of lollies and crisps, nuts and soft drinks. Children ran around the forecourt laughing and playing while their parents readied themselves for recreational battle under famishing aromas of barbeque meats adding to a smorgasbord feast all in the while being serenaded by a sound system playing old favourites and the latest hits.

In the gaming chamber wales from different parts of society and the globe arrived via watery backdrops and cascading light, their eyes lit like fireworks on entering where they sat in complete comfort. Politian's, entertainment stars and sporting personalities sat drinking alcoholic beverages—smoking cigarettes and watching half naked hostesses serve sandwiches and drinks giving away compensated gambling chips.

The fresh smell of carpet had been replaced by a scent of money—liquor and sex.

Violino sat at one of the gaming tables with Tammin—Mario and Salvatore on either side of them, flutes of Barolo rested between their fingers while the older statesmen enjoyed cigars.

Deli and Vito were seated at the bar with Seppi; smiles of celebration lit their faces as accomplishment filled the atmosphere—the Bruglioni family name had been publicly cleared of suspicion, as television station after television station focused live feeds to news breaking around the Gold Coast area.

"Do you believe this shit?" One of the wales commented, throwing sarcasm Violinos way. "All this Mafia shit, people really do eat this stuff up!" (His fingers pushed gambling chips in front of his poker hand, eyeing an attendants' ample cleavage.)

Violino found a new comfortable position responding to the comment made.

"Fucking Mafia—there's no such thing anymore . . . once—shit yeah! But drugs fucked the system destroying the Omerta—*code of silence.* Now it's all a bunch of wankers playing cowboys and Indians," he laughed, happily sliding his hand between Tammin's legs. (A smile coloured her face and eyes under twitches and tingles of an earlier encounter, all while watching an attractive brunette newsreader breaking Gold Coast news on a live feed.) Exclusive pictures were broadcast in a computer generated window beside her face with a tag line running constant particulars across the bottom of the screen. Cheers and gears erupted when two uniformed officers appeared escorting the most powerful figure in Queensland organised crime, Capofamiglia Eduardo Cavalieri to an awaiting squad car in handcuffs. (The brunette newsreader recapped the breaking story.) *If you've just joined us* her voice was lost in an echo of gamblers whistles and clapping. (Violino shushed them, pointing his palms toward the floor while asking Seppi to turn the volume up.)

"There are extraordinary events . . . tonight a series of raids occurred on Mafia businesses and private addresses in the Gold Coast area. Cavalieri family members and associates have been taken into custody after a string of deaths held the Gold Coast in fear. Drug cartel members and their associates have been charged and taken into full custody.

With me is Chief Inspector . . ." (The newsreader broke off pressing her ear-wig against her ear, nodding understanding from a voice speaking via the monitoring room at the station.) "Oh sorry—due to security reasons I cannot give his name: Here with me is the Chief Inspector who had been working with a team of detectives on the case . . . Good evening sir. Can you explain to our viewers what has happened here tonight?"

The Chief Inspector smiled into the television camera responding.

"Good evening Sarah. Well—to put it simply . . . an investigation on mafia figures has been proceeding for the last four years or so, after major rumblings in the trade unions and drug cartels signalled trouble to undercover officers working within' their ranks . . . and in the course of investigation and procedure, family figures and associates within' the mafia were taken out."

Sarah asked *by taken out, you mean killed?*

The Chief Inspector nodded his head stating *that is correct. There were multiple killings . . . a mini war.*

Fixing a finger to the earpiece, she echoed a question asked via the headset. "We understand that this investigation came to loggerheads three days ago from events in the Mount Tamborine area?"

The Chief Inspector looked into the television camera tilting his head giving the statement full focus before commenting. "That's right Sarah. On that occasion two undercover officers were taken out in a brazen attack. The assailants were captured and placed into custody where our interrogation techniques yielded information to process arrest warrants. Further evidence and information came from forensics. The rest as they say will be history." (Law enforcement officers could be seen milling around the crime scene under flickering police car siren lights.) The newsreader asked one more question.

"Will what we are witnessing tonight be replayed within' other known family cartels in Queensland?"

The Chief Inspector acknowledged the question with a brief pause.

"Arr, to this stage of the investigation it would be irresponsible to directly answer that question Sarah. But, so far as to say, our investigations into mafia practices and all origins of organised crime are continuing."

The television newsreader broadened her question *so our television screens will not be full of Bruglioni family members being arrested then?*

The Chief Inspector adjusted his stance, as another officers' face came into full view.

"Well, Sarah. A full investigation has been done concerning the Bruglioni family and interests. And where in the past, certain things have appeared to be questionable, nothing in recent investigations points to any wrong doings. As far as state law services are concerned at this stage . . . the Bruglioni family and all of its business interests are legitimate . . ."

(The Chief Inspectors aid took his attention and Sarah thanked him for his time, ending the interview and turning her attention to recaps of the breaking story while standing in front of Eduardo Cavalieri's private address.)

Violino saluted his father, as other family members joined the table.

Seppi with a tray of shot glasses and bottle of Sambuca, half filled each portion—stabbing delight colouring his voice, as he celebrated *legit . . . did you hear that! Fucking legit!* (Echoes of response spoke in the background to Violinos father while Seppi scuttled around the chamber with glasses and bottle delivering the complimentary salute.)

And then the young Don stood charging his glass toward the refrigerator saying *best investment we've ever made in entertainment* throwing back another shot. (The chamber stood and saluted the refrigerator with him,) when Holly's face appeared on the screen leading head shots of Donna, Ronato, Eric and Sergeant Sugar, their names scrolled the tag line beneath—under officers killed in the line of duty.

Violino strolled around the chamber with bottle in hand filling glasses and saluting his guardians under companionship with Seppi and Salvatore, sharing the pride and love he had for them and then toward Tammin pulling a box out of a trouser pocket.

Seppi and Salvatore ran to the bar replacing Sambuca with Champagne and wine flutes, while Tammin's eyes glazed under the attentions and focus of Violinos.

The young Don said, embracing her.

"And to this lady who has stuck by my side through thick and thin . . . who has taken my worst and forced out my best. If you will have me, will you be my bride?" (Champagne corks popped spilling sweet foam onto the carpet.)

Seppi and Salvatore started supplying the patrons while Mario served the table, glee adding a wobble to his voice, as he stated. "Full circled kid! Remember what your father said! This thing will turn full circle—maybe not in my life time but certainly in my sons. And look, he was right! The fucking thing has..!"

The refrigerator came alive from a run of commercials to live pictures of Capofamiglia Eduardo Cavalieri being escorted and placed into the back seat of a police car—a tag line ran the bottom of the screen reading *all his businesses had been raided and personalities under association arrested* while the attractive newsreader recapped the breaking news.

"After a string of arrests in the Brisbane and Gold Coast areas, Mr. Eduardo Cavalieri; said to be the leading figure of organised crime in Queensland was arrested in suspicion of the murders of investigating officers into organised crime.

Violino stood with a blank expression of reminiscence wearing his face watching head shots of the fallen officers and their names scroll across the screen. A feeling of empty sickness dried the back of his throat and tongue momentarily before directing thoughts back to the future, the lady sitting beside him and his guardians and wishing his father could be there to share his joy, knowing he would have approved of Tammin, for she proved her loyalty and that she genuinely loved him.

Looking around the gambling chamber once more, he took a long sip of his sparkling white lifting the flute skywards voicing *to the future!*

To be continued

9 781450 093477